THE DOCTOR'S DAUGHTER

THE
DOCTOR'S DAUGHTER

A Novel

HILMA WOLITZER

BALLANTINE BOOKS

NEW YORK

Copyright © 2006 by Hilma Wolitzer

Published in the United States by Ballantine Books,
an imprint of The Random House Publishing Group,
a division of Random House, Inc., New York.

BALLANTINE and colophon are registered
trademarks of Random House, Inc.

Library of Congress Cataloging-in-Publication Data
Wolitzer, Hilma.
The doctor's daughter: a novel / Hilma Wolitzer.
p.   cm.
ISBN 0-345-48584-X
1. Fathers and daughters—Fiction. 2. Children of
physicians—Fiction. 3. Parent and adult child—Fiction.
4. Adult children of aging parents—Fiction. I. Title.
PS3573.O563D63 2006
813'.54—dc22   2005048142

Printed in the United States of America on acid-free paper

www.ballantinebooks.com

2 4 6 8 9 7 5 3 1

FIRST EDITION

Book design by Dana Leigh Blanchette

To those good doctors,
Julia Smith and Frances Cohen,
keepers of body and spirit

THE DOCTOR'S DAUGHTER

1

The moment I awoke I knew that something was terribly wrong. I could feel it in that place behind my breastbone, where bad news always slides in like junk mail through a slot. It was there that I first acknowledged my parents would die someday ("Oh, sweetheart, but not for such a long, long time!"); where I knew I was ugly and would never be loved; where I suffered spasms of regret about my marriage and my children, and fear of their deaths and of my own. God knows there were plenty of things wrong in the larger world I could easily have named, and that aroused a similar sense of dread, but whatever was lodged in my chest that April morning was personal, not global. I knew that much, at least.

Was it something I'd done, or forgotten to do? There was a vague suggestion of amnesia, of loss, but when I tried to pin down its source, it proved to be elusive, a dream dissolving in daylight. In fact, I'd had a dream just before waking, but the content was obscured by a kind of white scrim. The only thing I could remember was the whiteness. And I couldn't discuss any of this with Everett—we'd quarreled again the night before and were being stonily polite. And what if my awful feeling turned out to be about him?

So I put it all aside while we ate breakfast, chaperoned by CNN and the *Times,* and chatted about Iraq and the weather and the eggs on our plates. I told myself that this was what long-married people do, even when things are good between them. Then I had a flash of my parents in their night-clothes, slow-dancing to the radio in their Riverdale kitchen.

After Ev left for work, I grabbed my bag and left the apartment, too. I had to go to the bank, and then I was going to buy a sandwich and sit near the East River to read manuscripts. Maybe the bank would be my last stop—it wasn't safe to walk around this crazy city with that much money.

Our doorman and the doorman from the building next door were outside in the sunlight, taking a breather from the bell jars of their lobbies. It must have rained the night before; the drying pavement gave off that sour-sweet musk I love, and up and down York Avenue, the ginkgo and honey locusts were suddenly, lushly budding. At fifty-one and with everything I knew, I was still such a sucker for spring. I probed for that sensitive spot in my chest as I walked, almost jogged, along in my jeans and Reeboks, out-pacing kids in business suits, and it seemed diminished by then, practically gone. It probably really was only the residue of a bad dream.

Outside Sloan-Kettering, patients tethered to their IVs were smoking, the way my girlfriends and I used to smoke near our high school, looking furtive and defiant at once. My father drove by in his Lincoln one day and caught me. "Alice!" he yelled. "What the hell do you think you're doing?"

"Oh, shit," I muttered, feeling my face and neck blotch, that curse of redheads. I dropped the cigarette—a stylish, mentholated Kool—and tried to make a run for it. But he grabbed my arm and pulled me into the car, where he bellowed and shook me, while my friends gaped at us through the tinted windows as if we were fighting fish in an aquarium.

It was the worst thing I could have done; my father was a surgeon, the venerated chief of surgery at Mount Sinai Hospital. He drove me directly there that day, and waved lurid photographs of cancerous lungs in my face, and made me look through his microscope at cells gone amok, like adoles-cent girls.

That wasn't the first time I'd disappointed him. I wasn't a boy, to begin with; I wasn't even the next best thing, a girl with an aptitude for science. And I didn't look like my mother. That day in the lab, I gravely promised him I'd never smoke again. "Daddy, I won't, I swear," I said. "I don't even *like* it." I think I even coughed a few times, for dramatic effect. Sin upon sin. In truth, I loved smoking, the deliciously acrid taste and how worldly I thought I looked with a cigarette drooping from my ragged, ink-stained fingers.

I was fifteen years old then and I still called him Daddy. I never stopped calling him that. And my Mother was "Mother," always, like the benevolent queen in the Grimms' fairy tale "The Goose Girl," which she often read to me at bedtime. I'm still haunted by its recurring lament:

Alas! Queen's daughter, there thou gangest.
If thy mother knew thy fate,
Her heart would break with grief so great.

As a child, I didn't really get all that archaic usage, or other words in the story, like *cambric* and *knacker*. But listening to my mother read "The Goose Girl" aloud as she lay next to me at night initiated my lifelong romance with language. The plot was electrifying, with its drama of switched identities, talking drops of blood, and a decapitated horse's head (also verbal) more than a century before Mario Puzo. And the message, that children, especially girls, are responsible for their mothers' happiness, was profound and unsettling. I became determined never to break my mother's heart, any more than I would break her back by inadvertently stepping on a sidewalk crack. And I meant to keep my promise to my father about not smoking again.

Passing the Mary Manning Walsh home at 71st Street, I thought of him, imprisoned since early winter in that other place, the one he'd always called, with a theatrical shudder, the "Cadillac" of nursing homes. "I'd rather be dead, Alice," he once said, pointedly, as if he were extracting another, unspoken promise. The Hebrew Home for the Aged isn't very far from the house where we once lived, although since his confinement my father didn't remember that proximity or appreciate the sad irony of it. He didn't remember a lot of things, including me most of the time, a likely source of misery in any grown child's breast. But somehow I knew it wasn't the source of mine. Maybe that was because I'd had several months to deal with the gradual death of my father's personality, a dress rehearsal for the big event.

Occasionally, he would still ask after my mother. "And how is Helen?" was the way he'd put it, a ghost-like version of his old courtly self. The first time he asked, I was so dismayed I couldn't speak. After that, I tried telling him the truth, but he always received it as fresh, agonizing news, and he'd grieve for a few awful moments before he went blank again. I couldn't keep putting him, and myself, through that, so I began to simply say, "She's fine." But once I saw him flinch when I said it, and I amended my lie to reflect his absence from home. "Getting along as best she can, Daddy," I said.

"But who's taking care of her?" he asked, with the perseverance of demented logic.

The worms, I thought, but I said, "Why, I am. And Faye, of course." And he finally sank back in his wheelchair, assuaged. Faye had been our family's housekeeper during my childhood—if he could bend time, well, then so could I. As I crossed East End Avenue to enter Carl Schurz Park, I realized that I hadn't visited my father in almost two weeks. I had to go and see him soon, but not on such a perfect day.

There was the usual pedestrian parade in the park. Runners went by wearing wristbands and earphones. Babies were being pushed in their strollers and the elderly in their wheelchairs, like a fast-forwarded film on the human life cycle. The pigeons paced, as if they'd forgotten they could fly, and dogs circled and sniffed one another while their owners, in a tangle of leashes, exchanged shy, indulgent smiles.

The homeless man who screamed was quietly sunning himself on my favorite bench, so I sat a few benches away, next to a woman absorbed in a paperback. I glanced at the cover, expecting a bodice ripper or a whodunit, but she was reading Proust, in French. *Touché.* The river glittered and flowed on the periphery of my vision as I took the manuscripts out of my bag. I was sure they would distract me from whatever was worrying me; they always did, even when I knew what was on my mind. There were four new submissions that day, three nonfiction proposals and a few chapters of a novel in progress. I began to read, and quickly set aside, the first three submissions. After all this time, I can usually tell before the end of the first paragraph if a writer has any talent.

My training began in 1974 at the literary publishing house of Grace & Findlay, where I mostly answered the phones, typed and filed for the editors, and read through the slush pile. It was only a summer internship, between Swarthmore and an MFA, and before I knew it some lowly reader at another publisher was going to discover *my* novel in their slush pile and make me rich and famous. That never happened, though. All I ever received were standard letters of rejection, the ones that say "Thank you for thinking of us, but your manuscript doesn't meet our needs right now," with the hidden subtext: *This is precisely what we hate. Do try us again when hell freezes over.*

A few years later, I joined the enemy, becoming an assistant editor at G&F, and I was still there, in a senior position, last June, when they merged with a multinational communications group and let me go. I understood that my firing was merely a fiscal matter, and I saw it coming, like a storm darkening a radar screen. But I felt shocked and betrayed anyway, even with the generous severance package.

At first I missed everything about my job—the physical place, my colleagues, my daily sense of purpose, and especially the work itself—with an ache akin to mourning. I decided that this was what it would be like to be dead, but still hovering restlessly at the edges of the living world. There were a few job offers at less prestigious houses, with lower pay and reduced status, and I swiftly, scornfully declined them. Ev says that I went nuts for a while, and I suppose he's right, if crying jags and episodes of misplaced rage are valid clinical signs. "Al," he reasoned one night, "you'll do something else, something new." What did he have in mind—tap dancing? Brain surgery? Part of the trouble was that I believed he was secretly pleased.

He had been in competition with me ever since graduate school in Iowa, where we'd met in a fiction workshop. Even his strapping good looks seemed like a weapon then. To be fair, I was pretty critical of his work, too—a defensive response, really. Everyone there was madly competitive and ambitious, despite the caveats of our instructor, Phil Santo, a mild-tempered, mid-list novelist who kept reiterating that he wasn't running a writing contest—there would be no winners or losers—and that we only had to compete with the most recent drafts of our own stories. "Make it new!" he exhorted us. "Make it better!"

Of course, there were winners; soon after graduation two of the men in our workshop went on to capture the fame and fortune we had all craved. And the rest of us, accordingly, became losers. Ev never published anything, either, but I think we both knew that I had come out ahead. At least I'd become a handmaiden in heaven, while he ended up at his family's printing firm, Carroll Graphics—brochures, letterheads, that sort of thing.

So, right after my dismissal, which my friend Violet Steinhorn wryly referred to as my "fall from Grace and Findlay," I read all of Ev's unexpected kindnesses to me, like the freshly squeezed orange juice and impromptu foot massages, as condescending and, at heart, unkind. In return, I withheld my sexual favors for a while, or gave them robotically, until I was proved to be right.

At Violet's urging I went into therapy for a few months, where I mostly wept while the psychologist, Andrea Stern, passed a box of Kleenex to me and crossed and uncrossed her legs. I stopped seeing her soon after she pointed out, and I agreed, that I was avoiding any reference to anything else in my current or past life besides my job. "I can't right now," I said. "Everything hurts too much." And she invited me to come back whenever I was ready.

Then, slowly, I began to recover on my own, to actually enjoy my new-found freedom to read just for pleasure, and go to museums or the movies in the middle of the afternoon. One day I made a lunch date with Lucy Seo, a book designer at G&F I'd stayed in touch with. She was full of industry chatter, and she kept looking at her watch because she had to get back to work. I guess it was contagious or still in my blood, because I became just as restive. I had to work, too. That's when I came up with my brainstorm, and placed ads in *The New York Review of Books* and *Poets and Writers*. "The book doctor is in. Seasoned editor will help you to make your manuscript better."

The response was immediate and enormous. Some of the letters, of course, were from the kinds of crazies and lonely souls I used to hear from when I was a reader at G&F: people burning to write about their abductions to other planets, or paeans in verse to their departed pets. But there were serious, interesting proposals, too—more than I could handle—and the recovered satisfaction of doing something I liked that was also worthwhile.

The ad was a little precious, and I couldn't help thinking how disdainful my father would have been if he'd seen it. He didn't believe even PhDs had the right to call themselves doctors. Violet, another physician's daughter, teased me about practicing without a license. And she was right, it did seem slightly illicit. But as the more open-minded Lucy pointed out, editing is actually analogous to medicine, with its orderly process of diagnosis, prognosis, and treatment.

I never made any promises to my clients about publication, but most of the projects I took on seemed to have a decent shot, and by choosing carefully I still allowed myself lots of time for personal pursuits and for my family. After I left the park that April day, I was going to go up the street to the ATM at Chase and withdraw five hundred dollars from my private money market account. In a day or two I would give it all to my son Scott, who had asked me for a loan.

He'd said that it was just a temporary cash-flow problem, but he hadn't paid back the other, smaller "loans" I'd made to him in recent months. "This isn't for drugs, Scotty, is it?" I asked, and he held both hands up as if to halt oncoming traffic. "Hey, whoa!" he said. And then he explained that he'd just gone overboard on some things he needed, clothes and CDs, stuff like that.

If Ev knew what I was up to, he would probably have killed me. Our quarrel the night before had been another version of the usual one about Scott, with Ev accusing me again of spoiling him stupid, of encouraging his dependency. "Someone has to make up for your coldness," I said, already weary of our Ping-Pong game of blaming. Which one of us should take the credit for the two children who had turned out so well? Then Ev said, "Don't try to throw this onto me, Alice. You're the enabler here." God, *that* psychobabble again—no wonder he couldn't get published. The money I was about to squander was mine, some of it inherited and some of it earned. I didn't need Everett's or anyone else's permission to help my own child.

It was soothing to sit on a bench in my new, vast outdoor office, with a roasted vegetable sandwich in my hand and the sun beating down like a blessing on my scalp and eyelids. That uneasiness I'd felt since awakening was definitely gone. A Circle Line boat glided by in the distance; for good measure, its passengers waving gaily to those of us on shore, and I waved back. The pages fluttering on my lap were by a first-time novelist, a thirty-six-year-old machinist in Pontiac, Michigan, whose cover letter had simply stated, "I really need help with this." But the opening paragraphs were exceptionally good.

The woman next to me reserved her place in her book with one finger and glanced surreptitiously sideways, as I often do on buses and the subway when I want to see what my seatmate is reading. I imagined that she'd sensed my pleasure in the manuscript and was merely curious about it. She caught me catching her and smiled. "Are you an agent?" she asked, and her smile became wolfish. She probably had her own unpublished six-hundred-page novel stashed behind the gin in the cupboard.

No, I wanted to say, *I'm a doctor.* Or, *I'm a writer, like you, only better.* But that would have been unreasonably mean, and a lie, besides. "An editor," I finally answered, a half-truth, tilting the manuscript out of her line of vision, like a grind hiding the answers to a test, and she nodded brusquely and went back to Combray.

I resumed reading, too, and as I turned the ninth or tenth page I was suddenly infused with joy and envy, the way I used to be in Iowa when someone presented a wonderful piece in the workshop. I hadn't even finished the first chapter and the voice of this writer—this Michael Doyle—was singing in my head. The story line, written in the first person about a young man's search for his missing sister, was fairly simple, even familiar, but the telling was unexpectedly vivid and complex. And it was funny, in a dark, yet sympathetic, way. Who did he remind me of—Salinger? Grace Paley? No, no one at all—that was the thing.

Now I wanted to thrust the manuscript on the woman sitting next to me and say, *Here, you have to read this!* Of course I didn't; I just kept on reading it myself, wondering why this naturally gifted writer thought he needed anyone's help. By the middle of the third chapter, though, his narrative began to flag and flatten, as if he'd lost his way in the story, or maybe just his nerve. I felt deflated for a moment or two before the old excitement took over—this was where I came in, wasn't it?

Then the homeless man began to howl his familiar aria of despair, and that disturbance in my chest came back, full force—*something is wrong*—and I wondered if it was only the renewable pain of failure, in art and in life. Hastily, I gathered the pages and the sandwich wrapper and shoved them into my bag. As I walked away from the bench, the Proust woman called after me, like someone having the last, triumphant word in an argument, "Have a nice day!"

2

The first word Scott ever said was "no," accompanied by a vigorous head shake, which I probably should have taken as an omen. But I was thrilled. He was so precocious—not even ten months old—and boys usually start speaking later than girls. I had just asked him one of those dumb rhetorical questions people ask babies, something like, "Does Scotty want to go bye-bye?" And he clearly, forcefully, said, "No!" Then he said it again, appearing as thrilled as I was with his new ability to communicate.

How I admired that feisty show of independence. A couple of months earlier, before he could walk or even properly crawl, he'd managed to get across the entire living room on his belly to reach a toy. Ev, who had organized an antiwar rally when he was at Bard, remarked fondly that Scott looked like a combat soldier making his way under barbed wire. He called him "little scout" and "GI Joe."

On the news, mothers of rapists and murderers always say, with apparent sincerity and bewilderment, "He was a good boy. He never hurt anybody," momentarily forgetting, I suppose, the little sister he molested and the immolated cat. But I knew that Scott truly *was* a good kid, just misdirected and lazy. It probably had something to do with being the baby of the family, coming as a happy surprise when Suzy was seven and Jeremy five. And his "crimes" were petty—smoking pot and pushing a little of it in high school, mostly to his own friends.

There were also a few minor incidents of shoplifting. The stupid things he took! A Mets key chain, when he was a die-hard Yankees fan. A roll of Tums. He said he'd thought they were LifeSavers, that they accidentally fell into his pocket, that his friend Kenny had dared him to do it.

The good thing was that he always eventually admitted his guilt, although he tended to put a little spin on the circumstances. And lots of teenagers commit those sorts of senseless infractions. Even Dr. Connelly, the psychologist at Fieldston, conceded that when she interviewed Ev and me right after Scott was suspended. But then she reminded us that he was also underachieving scholastically, failing two subjects and just squeaking by in the others. We didn't need to be reminded. Ev had said gloomily the night before that he just couldn't picture Scott in college. "You were sure he'd never be toilet trained, either," I said.

"We know, believe me, and we're on top of it," I told Dr. Connelly, an earnest, heavyset young woman with a faint blond mustache. "He's being tutored in math and science, and we've grounded him until his grades pick up." Ev had insisted on that particular punishment, and I suppose it was the most practical way to focus Scott's attention on his schoolwork. But I hated the word *grounded* almost as much as he did. It made me think of a bird cruelly deprived of flight.

Dr. Connelly nodded skeptically and proceeded to grill us about Scott's emotional history, starting with my pregnancy and labor and working her way up to his present difficulties. She seemed to be reading from a checklist on her pad. I assured her that his birth wasn't particularly stressful—not for him, anyway. The protracted deliveries of my older children had eased his entry into the world, just as Jeremy's academic success would later ease Scott's entry into that expensive but desirable private school. Suzy got into Brearley on her own merits.

"Has Scott ever tortured an animal?" Dr. Connelly asked—a startling shift of subjects—but we were able to answer, in complete honesty, that he hadn't. He loved animals; in fact, he was the only child in his kindergarten class who'd cried when their pet snail died.

Dr. Connelly continued. "Does he suffer from sleep disturbances, like night terrors or insomnia? Has he ever done any sleepwalking?"

I stared at her for a moment, fixated on her mustache, but Ev laughed. "I only wish I could sleep as well as Scotty," he said. "That's never been a problem for him."

This was true, as well. When the children were young and we went into their rooms to check on them before we went to bed ourselves, Scott lay so still, I was sometimes compelled to lean down and listen for his breathing.

"How about his siblings?" Dr. Connelly said. "Does he get along well with them?"

I thought of the physical fights between Scott and Jeremy, and the name-calling: pizza-face, peanut-breath, dickhead, fag. And of all the times Suzy said, after Scott had offended her—by deliberately burping at the dinner table, or by mimicking her telephone voice—that she wished she'd been an only child, like me.

"Oh, but you'd be so lonely, Suzy Q," I once cooed, and she gave me the dirty look I deserved.

"The typical love–hate relationships," I told Dr. Connelly.

"More love than hate, though," Ev added, and I gave him a grateful glance as she bent to scribble something into her notebook. Then she looked up again, her pen poised over the page. "Would you say that he's changed lately?" she asked.

Tell me, Mr. and Mrs. Samsa. Have you noticed anything different about Gregor? Actually, there wasn't any particular moment of profound change in Scott, no distinct sense of before and after. So much of what boys that age do is clandestine, anyway, and so much of ordinary adolescence seems like madness. The closed bedroom door with the thumping music behind it, like a heartbeat out of control; that harsh, barking laughter; the simultaneous eruptions of acne and anger.

Suzy and Jeremy had each gone through a similar stage. That's how I thought of it then, as an unfortunate but necessary stage on the road to maturity. Jeremy and Scott had shared a bedroom until Jeremy went off to Oberlin, and it was a continuous mess in there, with an aggregate boy-stench of feet and farting and dried semen and pot.

In the cab on the way to work after our meeting with Dr. Connelly, I was checking for messages on my cell phone when Ev said, "Well, I hope you're satisfied."

"What is that supposed to mean?" I demanded. I thought that things had gone pretty well, considering the circumstances. We had put up a united front of concerned parenthood, but not *too* concerned, and I had just been about to make a little joke about sending Dr. Connelly a thank-you gift of a bottle of Nair. I peeked at my watch; I had canceled two morning appointments with authors and there was a meeting about the fall list in the afternoon that I had to make.

"You know exactly what I mean, Alice. You indulge that kid," Ev said. "You let him get away with murder."

There was some truth in that; I did often try to ameliorate the tensions in Scott's life that seemed to overwhelm him, from social hassles to too much homework. But that's what parents do, isn't it? They help their children to endure in a difficult world. "Look," I said, "I'm not trying to white-wash this—Scotty has problems and we're dealing with them. But we're not talking about the Son of Sam here."

"That'll be next," Ev said grimly.

"If *you* say so," I snapped back. And that was the way it went. We hunkered down in separate corners of the cab and fired shots at each other until we got to Ev's office, where he thrust a few bills at the driver and got out, without giving me even a cursory kiss goodbye.

That was four years ago. As Ev had predicted, Scott didn't go on to college—not yet, anyway. But he didn't become a serial killer, either. He managed to graduate from high school, six months behind his classmates, and we all agreed that he needed some time off after that. So we helped him find a share in a low-cost apartment and a job in the mailroom at a small publishing house. Minimum wage, of course, but we thought he could work his way up if he made a genuine effort.

Scotty was always an enthusiastic reader—sometimes he even poked through a manuscript I was editing—and he'd written some funny little essays for school. I confess that I daydreamed about a writing or editorial career for him. When he lost the mailroom job, a few months after getting it, for coming in late too often, I was disappointed, but not crushed. And he found something else on his own in a couple of weeks, in the stockroom at Tower Records.

We supplemented his income, as we had supplemented Jeremy's and Suzy's when they first started out on their own. Before long Jeremy was supporting himself modestly, playing the French horn in a chamber orchestra in Philadelphia and sharing household expenses with Celia Peretti, his violist girlfriend. Suzy would probably be able to support all of us in grand style one day, when she made law partner at Stubbs, White, Kline and Moomy, where she was the newest associate. I had quietly upped the monthly ante for Scott a while ago—the cost of living had risen faster than his meager income—and Ev was annoyed when he found out. He'd worked out a careful budget with him, so much for rent, for food, for laundry, for haircuts. Scott's hair was longer than mine then.

"I don't know, Dad," Scott told Ev, frowning at the numbers, as if they were written in Sanskrit. "Like, expenses fluctuate."

"And you allow for that," Ev said flatly, "by putting something aside when you're flush." He kept underlining the final figure in the budget until his pencil broke.

Now Scott was coming to the apartment, on his day off, to pick up the money I'd withdrawn for him behind Ev's back. At first he was reluctant to meet me there; he and Ev weren't speaking, and I had to assure him that his father would be at work. The thought of Scott's company cheered me, a diversion from that determined trumpeting of doom in my chest.

"Come for lunch," I coaxed. "I'll make soup, and those cheesy corn dogs you like," wondering when the balance of power between parents and children shifted. Once, Scott was our devoted shadow, and now he lived with two roommates in a tenement in Alphabet City, as far away from us as he could get without falling into the river.

I wasn't going to go down there carrying five hundred dollars—why did he need that much, anyway? And Scott refused to take checks, which he claimed, vaguely, weren't his "thing." Maybe no one would cash them for him, or maybe he just liked the feel of a big roll of bills on his person. It would have been much easier if he'd had a bank account, so that I could simply transfer funds from my own, but bank accounts apparently weren't his thing, either.

I hadn't seen him for a couple of weeks and I was both eager and apprehensive right before he showed up, almost an hour after he'd promised he would. I've always loved his looks, so much like the young Ev's—the mass of dark curls and that sudden, witty smile. But I wondered if he would be wearing sunglasses to hide dilated eyes, and I worried that he would appear ill in some way, too thin or too pale. He's slightly built and he's my shortest child, probably a recessive trait from my father's side of the family, since Ev and I are both tall.

When he was fourteen, Scott sent away for a stretching contraption he saw advertised in the back of a comic book. It was called the Big Boy and it looked like some torturous sexual device, all black rubber tubing and metal rings. I was completely baffled after I found it under his bed, until I discovered the instruction booklet in his nightstand drawer. ADD UP TO SIX INCHES IN TWO WEEKS! There were side-by-side photos, ostensibly of the same man, looking like Hervé Villechaize in one and Wilt Chamberlain in the other.

Scott must have had the Big Boy delivered to a friend's address; I'm sure I would have noticed a package like that. And he'd probably sent cash through the mail for it, cash taken from my purse. That knowledge was retrospective, though. All that occurred to me then was a surge of pity for my secretive, undersized boy.

The doorbell rang, and I was relieved to see that he looked handsome and healthy in a clean pair of jeans and a Phish T-shirt, and the embrace he gave me was sweetly affectionate. "Ma," he said. "Whassup?"

Something awful, I might have replied, and the worst part is that I can't figure out what it is. He was the child of my heart, after all, and empathy had always run back and forth between us like an electrical current, but I knew it hadn't been a serious question. "Oh, the usual," I told him. "We're plugging along. Dad's working too hard." As if he'd asked about Ev, as if he cared.

Scott handed me a Tower Records shopping bag—why was he bringing me a present when he was so broke?—and then he went through the foyer into the living room and looked around, his thumbs hooked into his front jeans pockets. I had an abrupt, uncomfortable notion that he was casing the place. We'd accumulated some good things over the years—the Chinese rugs, a couple of Jacob Lawrence drawings, Ev's collection of antique glass paperweights. I felt a little light-headed; what kind of mother has such thoughts? I opened the shopping bag and saw that Scott had brought me a couple of old CDs I liked, but wouldn't have thought of buying for myself: *The Supremes' Greatest Hits* and Jimmy Cliff's *The Harder They Come.*

We ate lunch together in the sunlit kitchen, the way we did when Scott was little, and afterward I handed him the first chapter of Michael Doyle's manuscript. He started reading it at the table while I cleared our plates and loaded the dishwasher. He laughed a few times as he turned the pages, rapidly it seemed. "This is great," he said at one point, without looking up. "Who is this guy?"

"America," I said, "and I'm Christopher Columbus."

"Cool," Scott said, and continued to read.

I'd written an e-mail letter to Michael Doyle that morning, asking him to send me any other pages he had. Like his novel's hero, he worked on the line at GM, and for the first time I offered a reduced, flat fee for my services. In my comments about his writing, I was careful not to be too flattering or too critical. I told him there was considerable work to be done to pick up the energy and charm of his earliest pages, and that literary first novels aren't most publishers' first priority. The list leaders at Grace & Findlay during my last season there were, oddly enough, a celebrity cookbook and the memoir of an anorectic.

When Scott had finished reading the chapter, he asked me what the novel was going to be called. The title page simply said "Untitled."

"What would you call it?" I asked him.

He thought for a moment and then he began shuffling through the pages until he came to the passage he was looking for, where the hero, Joe Packer, says that he's been searching so hard for his sister, he feels as if he's been walking to Europe. "That's it, right there," Scott said, tapping the page. "'Walking to Europe.' It comes out of the guy's own mouth and it sounds really weird, but in a good way. I mean, people would remember it."

He was right: people would remember it, because it would remind them of everything difficult in their lives that they tried to change, against the odds. Like my marriage, for instance. I went into the bedroom to get the money for Scott from my hosiery drawer, thinking it was practically a reward now for coming up with that title. Under my panty hose in the drawer, there was a pair of black mesh stockings that I wore only in that room, usually with nothing else. When I saw them, I had an immediate, uncanny sense of Ev's presence, and I glanced at the bed as if I expected to see him lying there, watching me with heavy-lidded eyes. The patchwork quilt was smoothly, chastely tucked in, the pillows plumped.

My mother's old Lucien Lelong perfume bottle, filled with pink-tinted water now but still retaining a trace of its scent, was in the center of my dresser top. My father had given it to her for one of their wedding anniversaries when I was a child. It's an extraordinary object, with the figures of an eternally embracing couple floating inside the glass, and a winding stem on the bottom. When you turn it, as I did then, a tinkling version of "La Vie en Rose" plays and the couple begins to dance.

On my night table the digital clock greenly pulsed the seconds away, then the minutes. I sat down on the edge of the bed and tried to think of when Ev and I had last made love. It had to have been a couple of weeks ago, and it was strenuous, I remembered, but not exactly what anyone would call loving.

The physical attraction between us was powerful from the beginning — we had made three children with it — and it had retained a surprising amount of its original vitality, until I lost my job and this business with Scott and the money started. Then, I don't know, something like the old workshop competition took over, and the friction of sexual love became more like the friction of animus. To put it bluntly, we mostly got off against each other, fiercely and swiftly.

And we didn't speak about it later, just as we never really spoke of what had driven each of us in the unforgiving criticism of the other's writing. I lay beside him afterward, but distinctly separate, as if we'd been severed by surgery, and I missed our old postcoital friendliness — the sleepy conversation, those murmurings of love. But as sad and unpleasant as this contemplation was, I knew it wasn't the emotional secret I was keeping from myself.

All that time, Scott waited patiently in the kitchen for his money. He didn't come in to see what was keeping me, as he used to come in as a child when he intuited somehow that his father and I were doing something that excluded him, that excluded everyone. I guess Ev and I never mentioned that little habit of Scott's to Dr. Connelly, when she'd asked us about his early sleep patterns, because we'd found it more touching than exasperating.

And I had experienced the same impulse myself when I was a little girl, although I hadn't thought about it for years. My mother and father in their bedroom, their *bedchamber*, with the cream satin coverlet and the tufted headboard and that funny smell even her Lucien Lelong couldn't disguise. How pleased he always looked, how uncharacteristically rumpled. One time, I paused in the doorway, a timid actor waiting offstage for a cue. "Come here, goosey girl," my mother said, opening her white arms like wings to take me in.

I got up and opened my dresser drawer again and took Scott's money out. Ev's specter seemed to have vanished from the room, but just before I closed the drawer I put three hundred dollars back. I went inside and explained to Scott that I was having a little cash-flow problem myself, and he didn't look very happy about it, but he pocketed the two hundred and prepared to leave.

I felt a pang of remorse for holding out on him and I didn't want to let him go yet. "I've got an idea," I said. "Why don't we go see Poppy in the Big House? I know he'd love to see you. We can take a cab," I added, as further inducement. My father did love to see Scott, who'd always amused him, even now when he confused him with one or another of his nursing aides, covering himself by calling them all "young man."

Scott looked at the watch I'd bought him in February for his birthday, one of those oversized, complicated mechanisms that tell you the time in Tokyo and Paris and is guaranteed to function sixty fathoms under water. "Sorry, no can do," he said. "I have to be downtown." Like a man with urgent business elsewhere.

A few days later Ev asked me if I had seen his blue-and-white swirl paperweight. It was a mid-nineteenth-century miniature Clichy that he'd picked up in Paris five years ago, and one of his favorites. I had often seen him gazing into its layered depths as if it held the answer to some cosmic question.

Ev had always treated his collection of paperweights in a casual and generous way, sort of like public art. He let the children and guests handle them, and he didn't keep them in one place or organize them in any formal way, by color or artist or period. Instead, he set them almost randomly on shelves and tables around the apartment, where they didn't have to vie for glory, and each one became an individual beacon of light and beauty.

My first, unbidden thought when Ev asked about the missing Clichy was of Scott standing in the living room the other day, looking around as if he were seeing everything there for the first time. "Oh, I don't think . . . ," I began, and then stopped myself, flustered and perturbed. I could feel the color rise in my neck, like mercury in a thermometer.

"You don't think what?" Ev said, and when I didn't answer, "Hello? Alice?"

"I don't know. I've lost my train of thought."

"What's wrong with you? You never finish a sentence anymore."

"Something's been . . . never mind," I said.

"What?"

"Nothing."

"Al, *what*? Talk to me."

"I told you. *Nothing*. I'll ask Esmeralda about the Clichy on Thursday. Maybe she moved it when she dusted."

3

"Have you noticed anything different about me lately?" I asked Violet. We were sitting across from each other in a small, crowded diner a few blocks from the Met. All around us, silverware rang against china, and other women, surrounded by shopping bags and oversized purses, leaned forward into their own intimate and animated conversations. Shrieks of laughter erupted periodically, like jungle birdcalls, around the room.

"Somebody ought to write a book called *The Bitches of Madison Avenue*," Violet remarked.

"Well, have you noticed anything different or not?" I said.

She peered suspiciously at me over her menu. "Like what? You haven't had anything done, have you?" My friend Violet is what the French call a *jolie-laide*, and what Americans mean when they say that a woman looks interesting—a measured compliment in any language. Her mother had tried to talk her into a nose job when she was a teenager, but Violet refused, insisting that her nose was an important part of her true self, and she was right. Now her longish nose suited her longish face and wide mouth, all of it softened by that nimbus of frizzy dark hair.

I picked up a teaspoon and looked at my own distorted, inverted image in its bowl. My pale neck stretched out like the original Alice's after she'd eaten that piece of cake. I put one hand to it. "No," I said, "but maybe I should."

"So what is it, then?" Violet asked, too loudly over the general din. "Are you having an affair?"

A woman sitting with her back to Violet turned around and gave me the once-over before going back to her salad. "Yeah, right," I said sourly. But I fanned my face with my menu until the waitress came by a few moments later and took it, along with our orders.

"What's the matter with you?" Violet said. "You look like a boiled beet."

"It's just . . . well, do I seem a little *off* to you?"

"In what way?"

I wasn't sure how to explain it. Given her psychoanalytic leanings, Violet might interpret my complaint as a simple panic attack, but I'd had a couple of those in college—with mild tachycardia and vertigo—and this was different, less transient for one thing. So I said, "It's just . . . well, do I seem more forgetful?" Which was only a skewed and inadequate way of saying that I might have forgotten something essential, and it had come back to torment me.

"Uh-oh," Violet said. She raised her water glass and clinked it against mine. "Welcome to the seniors' club."

"Oh, are you losing it, too?" I remembered Violet's outrage when she received her first, unsolicited issue of *Modern Maturity* soon after she turned fifty. I think she mailed it right back to them.

"Not me. My memory's perfect, knock wood." She rapped twice on the table and immediately cracked, "Who's there?"

I'd told that joke to her in the first place, a long time ago, but I laughed dutifully, before I said, "That's how my father started, you know, by forgetting little things. First, he couldn't find his keys. Then he couldn't remember what doors they opened. Now I don't think he even knows anymore what keys are *for* . . ."

"Alice," Violet said firmly. "That's not happening to you."

"Oh, yeah? Well, this health magazine I bought has a memory quiz, but I keep forgetting to take it. Don't laugh, I'm serious."

"Aside from the fact that you're crazy," Violet said, "there's nothing wrong with you."

"How do you know?"

"Because I just do. What are you working on, Doctor?"

"A few things," I said.

"What?"

"Well, I'm still editing that elderly ex-debutante's memoir. It's completely irreverent, but it's quite amusing and *very* dishy."

"Can she write?"

"No, but I can, and she'll go to some vanity press, anyway, and distribute copies to all her new enemies. Oh, and I've got some hotshot scientist's proposal for a popular book on bioethics, fascinating stuff if it were only readable."

I took a long sip of water. "Then, there's this first novel," I said, as offhandedly as I could. Michael Doyle's book was on my mind much of the time lately.

"Aha!" Violet exclaimed. She knew my weakness for debut fiction, for discovering new writers. She'd once said it was the way I compensated for never having been discovered myself. Violet wasn't known for her diplomacy. "Is it any good?" she asked.

"More than that, actually," I said. Michael—we were now on a first-name basis in our e-mails—had sent another fifty pages, with some of the same virtues and the same problems as the first batch. He seemed to start dragging his feet whenever the tension really built around his protagonist, Joe, and his missing sister, as if he didn't know or like where it was heading. But he'd included a lingering sexual scene between Joe and an older woman he meets in a bus station that was hotter than anything I'd read since *Endless Love*. "I mean it's still pretty rough," I told Violet. "But I think he's the real thing. You know—the writing is funny and it's very wise and sexy." I sounded like a dust-jacket blurb, like an imbecile.

"Oh, so *that's* your affair." Violet said, and my face grew hot again. I hadn't just admired those pages, I'd been turned on by them. Why did Violet always know things about me faster and better than I did? I suppose it's because she's my oldest and best friend, if that latter designation is still applicable at our age. But we've shared far more than the experience of years between us. We've been each other's confidantes in all matters of the heart and spirit since childhood.

She was the first to learn, in a breathless letter, about my sexual initiation, soon after it happened, like a news bulletin from a war zone. "It was okay," I wrote, "but I don't think I'll do it again." Actually it was terrible and amazing and a little blurry because both Stuart Rothman and I were both pretty high at the time. It was August and we were junior counselors at Camp Winnetoba, which was alleged to mean "rustling pines" in Chippewa. I bled like crazy on a bed of pine needles—God, would I need stitches?—and for a moment Stuart thought *he* was the one bleeding, and all was almost lost. Afterward I reached out to embrace him, because I thought that's what you did, and he shook my hand instead. Mission accomplished.

That same year, I tried out my first, embryonic short stories on Violet, who loved them completely, as I had known she would, a cushion against all subsequent criticism. In turn, she showed me her paintings, and I said that I loved them, too, although in fact I found them harshly ugly and disturbing. They were dark and vaguely figurative, as if the figures were skulking in the painted shadows.

We pledged to become lesbians and live together if neither of us ever found anyone we liked as much as we liked each other. Years later Violet called from New Haven to tell me about Eli Kahn right after he proposed, and she was the only one from home to know about Ev when I was still afraid to tell my father.

Our parents had been good friends before we were born. They were neighbors in Riverdale, and Violet's father, Leo Steinhorn, retired now, was on the staff at Mount Sinai with my father. Both men were renowned in their fields—Leo was a hematologist—and our mothers had been consummate doctors' wives. Gracious hostesses in the dining rooms, first ladies at awards ceremonies, keepers of their husbands' flames. Violet's mother,

Marjorie, continues to play that supporting role, with considerable flair, to a diminished audience.

Violet's birthday and mine are two weeks apart, in November, and she was my first playmate. There's a faded photograph in one of my mother's albums of the two of us, in bonnets, facing each other in a baby carriage, like Siamese twins joined at the sternum. "At least you've always had Violet," people used to say in comforting tones, on the popular assumption that it was lonely being an only child. I tried to perpetuate that myth myself when Suzy complained about her brothers, but when I was young I never really suffered an absence of siblings.

I didn't have to share my room or my toys—except on the occasion of a friend's visit—or my parents' ardent attention, ever. And the relative solitude of my early life probably served to stimulate my imagination. I held frequent conversations with myself, not with a pretend friend, as my mother liked to think. "What's her name, dear?" she once asked, trying to join my game, and I said, "Alice, of course." I heard her whisper something about this episode to my father later, followed by little bursts of conspiratorial laughter.

My parents were devoted to each other, with the particular, exclusive intimacy of childless couples. They had already sadly accepted my mother's barrenness when I showed up, thirteen years into their marriage. Violet's mother once told me that their names were joined on everyone's tongue: Sam and Helen, Helen and Sam. I couldn't help thinking: Ev and Al, Al and Ev, and that our gender-bending nicknames just didn't have the same cachet. "He worshiped her," Marjorie Steinhorn said, in that stage whisper she still uses for dramatic effect. "They worshiped each other."

But she didn't have to tell me; I'd seen it for myself. The way Helen fed Sam tidbits from her own plate; the way they always kissed fully on the lips, and not just in greeting or farewell. The romantic gifts he gave her: volumes of poetry; exotic flowers and diaphanous scarves, pulled from their boxes with a magician's sorcery. My parents may have wanted a child, but they didn't really *need* one. Still, when I was born, they opened their magic circle to let me in. And if my mother was the queen of that household, then I was nothing less than the crown princess. To the rest of the world I was the doctor's daughter, with all the material benefits and reflected glory that title bestowed.

My bedroom suite in our Riverdale house was once featured in *House & Garden*. "The eminent New York surgeon Dr. Samuel Brill, and his socially prominent wife, Helen, have created a suburban Wonderland for their seven-year-old daughter, Alice." My playroom had the requisite doll corner, with an array of authentically costumed international dolls, and the more unusual (especially for a girl) science corner, where my father had set up a miniature laboratory for me. To his frustration, I mostly used it for concocting "food" to be served in the doll corner.

In my bedroom I had a canopied bed draped in white eyelet and a skirted, mirrored dressing table, where I could despair of my looks in absolute privacy. I searched for a resemblance to my dark-haired mother, who herself slightly resembled the actress Hedy Lamarr and was named for the charmer who'd brought down the city-state of Troy. For a while I believed that my own name came from the only book I earnestly disliked, about that eponymous girl with no control over the frightening dreamscape of her life. Later I learned that Alice had also been my paternal great-aunt's name.

I had my mother's cheekbones and her long legs, but I had my father's red hair, his pallid coloring that flared too easily with emotion and was patterned with freckles, the blind look of blond eyelashes; I was the negative of her vibrant positive. I sat at my little white Sheraton desk—a miniature of the one in my parents' bedroom, where my mother wrote poetry by hand—and knocked out my sappy verse on a shiny silver Olivetti. Some of my poems were, predictably enough, about my beautiful mother and brilliant father, while others dealt with being an orphan or a starving refugee.

My parents encouraged me to recite them, hot off the press, to their poor friends during the cocktail hour in our living room. "Far from my native land, I've come across the sea / for a crust of bread in my hand, and a smile from Lady Liberty . . ." I can still see the frozen smiles on their faces and hear the polite smattering of applause, like a brief summer shower. After my performance, I walked happily around the room behind Faye, receiving compliments and passing out the stuffed olives and the *rumaki*.

What an affected little prig I was; it still pains me to think that none of my children would ever have chosen me for a friend.

My mother kept her own poems, which were mysterious to me, yet mysteriously lovely, mostly to herself—at home, anyway. Even my father didn't know that she was sending them out until she received an acceptance letter one day from an obscure literary magazine in Eureka, California, and released a little yelp of surprise, as if someone had stepped on her foot.

He was so proud of her. He waltzed her around the room, calling her his "poetess laureate," and at one of their next dinner parties there was a copy of *The Jumping Frog Review*, with my mother's poem in it, rolled like a diploma and tied with red satin ribbon, at everyone's place setting. I'd helped him to lay them out.

"Violet," I said now, "I feel terrible."

"What? You're not sick, are you?" She grabbed my wrist, as if she were about to take my pulse.

"No. At least I don't think so." We had both always enjoyed the informed hypochondria of doctors' children. "Feel my head," we used to say giddily to each other. "I'm burning up!"

"Then what's going on?" Violet asked.

"Well, plenty. I mean, the usual. Scotty, my father, terrorism . . ." I was acutely aware of having left Ev off my list of vital concerns.

"Yeah," Violet said. "But what's really getting to you?"

"That's the trouble, I'm not sure." My hand went to my breast and then sank to my lap. "I just have this *sense*, not a foreboding, exactly; it's as if something very bad has already happened, but I haven't found out about it yet."

"Ah, the secret life of the unconscious," Violet said, as I'd been afraid she would. "So go to a therapist. I'll get you a name."

Violet was always pushing psychoanalysis—the unexamined life, blah, blah, blah. You'd think she was getting a kickback from the Freudian Society. Violet had gone into analysis, herself, after she and Eli separated. It took six years to complete, but she claimed that it saved her life, if not her marriage. That would have been really difficult to do, since Eli had fallen in love with someone else. Since then, Violet took love wherever she happened to find it, usually in brief affairs, and most recently with a married doctor she'd met at the Whitney. What would her analyst have said about that?

I had long been resistant to the parsing of my own psyche, especially when I was writing and feared the intrusion of interpretation. I'd been in short-term therapy twice in my life, though—that time after I lost my job, and earlier, when I was about ten years old and had developed a nasty little blinking tic.

Dr. Pinch, whose psychiatric practice was on Park Avenue, was a colleague of my father's, making him suspect to me from the start. Each time I left his office, I imagined him picking up the phone and reporting to my parents, verbatim, everything I had just said. Not that I ever said very much. I knew I was there because of my new "habit" of blinking, but, strangely, Dr. Pinch didn't refer to it, and neither did I.

This was completely unlike any of my previous medical experiences. When I had an earache, my jovial pediatrician always asked me where it hurt, and then looked into the offending organ with a lighted probe. Our family dentist, appropriately, examined my teeth. Dr. Pinch, on the other hand, never mentioned my eyes.

I was a very literal-minded child; his Dickensian name made me nervous, and why wasn't I going to an eye doctor in the first place? He asked me seemingly irrelevant questions about magical wishes and dreams—did I ever think I didn't live with my "real" family, did I ever daydream about having a twin?—and I blinked madly at him and mumbled grudging, monosyllabic replies. Sometimes I merely shrugged, meaning: *I hate you, I don't know, leave me alone.*

I might have told Dr. Pinch, if he'd ever asked me directly, that I blinked because I couldn't stand looking at anything very long. But he never did ask. After several weeks, during which my parents intently ignored my tic—although my mother lost control at breakfast one morning and cried, "Sweetheart, why are you doing that to your pretty face!"—it simply went away.

"You know I tried therapy a couple of times," I reminded Violet, "and it didn't do me much good. I guess it's not my thing," I added, realizing how much I sounded like Scott.

"How's Ev doing?" Violet said then, and I felt alerted in a prickling sort of way. What was she really asking or implying with that non sequitur? Had he said something to her about us? She and Ev had always liked each other, making it difficult to ever complain to either of them about the other one. When Ev and I eloped, Violet flew to Iowa to be our witness, and Ev sometimes referred to her as his best man.

"He's okay," I said. "He's fine." *We're* not, though, I thought, but didn't say. Violet was likely to take Ev's side, and point out that I didn't know how lucky I was. She'd already told me more than once that I clung to some foolish fantasy of perfection, that my parents' marriage was an impossible ideal for ordinary mortals.

Our waitress brought our sandwiches, and I smiled up at her and said, "Thanks, that looks delicious." As soon as she turned away, I burst into a torrent of silent sobs.

"Honey," Violet said. "What is it?"

"I don't *know.*" I blew my nose briskly on my napkin and took a bite of my tuna melt. "Maybe I'm just having a midlife crisis." What an easy way out that would be, to have something fleeting that everyone gets, like gas pains or nostalgia. I used a mocking tone when I said it, though, to ward off Violet's disparagement of such a wastebasket, pop-psychology term.

But to my surprise, she only said, "Why not? This is the crossroads, kiddo, when you're looking back at all the mistakes you made, and ahead, well, ahead to old age and death."

"Thanks a lot. I knew I could count on you to cheer me up."

The waitress came over a couple of minutes later to refill our water glasses and ask if everything was okay. Her name was Florence; it was embroidered in script just above her pocket. She looked something like Parksie—Eleanor Parks—my father's longtime surgical nurse. The uniform, I suppose, and that pillowy bosom. Her eyes, lined with smudged kohl, were filled with friendly sympathy. Whenever I visited my father's office, Parksie, who doted on me, or his secretary, the serenely glamorous Miss Snow, would sit me down at her desk and give me a fan of freshly sharpened pencils and recent copies of *Highlights*. Goofus and Gallant.

Hidden pictures. I carefully circled all the secreted items I could find: shoes in trees, monkeys in the kitchen—while my father, on the other side of the adjoining wall, illuminated X-rays to show his wary patients ominous, hidden shadows.

I told the waitress that the food had been great, that everything was fine, a seeming contradiction, I suppose, to my half-finished sandwich and blotchy eyelids. But she smiled as if she believed me, and cleared the table.

Then Violet and I took a taxi down to Soho, where a couple of her paintings were in a group show at a cooperative gallery. It was her turn to mind the show for a few hours, and I was going along to keep her company. Violet's work had become more abstract over the years but no less oppressive, with its sullen colors and heavy brushstrokes. It was as if she were deliberately hiding something more aesthetically pleasing under those dense layers of pigment.

Her paintings' lack of compromise and consolation always made me a little anxious, and I felt like a Philistine and a traitor because I didn't really enjoy looking at them. I couldn't lie to Violet about it, but I couldn't quite tell her the truth, either. When I commented at all, I used evasive, counterfeit words like *intense* and *labyrinthine.*

"There's enough beauty in the world," she told Ev and me, severely, at her studio one afternoon as she showed us some new canvases. "I don't have to add to it." Had she read my mind?

"But these *are* beautiful, Violet," Ev told her. "The way you are." His saying it at that moment, with such genuineness, made me feel immensely happy, as if he had said it about me.

Our children loved Violet, too; she was the closest they came to having a cool aunt. Their only actual aunt, Ev's brother Steve's wife, Karen, in San Diego, was very sweet to them. She never forgot birthdays, and she sent them greeting cards on every imaginable holiday, from Purim to Presidents' Day. But I knew that at one time or another each of them had told Violet things they weren't able to tell Ev or me. She always treated them seriously, even when they were small, when she'd let them do huge, messy paintings in her studio.

The show at One Art was an eclectic jumble of showy collages; almost invisible pen-and-ink drawings; whimsical wire sculptures; and Violet's big, somber canvases—like a family of foster children thrown together by cruel fate.

Soon after we arrived a man and woman came in, asked directions to another gallery, and left. I walked around the room, looking at the work, while Violet leafed through the guest book, reading some of the inscriptions aloud to me. Someone had scrawled, "Keep your day jobs!" across a whole page, which made Violet laugh. A few other people, from places like Georgetown, Texas, and DeKalb, Illinois, had written polite and positive remarks, or simply signed their names and addresses.

But the comments were mostly from relatives and friends of the artists. "Beautiful work! We're so proud of you! Love from Aunt Lil and Uncle Bernie." Art critics don't review co-op shows any more than literary critics review self-published books. It was a good thing that Violet *had* kept her day job, at a high-end art shop called Framework, on Lexington Avenue. And I suppose it was good that I was still working, even freelance, in my field. The major difference between us was Violet's steadfast commitment to her painting, to her art—as essential to her true self as her prominent nose.

Maybe not having children was the trade-off; look at Austen and Dickinson and Georgia O'Keeffe. Louise Nevelson had a son, but she handed him over to someone else to raise. I'm not convinced of the connection, though. My own kids were grown now, or nearly so, and the only writing I'd done in the past few years was in the journal I still kept in a spiral notebook, a grown-up version of my childhood diary. And even those entries were sporadic and sparse, and strewn with domestic effluvia: blue pants to cleaners, Total, milk, asparagus, Crest. I'd added a couple of hasty notes recently in my weird shorthand: "? Esm. & Scott re: Clichy." "Visit D.!"

Back when I still thought of myself as a writer, before I started tampering with other people's work, I carried a notebook all the time and wrote down almost every impression I received, as if I were a recording angel assigned to keep track of the mortal world. Aunt Lil and Uncle Bernie and the Hildebrands from DeKalb were surely not the audience Violet had envisioned for her work, but it didn't matter all that much; she painted for herself now.

"Write the story you'd like to read," Phil Santo used to tell us in the workshop, but we could hardly hear him over the roaring of our ambition. What happens to all that lost desire, all the language we never use? Why did the floor of my life suddenly seem to be made of glass that I might just crash through? And where was my mother when I still needed her? The room began to turn, like the dancers confined to her perfume bottle.

"Violet," I said. "Feel my head. I think I'm burning up."

4

My father didn't just lose his keys one day and forget what they were the next. His decline was gradual and followed an unremarkable pattern. At first he suffered from the usual complaints of the aging, like hearing loss, lethargic bowels, and hesitant urination, while his heart stampeded, although nothing much really excited him anymore. A hearing aid and a beta-blocker were prescribed, as well as medication for his prostate and blood pressure. He had retired from his surgical practice several years before, but he still did a few consultations. His reputation was intact even if his hands shook sometimes; he was, after all, the same man who'd written a landmark monograph, in 1968, on surgical intervention in bile duct blockage.

Then we noticed that he'd begun to grope for words—"senior-itis," he called it with a mirthless chuckle—or simply wound down in the middle of a sentence, to silence. After a while the phone calls started. My father had never cared much for the telephone; I think he considered it a "feminine" instrument, like the hair dryer and the vacuum cleaner. He'd almost never answered the phone at home; either Faye or my mother did that, and at work it was the job of switchboard operators and medical secretaries, like his own Miss Snow, the pretty post-deb blonde who wore demure pastel twin sets and pearls, but aggressively guarded his door and his telephone extension.

When I began to call him regularly, after his retirement, our conversations usually resembled a celebrity interview—I'd ask probing questions, and he'd give abbreviated, evasive answers. "Daddy, tell me what you did today." "The usual." The sense I got was that he was busy, which was good, and that he wasn't too lonely, which was even better.

My father did write letters over the years, though, and I've saved the ones he sent to me when I was away at summer camp and college. They were all handwritten on his professional stationery, and they were chatty and affectionate, and invariably signed "Your Daddy." On my nineteenth birthday he sent greetings on a page from his prescription pad. "Rx for Alice Marion Brill, age nineteen: Take one heaping dose of happiness every day."

So when the telephone calls began, about three years ago, I was startled at first, and then I grew concerned. The first one came while I was at work. He'd called, it seemed, to ask me the time. He had a wonderful restored Breitling watch that my mother had given him, and a silver desk clock, with imposing Roman numerals, in his consultation room at the hospital. A cherry-wood grandfather clock reliably chimed out the hours in the vestibule of his home. Why was he asking me the time? I was busy when he called and decided that, oddly enough, he was just checking his watch's performance.

There was no discernible reason for the other calls, though, especially in the middle of the night, when he didn't say anything for long seconds while I shouted "Hello! Hello!" against the possible onslaught of bad news. Once, he said, rather formally, "Forgive me, I must have the wrong number," and hung up.

Twenty-seven years before, not long after my mother died, people tried to fix my father up with various widows and divorcées. A couple of infatuated patients pursued him themselves. But he didn't want to date at all; the term itself seemed distasteful to him. Marjorie Steinhorn said he'd told her that he still felt married. He continued to play bridge and have dinner with old friends, and he kept renewing his subscription to Alice Tully Hall, taking me with him, or one of the children when they were old enough. I believe that Jeremy's interest in music began with those Sunday-afternoon concerts. He would reread the programs in bed the way Scotty reread his favorite comic books.

It was my father's own idea to sell the Riverdale house and move into the town house in Scarsdale. Faye had retired and gone back to North Carolina, and no one else he hired seemed to please him. He was between housekeepers when someone broke into the house while he was at the hospital. They were sophisticated thieves who'd managed to disarm the security system, and they stole many of the things he cherished, including a portrait of my mother by Alice Neel and the Egyptian prayer rugs they had bought on their honeymoon. It was as if my mother had died again—he suffered a similar impotent wrath, the same crushing grief.

Ev and I agreed that a new, smaller place was appropriate and we helped him to settle in, with enough of his old belongings to make it feel familiar and comfortable. He especially wanted to keep his bedroom furniture and his collection of antique surgical instruments. But he relinquished other possessions with seeming ease, and he finally gave me several things that had been my mother's, including her perfume bottle, some books and jewelry, a file box containing Faye's recipes, and an accordion folder filled with literary memorabilia.

One day last year I was in the office with a client when my phone rang. It was a police officer in Scarsdale, and he asked me if I knew a Samuel Elias Brill. My first gasping thought was that he had died—the somber way the officer said my father's full name, he might have been reading it from a death certificate or a tombstone—and I realized that on some level I had expected this call for a long time, the other dropped shoe. But it was something worse. My father had left the town house in his pajamas in the early morning and wandered around his neighborhood, where he was discovered, chilled and confused, by some children waiting for a school bus.

Even then, I managed to find benign explanations. Bad dream. Bad medication. But the confusion came and went as erratically as his moods—

rampant rage one day, utter sadness the next; two sides of the same coin. Against all of his arguments, I hired a twenty-four-hour home attendant for him, and the loss of his independence only seemed to make things worse. He told me more than once that he wished he were dead. "He's being a drama queen again," I'd complain to Ev, but I felt sorry for my father when I was with him.

"You don't really mean that, Daddy," I said one day. "I know this is hard, but there are still lots of things you enjoy. Your music, the children . . ." I looked around his living room for further inspiration, and all I noted was the ticking clock, the silent carpeting. I gestured toward the window, the gray winter sky. "The *world*," I said finally, and he said, "I'd rather be with your mother."

Maybe it was a mistake getting a man to care for him; someone with the same general responsibilities, but who looked like Faye, soft-eyed and brown-skinned, and wearing an apron, might have been more acceptable. Ralph Spear was a short, muscular white man with a shaved head and multiple tattoos. He reminded me of a circus acrobat. My father referred to him bitterly as "that thug" or "my keeper." There was unarguable truth in the latter. Ralph cooked the meals and did the laundry, and he took my father to his various medical appointments. They even played chess together some afternoons, but his primary job was to keep my father safe. And one day he failed to do that.

Ralph was making grilled cheese sandwiches for their lunch when my father said that he felt tired and was going to lie down until the sandwiches were ready. Then he went into his bedroom and locked the door behind him. Ralph heard the click of the lock all the way in the kitchen and rushed down the hallway to the bedroom. As he beat on the door, yelling, "Open up, Doc! Come on, open up!" my father took a case of old surgical instruments out of his closet, sat down on the bed, and, with a primitive scalpel, neatly cut his left wrist. My instinct to hire a strongman saved his life; Ralph broke the door open and, a few minutes later, I received that heart-stopping phone call.

Sometimes Ev or one of the children reluctantly accompanied me to the Hebrew Home for the Aged to see my father. Violet went there with me only once, and then begged off from future visits, saying she preferred to wait until it was her own turn to be addled and incontinent. We were back in Manhattan, at a Starbucks, rewarding ourselves with coffee and pastries, and I said, "Imagine, Violet, *my* father—my famous, fastidious father—in diapers! If that ever happened to me, I'd want to be shot." Violet sipped her coffee and said, completely deadpan, "Not me, I'd want to be changed." Then we both laughed so hard, coffee went up our noses, and we kept bursting into nervous laughter that whole afternoon for no reason at all.

Most of the time I went to see my father by myself, dragging my feet all the way there. He had a few other visitors. Leo and Marjorie showed up about twice a month, close to their old schedule with my parents for bridge and dinner, and so did Parksie, who had to take the tram from Roosevelt Island, and then an express bus to Riverdale. Three of my father's former surgical fellows used to travel together to see him, in a sort of pilgrimage, but they stopped going after their personal god failed to recognize them. His ability to remember who people were ebbed and flowed, just like his orientation in time and to place, and his fits of agitation.

I felt guilty about staying away for three whole weeks, but I kept excusing myself from duty. I had so much work to do, I didn't feel too great—that ominous feeling in my chest had taken root there like a strangler weed—and I called the nursing desk on his floor nearly every day to check on him, in lieu of visiting. Mostly, I just wanted the uninterrupted routine of my own life, or to live in the more compelling world of *Walking to Europe*. Michael had taken my most urgent editorial suggestions seriously, and he'd sent some solidly revised pages that put me back under the spell of the manuscript.

Caitlin, his hero Joe Packer's sister, had been unemployed and living with a darkly moody boyfriend, one in a series of difficult men she was drawn to, when she disappeared. I could see the generic furnished room they'd shared, his transient's eyes already ogling the door, while Joe looked around for some evidence of where she might have gone, or that she'd even ever been there.

As I suspected, Michael loved Scott's title and wanted to know all about him. In my e-mail I only said that Scott was a terrific kid with an imaginative bent. I avoided mentioning his age, and knew it was because it might reflect on my own. I was so easily distracted from my father's needs; what would he think of me if he were able to think straight? He was very strongly principled about obligation. You did things because you were supposed to, not because they were pleasant, whether it was performing surgery on a malodorous, abscessed liver or sending a thank-you note to your great-aunt for that ugly hand-knit sweater. Attending to the father who had so faithfully attended to you was surely the embodiment of that law.

The Sunday after my lunch with Violet, I was sitting opposite Ev in the living room, doing the *Times* crossword puzzle, when he put down his section of the paper and said, "You can't keep putting it off like this."

Oh, yes I could. It was raining out, I wanted to go back to bed. I had been sneaking glimpses, over my puzzle, of Ev's broad hands on the newspaper, and the swell of his thighs in his pajamas, and thinking that I might invite him back to bed with me.

"Come on, Al," he said, pulling me up from the sofa. "I'll go with you." The strength of his grip and the sweetness of his offer aroused me further, but Ev went right to the phone to call Suzy and arrange for her to meet us in the main lobby of the nursing home.

Suzy's hours at Stubbs, White were erratic and long, and I knew that weekends were especially precious to her. She had a habit of being late for most occasions, but she was waiting there when we drove up, and I felt that familiar shock of happiness on seeing her, the way I used to when I'd spot her in a crowd of children swarming out of All Souls or Brearley. Could there ever possibly be a time when I wouldn't know my own, beautiful daughter? Like Scott, she has Ev's strongly defined coloring—Jeremy is the only other redhead in the family—and an original, heart-shaped face. "Mom! Dad!" she called, sounding equally pleased to see us, and we hurried across the lobby toward her.

When a child turns out well, you often think that it's just remarkably good luck, practically a miracle. So many things might have gone wrong and haven't. At other times you take too much pride in having successfully launched a person separate from, yet somewhat like, yourself. A new and improved version: intense without the neurosis, self-confident without the solipsism. Ev and I have always been at peace with each other in Suzy's company, perhaps because we were still so much in love when she was born. I felt safely flanked by the two of them as we rode up in the elevator to the Alzheimer's unit.

Whenever I went there alone, the dread set in even before the ascent began. The place itself is attractive and well kept; my father was right, irrespective of his contempt, in calling it the "Cadillac" of nursing homes. Ev and I had looked into a few other facilities closer to our apartment before committing him there. They were all pretty shabby and drab in comparison, and that reek of urine and cafeteria cooking assailed us as soon as we walked in the front door. Yet the day we brought him to the Hebrew Home I was filled with misgiving. All I could think of was the distinguished person, the *personage*, my father had been in his prime, and how revolted he'd always been by the idea of institutional life.

Ev had put his arm around me and said, "Remember how you and Jer clung to each other the first day of preschool?" But I brushed off his embrace and the comparison; that was a beginning and this was an end. I tried to tell the nurse on duty about my father, while the aides undressed him and put him to bed, and she said, "Oh, honey, everyone here was somebody once."

Despite the relative luxury of the Hebrew Home, and the comfort of having Ev and Suzy beside me, I felt that swooning aloneness as soon as the elevator doors opened onto my father's floor and the noise reached my ears. There were fewer men than women in residence—we outlive them, a doubtful blessing—but their commanding baritones dominated the sopranos in that chorus of the damned. "Help!" they called. "Jesus!" "Shitfuck!" "Mama!" Or they simply let loose a yowling of misery beyond language, like the homeless man in Carl Schurz Park.

And I could always pick out my father's voice, even from a distance. That day it was especially easy because he was shouting my name, over and over, and, feeling surprisingly lighthearted, I rushed ahead of Ev and Suzy to reach his room. He was in a wheelchair at the side of his tightly made bed, and he looked up sharply when I came in. "Alice!" he cried. "Where have you been?" The old impatience was evident, as if I were late for dinner again, and Faye was keeping the roast warm in the oven.

"Daddy," I said breathlessly. "I'm sorry, the traffic, but here I am."

His eyes were shiny from the drugs, but clear—he'd had cataract surgery on the left one a couple of months before—and I noticed that his hearing aid was in place. He tended to pull it out and toss it somewhere, under the bed or onto his lunch tray—it had already been retrieved from the kitchen twice. I didn't blame him; I'd want to shut off the din of that unit, too. Now he tapped the device and it beeped, so I knew I didn't have to check the battery. All of his senses were honed to receive the horror of his situation. And yet he seemed better, less frantic than the last time I was there. And he knew who I was.

Suzy and Ev came into the room, and she bent to kiss the top of his head, where the red hair had thinned and faded to a pinkish gray. "Hi, Poppy, darling," she said. "How are you?" His face registered pleasure, and a low, humming sound came from his throat, something like purring. I didn't know if he recognized her, or if he was merely enjoying the attentions of a fragrant young woman. Before I was born, he'd hoped for a son, preferably a son delivered with a stethoscope coiled around his neck. But he seemed ecstatic when he had a granddaughter, and he'd always preferred Suzy, his "little crêpe Suzette," to the boys.

Women had played one subordinate role or another all during his professional life. Parksie was his surgical nurse for thirty-eight years, until his retirement, and Miss Snow had come straight from a preppy sort of secretarial school to work in his office, staying until her marriage. There were various female clerks and technicians at the hospital, too, and female patients had dominated his practice. When I was a young girl and our family went to a restaurant or to the theater, it seemed as if some woman or another was always coming up to him, saying, "Dr. Brill? I'm so-and-so, you removed my gallbladder last May."

They were very excited about seeing him out of his usual context, and a little shy, as if he were an actor sighted offstage and they were about to ask for his autograph. My mother referred merrily to his adoring gang of gallbladders, appendectomies, and hysterectomies as "your father's harem." He called them, one and all, "dear."

Ev patted my father's shoulder, and my father grasped his hand and said, "Doctor, it's good to see you." Years ago, that might have been taken for sarcasm; he'd wanted me to marry a doctor. I was *supposed* to marry a doctor, if I couldn't become one myself, and I almost did. But instead of continuing a medical dynasty, I'd started an ordinary family, which wasn't easy for him to forgive, especially because of the covert way I did it. Still, I could tell that his greeting to Ev was only the result of his confusion, and that Ev had not been offended.

I glanced around my father's room, made clinical by the hospital bed and the bedside commode, despite those carefully handpicked remnants of his old life: the gray cashmere throw; his silver clock; a framed photograph of my mother and me taken forty years before in Chilmark; the certificate honoring him for his service as chief of surgery; a single medical book, illustrated with transparent colored overlays that peeled back to reveal all the invisible systems of the human body; the sparse jade plant that had once flourished on my parents' sunporch.

What was he doing here? I had a sudden, insane notion that I'd let him down long ago, and now he was letting me down in return. *Something is wrong.* Of course I understood that what had happened to him was purely mechanical. The neurologist had explained it carefully, as if he were peeling back sections of my father's deteriorating brain. He used an automotive analogy, I remember, citing a tired engine, a busted carburetor. My father the car.

I was just about to suggest that we all go to the solarium when my father said, "Tell me, how is Helen?" Suzy's hand went to her mouth, and she turned away. She was a grown woman, a lawyer who cleverly calculated the strategies of contracts and torts. But now she was reduced to uncertain girlhood. Ev didn't look very happy, either.

"She's doing all right," I answered, in the casual tone I'd perfected. "Listen, Daddy, shall we go to the solarium?"

"I worry so about her, you know," he said, and Suzy left the room. At that moment I was particularly glad she wasn't an only child. Not, as I had once coyly told her, because it was lonesome, but because someday she would be able to share the burden of failing parents, of Ev and me, with her brothers.

I came up behind my father's wheelchair and began to propel it through the doorway. Ev followed us out into the corridor, where other families pushed their elders in one direction or the other, or guided them, hand in hand, as they tried to walk. I'd thought the change of setting would distract my father, but he was stuck in that movie of his former life playing inside his head. "Is Helen coming, too?" he asked as we waited for the elevator. *Knock it off!* I wanted to shout, the way I used to when Scotty kept doing that maddening Woody Woodpecker laugh. "Is Helen coming?" my father asked again, a little louder this time, and I had a flash of Richard Widmark hurling his wheelchair-bound victim, screaming, down a flight of stairs.

My mother had been dead for so many years. She died when I was in graduate school, not in the unimaginably distant future, as she had promised. She'd developed breast cancer while I was still at Swarthmore, and my father told me about it in a phone call, at the end of finals week. The fact that he was using the phone at all should have alerted me, but somehow it didn't. "Mother isn't well," he began. His usually rich and sonorous voice had thickened and grown faint.

"What?" I asked, thinking distractedly of a cold or the flu. He sounded funny; maybe he'd caught it, too. But my mind was elsewhere, on some academic prize or social event.

"Alice, darling, she's in the hospital. She's had a mastectomy."

For a moment, I couldn't make sense of the word. Did it have something to do with the ear? But I held one hand against my own breast, where I'd already registered the news. "But why didn't you tell me!" I wailed. "I would have come home."

"We didn't want to upset you before your exams. She's doing very well," he said. "Harvey Wagner did the procedure." The *procedure*! I pictured a younger Dr. Wagner cutting precisely into a pink lamb chop at our dining room table.

She did do very well for what seemed like a long while, and I let myself be seduced into solace and calm. My father was a doctor, after all, and he loved my mother as fiercely as I did. I came home to see her and then went back to school, where I fell in love, with a series of books and boys and the possibilities of my own potential. I worried about her, of course I did. But she was on the borders of my concentration, not in its center. Only I resided there.

In the solarium a volunteer banged out sprightly show tunes on an upright piano, and for several minutes we were relieved of the burden of conversation. After the last number, a merciless rendition of "Everything's Coming Up Roses," there was some halfhearted clapping, like the applause in my parents' living room after I'd recited my poems. I was about to suggest we take my father back down to his room when he leaned toward me and looked into my eyes, more directly and intensely than he had in years. His speckled talon poked me in the chest. "You should take care of that lesion, dear," he said.

5

As soon as Ev left for the office on Monday, I put my mother's accordion folder on the kitchen table and reheated the coffee. I had looked into the folder from time to time since my father had given it to me, but I'd hesitated to really explore its contents. Privacy had always been a priority of my mother's—you knocked on closed doors, you allowed people the sanctity of their thoughts. And she'd become more discreet about her poems after that first publication. She kept writing, though, and after a while she began to publish occasionally in more respected journals, like *Poet Lore* and *Prairie Schooner.*

She was so modest, she didn't even mention those acceptances until copies of the issues with her poems in them arrived. My father had apparently taken his cue from her to be more low-keyed about her latest successes, too. There were no more delirious waltzes around the house, and no grand announcements or ribbon-tied copies of literary magazines distributed as table favors to friends. I can only remember his playful warning to her, after she'd been paid fifty dollars for one of the poems, "Well, Helen, don't spend it all in one place!"

I had been missing her with something like the old, pervasive longing lately, and I'd begun to associate that revived ache with the peculiar feeling in my chest. Was there a clue to the link between them, or at least some consolation, to be found in her writing? Or maybe there was no mystery at all; maybe it was just that the hole in my life could only ever be filled by her, and that things had just gotten worse since my father's emotional vanishing act. I was still troubled by the strange thing he'd said to me in the solarium the day before, and his calling me "dear" that way, as if I were one of his groupie patients.

After Ev and I came home from the nursing home, we went straight to bed and made love—you would think we had planned it in advance. Life against death. We took things more slowly this time and were less grasping than we'd been; for once we tried to please each other as much as ourselves. And I was fully there with him. Recently, helping myself to satisfaction, I'd had a fantasy about Joe Packer, the lanky, droll hero of *Walking to Europe.* That was the first time I'd conjured up a fictional lover since I was thirteen and Edward Rochester rode into my imagination on his black horse.

Sunday afternoon, Ev's and my kisses were leisurely and deep, rather than desperate, but when he began to caress my breast, I stilled his hand and hissed at him, "What are you doing?"

"I'm *touching* you, Al, that's all. God, you're so lovely," he murmured, and he lowered his mouth to my nipple.

Later, we talked a little, about my father's decline, how pretty Suzy had looked, our separate plans for the following day, and how we'd meet up again in the evening. Not love talk, exactly, more like married talk, which offers its own pleasures. In that domestic closeness, I told Ev that I'd asked Esmeralda about his missing paperweight, and that she said she hadn't seen it. She had seemed insulted by the question, as if I'd accused her of taking it, reminding me of how awkward I often am around household help. I still hadn't mentioned my evil thoughts about Scott and the Clichy to Ev.

I untied the black grosgrain ribbon on my mother's folder. There were handwritten copies of several of her poems inside, with words crossed out and replaced in red pencil, in the same small, neat, girlish hand, *her* hand. My heart knocked at the sight of it, at the thought of what remains, but I examined the poems themselves at first with a more detached editorial curiosity. Habit, I suppose. I've always enjoyed trying to follow the trajectory of a writer's revisions; why the specificity of "January" instead of "winter," the decision against alliteration in one poem and the indulgence of it in another. I noted all the references to nature, and looked for literary influences.

My father had given her volumes of poetry on occasions like Valentine's Day or their wedding anniversary. These were usually supplementary gifts, accompanying the main offerings of jewelry or furs. He had chosen books by poets like Elizabeth Barrett Browning and Sara Teasdale, or anthologies of love poems, and he'd written inscriptions on the flyleaves of most of them. "Darling Helen, let me count the ways." The ones she'd bought for herself included Cavafy, Bishop, Dickinson, and Larkin, and she'd annotated those pages with underlined passages, asterisks, question marks, and exclamation points. I began to see a contradiction among the things that had most moved or interested her—despairing irony and determined joy—and a favoring of interior rhymes and ambiguous phrases.

She'd kept a careful record in a green ledger of the submissions of her own poems, when and where they were sent, and returned or accepted. Some responses from editors were among her papers, including those that began, "I'm happy to inform you . . ." or "We'd like to publish . . ." The kinds of letters I'd once dreamed of receiving myself, though from more significant places.

There were a few standard rejection slips, but they were either hand-signed or had personal notes appended. "We're swamped now. Can you send these back in the spring?" "This came close. What else do you have?" I had sent similar notes in the past to young writers I'd wanted to encourage and cultivate, and even started long correspondences with a few of them.

My mother seemed to have had the same sort of vigorous exchange with someone named Thomas Roman, the poetry editor at a quarterly review in Massachusetts called *Leaves* that was now defunct. "Helen," he wrote in one letter dated in March 1972, "it's been a crappy winter, but I am considerably brightened by your latest offerings, which restore the possibility of greenness to me. I'm taking 'Mountain Day.' How is your back, love? Yours always, Tom."

The ease between them was so palpable, I felt like a voyeur. I touched my own lower back, as if I were testing it for vicarious pain. I wondered if my father had ever read that letter or any of several others from Tom Roman in her folder, and what he might have made of them. Well, I'd never be able to ask him now. He hadn't ever specifically spoken about my mother's work to me, although he did say, in a letter I received at college, that she was "still scribbling away."

I was reading a long poem of hers, either a first or final draft, because it was unmarked by her red pencil, when I found that my hand had crept inside my robe to touch my left breast, the breast Ev had bent to so passionately the night before. I continued reading while I lifted my arm and began the standard breast examination, moving my fingers in concentric circles, from the nipple outward. I did this once a month, usually in the shower, with wet lather on my fingertips to make the process smoother. That morning, two things happened at the same moment. I read a line in the poem that arrested me, and I felt a thickening under my fingers. The line was the final one: "Then the goose ate that feathery / thing and flew away." "Oh," I said, not certain of what I was responding to.

I got up from the table and went to the mirror in the dining room, where I opened my robe and peered at my breasts. They've held up fairly well, that midlife reward for the agony of underdevelopment in adolescence. I raised my left arm again, and retraced the area where I'd felt something before, but I couldn't detect it now. False alarm. "Alice," my father would chide, "you've let your imagination run away with you again." Whenever he'd said that, after a bad dream had seemed real to me, or my worry over something trivial grew out of bounds, I would picture myself eloping with some fabulous, multicolored creature. This seemed like a similar escalation of fear.

Closing my robe, I went back to the kitchen and my mother's poem. I didn't think she'd ever published it. In fact, it seemed so unpolished, she might not have even revised it. Unless she'd kept a later draft somewhere else. I poked deeply into the back pockets of the folder, searching for another version, but all I came up with was a small square envelope addressed to my mother from *The New Yorker.* I was immediately struck by the date on the postmark: November 18, 1963 — my own birthday, my tenth birthday.

Folded inside was a printed rejection slip for something she must have submitted to the magazine. She'd always subscribed to *The New Yorker,* but I hadn't known she'd ever tried publishing there. It seemed so uncharacteristically ambitious. Scrawled at the bottom of the slip, in pencil, was the single line: "Try us again!" and the initials "C. W." Had she? There were no signs of it, no further correspondence from anyone at the magazine. The paper looked fragile, especially at the crease, as if it had been opened and refolded innumerable times. It was really just another turndown, with the bonus of the handwritten postscript, but I had the sense of having uncovered a key piece of my mother's history.

Except for that final, cryptic line of the unmarked poem, it was fairly straightforward narrative verse about sitting near the lake in Central Park, feeding the ducks and geese. That was something she and I often did together when we went into Manhattan. Faye would save the crusts for us from the stale loaves she used in her banana bread pudding. The poem was untitled. I read it again and found myself trembling. I knew it wasn't poetic quality that had gotten to me, though — my mother had written much better stuff than this. It was the poem's particular content or its language that made me feel the way I did: troubled, anxious, as if I were about to receive unwelcome news.

The reference to Dickinson's "Hope is a thing with feathers" was easy enough to decipher; at some point my mother had experienced a loss of hope. I doubted that it involved a literary disappointment. When the goose ate it and flew away — that must have been when she'd first learned about her cancer. My hand went back to the opening in my robe, but didn't venture inside this time. Or was it when she realized that the treatments could no longer stem the disease?

The poem wasn't dated, so there was no way to really know. The hungry, honking geese at the lake, I remembered, had originally migrated from Canada. Their droppings were as big as a small dog's, and we had to scrape our shoes on the curb after we left the park.

I sipped my cooled coffee, and scanned the pages of the ledger, to see if there was any indication that my mother had sent this poem anywhere. Maybe she'd titled it later, after it had been taken. There were no probable matches among the recorded acceptances or rejections, though, and I didn't have copies of any of the journals in which her poems had appeared. I'd asked my father if I might have them after he'd moved to Scarsdale and downsized his possessions, but they seemed to have vanished during the packing or the move itself.

Suddenly, I lost interest in playing detective. It seemed futile now, and a little boring, but I took my notebook from my purse and jotted down a few things, anyway. "C. W. *New Yorker*, Nov. 18, '63," "Thom. Roman," "Central Pk." "Thing with feathers?"

Then I went to the refrigerator and pulled out a bagel and some Swiss cheese. I realized that I was famished and there were things I had to do: get a haircut; send Parksie some flowers for her birthday, the way my father always did; and then go to the park and work on the bioethics manuscript and on the latest installment of *Walking to Europe*. In the evening Ev and I were going to meet at a church in Chelsea, where Jeremy and Celia's chamber group would perform. I tucked everything neatly back into the accordion folder—making sure I put the note from *The New Yorker* just where I had found it—and carefully retied the ribbon.

I lingered in the shower, turning the hot water up a notch every couple of minutes, until the enclosure felt like a sauna. Without really thinking about it, I closed my eyes and lavishly soaped my breasts. Then I began to examine the left one in the usual circular pattern. *Bingo.* It definitely felt more like a thickening than a discrete lump. That was a good sign, wasn't it? Jesus. I started trembling again in the overheated stall, and all that steam was affecting my breathing.

I got out of the shower, wrapped myself in a bath sheet, and sat down on the closed toilet seat. My mother's mother, the grandmother I'd never known, had died of cancer, too, when my mother was eighteen. It was so widespread by the time it was discovered that no one was exactly sure where the primary lesion had been. The thought of the word *lesion* chilled me even further. Was my father confusing me with my mother when he'd used it the day before?

He had found her tumor himself, and I could only imagine the circumstances of that discovery—sexual delight turned to abject terror. She was a doctor's wife with a family history of malignancy; didn't she do regular self-exams? And why hadn't he found it earlier, before the metastasis? His fingertips were attuned to that kind of blind discovery. I wondered if there had been a rift between my parents, like the one between Ev and me, that was finally resolved in bed. I hadn't noticed any lapses in their paradise, but I was away at school most of the time then and, as I've said, fairly preoccupied. "Let me count the ways," he'd written to her, while she had underlined Larkin's "Beneath it all, desire of oblivion runs." My poor mother, my poor father.

No one can ever convince me that the term *a good death* is anything but an oxymoron. The last-ditch chemotherapies, a few years later, after the cancer had reached my mother's bones, offered their own, additional torments—neuropathies that numbed her hands and feet and left a perpetual taste of metal in her mouth, as if she'd been sucking pennies. She had no appetite, anyway. Faye or my father or I spoon-fed her broth and Jell-O, which she vomited into a basin soon after, while one of us held and stroked her clammy, bristly head.

"Sweetheart, you shouldn't be seeing this," she once said to me in her hoarse new whisper, but I couldn't take my greedy eyes off her. She had always tried to shield me from things that might be offensive or frightening. At scary movies she would cover my eyes with her own hand, that cool, fragrant blindfold, and I got into the habit of protecting myself, of turning away from things I didn't choose to see. Bad training for a writer, I suppose. Was the compulsive blinking I did at ten simply another manifestation of that?

Dr. Augustus Strange, my father's medical school mentor, had worshiped two deities: the preservation of life and the genius of research. The idea was to keep the patient alive until something was developed in the laboratories that could save her. My father was torn between love and love, his love for my mother and his love for the ethical precepts that guided him. He let her suffer longer than he should have, I was positive of it, and just as certain that the choices he'd made, and his flash memories of their consequences, incited his current bouts of anger and depression. Imagining her still alive was only a mitigating aspect of his dementia, a respite from all that oppressive guilt.

I was due for my yearly mammogram in June, only a few weeks away. I could probably move up the appointment if I called and said that I'd found something in my breast. Something that was most likely nothing at all. But my mother's oncologist, Jeannette Joie—oh, the paradox of that name!— had once told her that one should listen to one's body, that intimations of illness and disease are sometimes available to the patient long before any real symptoms. Was this what I'd been trying to tell myself since that disturbing April morning?

I flipped through my notebook, looking for something to support that theory, when I remembered that Dr. Joie was from Montreal—a Canada goose! I made a note of that, too. The appointment at East Side Radiology was at 10 AM on June 13, Friday the thirteenth, as it turned out, but I'm not superstitious. I'd made it months ago, and I knew the receptionist would become cross and difficult if I tried to change it. A couple of weeks probably wouldn't make a difference, anyway, and my own schedule was pretty busy.

Soon I was sitting in the park reading Michael's newest installment. Most of it was very good, although there was still an occasional sense of something vital withheld, or skirted. But the characters were consistently, divinely rendered, especially Joe Packer, and I did something I frowned upon when one of my authors did it—I started to cast the movie.

Joe would be played by Matthew McConaughey, who'd have to grow a mustache for the part, and that beautiful red-haired actress, Julianne Moore, would play his girlfriend, the older woman he meets in the bus station after she runs away from her unhappy marriage. I didn't write to Michael about any of this, for fear of sounding like some starstruck idiot, and because I didn't want to distract him from his own vision of his characters and their story.

He'd called unexpectedly one afternoon the week before, saying that he just wanted to hear my voice, to make sure he hadn't dreamed me up.

He sounded as appealing on the phone as he was on the page. "I figured I'd probably reach some suicide hotline," he said, "but that would just be pretty convenient." His voice was both rough and honeyed, the way I'd imagined Joe's would be. There was a lot of noise in the background, some kind of grinding machinery.

"You sound like you're in Michigan," I said.

"Everyone tells me that," he said, and we both laughed.

The relative intimacy of a telephone conversation after all that e-mailing made me loosen my reserve, and I told him more candidly how much I admired his writing. The revisions were strong, I said—and he'd addressed all of my smaller concerns, about oft-repeated words or similes that seemed forced—but it was important not to hold back emotionally, as he still sometimes tended to do. He kept saying, "Yes, I know. You're right about that. I'll fix it."

Then I explained how a novel had to be pitched these days, maybe in one compelling sentence, and how crucial the sales department was to the fate of any book. It wasn't my usual style to bring up commerce in the middle of a discussion about craft, but I felt a little reckless and giddy that day. "When the time comes," I said, "I might be able to help you place it."

Michael said that at the rate he was going, he'd probably have a draft done by the end of the summer. He proposed delivering it to me then by hand, and I warned him not to rush things, to let the writing follow its natural flow.

The evening of Jeremy's concert, Ev was already waiting in the church when I got there. To my surprise, Scott and Suzy were there, too. Jeremy had invited them, and I was elated by this evidence of our children's autonomy, and that they had outgrown the ferocious hostilities of childhood. They were still so different from one another—Suzy avidly read the program notes, while Scott went through some cards in his own wallet and then checked out a prayer book and the donation envelopes in a pocket in our pew—but now they were civilized beings temporarily bonded by music and family occasion.

A truce must have been called between Ev and Scott, as well, because I saw Ev lean over to whisper something in Scott's ear, making him laugh. Poulenc and Debussy were on the short program. My clone, Jeremy, blushing under the spotlight at the altar, gave us a shy little salute before the group started tuning up, just as he used to do at school concerts and plays. His girlfriend lifted her bow and waved, too. Scotty and Suzy sat between Ev and me, separating and uniting us, as they did on Sunday mornings in our bed when they were children, and we smiled at each other over their heads as the music began.

6

My uneasiness around household help was probably a throwback to my childhood, when it began as a kind of love affair. Faye Harriet White was born in Beaufort, North Carolina, and came to New York City in search of work when she was thirty years old. My mother had just been confined to bed with the threatened pregnancy that was to result in my safe delivery, and so it was my father who hired Faye, through the auspices of the Maid-Rite Employment Agency (renamed Domestic Arrangements in a more politically correct era), to replace their part-time cleaning woman, to live with them and run their household.

When the story of Faye's hiring was first related to me, I pictured something like an adoption agency in a Shirley Temple movie, with various orphaned maids lined up, each one yearning to be picked, and my father, with his infallible eye and knowing heart, choosing the one shining person in their midst.

Faye was securely in place when I was born, so I can't recall a time before her presence in my life. Our three-story, gray gabled house in Riverdale required a great deal of maintenance. There were gardeners and yardmen, and men who came in on a regular basis to do the heavy work, the window washing and floor polishing. Some of the laundry—like my father's white lab coats, our bed linens, and the curtains—was sent out to a professional service, but Faye attended to everything else inside the house.

I remember doing my homework at one kitchen counter while she chopped onions or punched down bread dough at another, and I can still hear the sputtering hiss of her steam iron in the basement, where she smoothed out the tangles of our personal laundry. But my sharpest memories of Faye involved her care and feeding of me, and served to strengthen the conviction I held then that she was, somehow, exclusively mine.

I was almost ten years old and in the fourth grade at the Chapin School in Manhattan, to which I commuted every day, along with Violet, in a yellow school bus. My study group was doing a unit that term on the Civil War, and our progressive textbooks were filled with hard facts about slavery in easy-to-read language. I examined the illustrations of a slave ship, with its shackles and chains; of an auction at a slave block in South Carolina, where a half-naked woman stood, bound and disconsolate, on a platform, while a man in buckled shoes raised one finger in chastisement or to place a bid; and of the separate, minimal slave quarters on plantations.

Faye, of course, lived right in our house with us. She had her own room and bathroom, off the kitchen. I wasn't permitted to enter her room—another fallout from my mother's commitment to privacy. But sometimes Faye left the door ajar and I could see her single bed with its pebbly chenille cover, the small white television set on her dresser, and one arm of the pink linen lady's chair my mother had had moved in there when she redecorated her own sitting room.

It was a Friday afternoon, and Halloween. Our jack-o'-lanterns had been carved and set on the porch steps, awaiting darkness and their candles. I was going to be a fairy princess again for trick or treat, and Violet, who lived a few streets away, was going to be the Headless Horseman. She had designed the costume herself, and executed it with the help of the Steinhorns' maid, Mattie. It was composed of a folded oak-tag frame that sat across the top of her head, and would serve as a pair of broad shoulders when one of her father's jackets was hung on it. Mattie had sketched in a black hole with Magic Marker, where the head should have been, and Violet drew a shirt collar and tie on the front of the oak tag, punching out airholes and eyeholes with a pair of Mattie's sewing scissors. She intended to tip her father's gray fedora to her invisible head when we went door-to-door that evening.

My mother had gently urged me to try something different and more creative this year, like Violet, but I stuck to the role I loved best, although I knew it was babyish and unoriginal. And I'd requested, and received, a particular store-bought costume that was so puffy and stiff and sparkly, it seemed to transform me. When I came home from school that afternoon and tried it on, complete with tiara and star-tipped wand, I shed glitter everywhere, like fairy dust.

Faye was doing the laundry in the basement and my mother was out shopping for trick-or-treat candy. My father had just returned from performing several hours of surgery at the hospital. He was relaxing in his study the way he loved best, reclining in his brown leather chair in a dressing gown, and listening to a Beethoven symphony on the stereo system. I had taken my social studies book home with me, and I went upstairs and sat at my desk, with some discomfort, in my princess outfit, reading about the destruction of slave families, about children being sold off separately from their parents, and husbands and wives torn from each others' arms.

After a few minutes I became hungry and I went downstairs again, carrying my wand, to look for a snack. The door to Faye's room was wide open. There was a book on her bed—the Bible, I saw with disappointment, as I got closer. From that angle in the doorway I could see her night table, too, with its blue china lamp and a small picture frame. I wondered if it held a photograph of me, like the ones on my mother's dressing table and on my father's desk in his consultation room at Mount Sinai. I crossed the threshold of Faye's room; it took only two or three baby steps before I was inside. The framed photo on her night table was of a skinny black boy about my own age, squinting into the sun in front of a bright green, shingled house. I had never seen the boy or that house before.

I looked down and there was telltale glitter at my feet on the braided bedside rug. I tried to pick some of it up between my close-bitten fingernails but only managed to disseminate more of the stuff onto the rug and the bed. I knew I'd be in trouble with my mother if she saw it, and I was about to go and ask Faye for help when she came to the doorway with a stack of folded towels in her arms. "What are you doing in there, Alice?" she asked.

"Nothing," I said. "Hey, I'm your fairy godmother," I added, waving my wand at her.

"You're my fairy messmaker, you mean. Set that thing down now."

I lay the wand on her night table and picked up the boy's photograph. "Who's this?"

"That's Roger," Faye said. "That's my baby." She took the photograph from me and gazed at it with the melted expression I had always associated with myself, with a time when she still bathed me, and I'd enter a kind of trance as the warm washrag sloshed across my shivery shoulders and down my spine.

"What do you mean?" I asked in alarm.

"He's a lot bigger than that now," Faye said, "but that's my son." She replaced the photo on the night table and swiped at the glass with the corner of one of the towels she still held. "Now I've got to clean up in here, and you've got to get that dress off."

"It scratches," I whined, in a pathetic bid for sympathy, and then I said, "But where does he live?"

"Roger? In Beaufort, with my mother."

"But . . . but . . . ," I stammered. I had so many questions I couldn't formulate any of them. I knew that Faye had a family in North Carolina. Letters and phone calls came periodically for her from them, and every summer, during the two weeks my father joined my mother and me at the rented house in Chilmark, she went down south for her vacation, and to "see everyone." I had envisioned those reunions as a kind of pastoral mob scene, with cousin-friends and aunts and uncles, everyone hugging and smiling, but no one especially close or important to Faye.

This was the most stunning news I'd ever heard. It slid into place in my chest so decisively, I knew it could never be removed. Even more extraordinary was the sight of Faye herself right then, casually arranging towels on the rack in her adjoining, pink-tiled bathroom.

I grabbed my wand and ran out of the room, through the kitchen, and down the hallway into my father's study. The symphony had just reached a crescendo and I had to really shout over it to be heard. "How could you! How *could* you!" I cried. And I stamped my feet as hard as I could on the Oriental rug beneath them.

His eyes were closed and he didn't respond for a few moments, but I knew he wasn't sleeping by the way his pale, beautifully tapered fingers kept time with the music on the armrests of his leather chair. Then his eyes opened and he said, irritably, "What is it, Alice?"

"It's you, Daddy!" I yelled. "You're a mean, terrible slaveholder!"

"What!" The music continued relentlessly over our heads.

"You sit here listening to your precious stupid music while your poor slave works her fingers to the bone," I said, shaking my wand at him until fairy dust was scattered across his paisley dressing gown like dandruff. But my father refused to disappear.

He hoisted himself up with effort from the depths of his chair, and brushed his hands ineffectually at the clinging silvery glitter. "What in hell are you talking about?"

"You know perfectly well. Faye! *Faye!* Who you brought here in chains and she can't see her own child! You slaveholder, you! Oh!" And I burst into furious tears.

"Alice," my father said through his teeth. "Go to your room. Right this minute!" I watched the changing patterns of rose and white bloom on his angry face. "Do you hear me?" All of Riverdale could hear him. I stood my ground for a second or two and then I flung the wand at him and fled.

Up in my room, the room that had once been featured in *House & Garden*, I flounced around in helpless rage for a while before I went next door to my playroom and with great deliberation took a couple of Erlenmeyer flasks from the science corner and threw them against the wall. I didn't know what to do with myself after that, so I tossed a couple of Bulgarian dolls after the flasks, which had satisfactorily shattered. Then I marched back to my bedroom, plopped down at the desk, and scrolled a sheet of paper into my Olivetti. "Far from my native state," I rapidly typed, as if I were plunking out an exercise on the piano, "I've come across this land / to find my poor slave fate, at a cruel, cruel master's hand." *There.*

As soon as I finished typing, my mother opened my door, without knocking—didn't *my* privacy count?—and strode into the room. "Alice," she said. "What can you have been thinking?"

"What do you mean?" I asked, evasively.

My mother sank onto my bed. "Sweetheart," she said. "You have deeply hurt your father's feelings."

"Well, he deserves it," I said, although everything that had happened was a little muddled in my head now.

"Oh, you don't mean that. Daddy is a wonderful man. And Faye is certainly *not* a slave. Where did you ever get such an idea?"

I shrugged.

"Your father pays her a handsome salary," my mother said. "And we both care about her very, very much."

"But she doesn't live with her little boy!" I cried.

"That's true," my mother agreed. "But that isn't Daddy's fault." She paused. "There are many difficult things in this world," she said, "and nobody to blame for them."

"I broke my flasks," I said, needing to claim responsibility for something.

"You did? Let me see."

We went into the playroom together, and all my mother said when she saw the costumed dolls lying among the shards of glass, like the victims of a Balkan war, was "Please don't walk barefoot in here, Alice." Then she crouched to pick up the larger pieces of glass. "Oh!" she cried out a moment later. She had cut her finger, and I marveled at the crimson brilliance of the blood that welled up, like the blood on the cambric the queen gives her daughter in "The Goose Girl."

It's established in the first paragraph of the story that the king is dead, and that the widowed queen has sent her beautiful daughter out on horseback, accompanied by a waiting-woman, to meet the prince to whom she's betrothed. But soon after they start out on their journey, the waiting-woman forces the princess to exchange places with her. This was one of my favorite parts, because it meant that we aren't bound forever by what we appear to be. But it was terribly sad, too. I could almost hear the blood drops on the cambric intone, "Alas queen's daughter, if thy mother knew thy fate . . ." and the blood inside my head thudded in response. What if, in some unrecoverable instant, I had managed to coerce Faye, an African queen's daughter, a true princess, to switch places with me, and become my indentured servant?

After my mother put a Band-Aid on her finger, she told me that my father had petitioned her for leniency toward me, which I doubted; it was probably the other way around. She said that I had to go downstairs and apologize to him for my rudeness, after which I would be allowed to have supper at Violet's, as planned, and then go out trick-or-treating, with Mattie as our escort.

We went downstairs to my father's study. The music was off now and he was back in his chair, sipping a Gibson. Sometimes he would offer me the little pickled onion. I approached him slowly, propelled by soft nudges from my mother, right behind me. Then I stood there, not saying anything.

"Alice wants to say she's sorry," my mother said.

"Oh? And are you her ventriloquist, Helen?" my father asked. But he sounded amused, and his face was all one neutral shade again.

I stepped a little closer to him, on my own now. "I'm sorry, Daddy," I murmured.

"For what?" he prompted.

"You know. For saying mean things, for being rude."

"I see," he said. "Not exactly royal behavior, was it?" He reached out and straightened my tiara, which must have slipped during all the excitement. I could smell the soap on his hands and the gin on his breath. When he finally proffered the onion, I snapped it up, the way a dog takes a treat.

I was lying on my bed later when Faye stuck her head in. "You sleeping?" she asked. I shook my head, and she came all the way in, dragging the Hoover behind her. She went past me into the playroom and vacuumed up the remaining splinters of glass. They made satisfying little popping sounds, like firecrackers. Faye came back through my room on her way out. "Do you want some tomato juice, girl?" she asked, and I shook my head again. I didn't look directly at her, but I could still see her neatly plaited hair, her bosom rising and falling under the flowered field of her housedress.

As soon as she left, I went to my desk and tore the poem I'd written about her into pieces almost as small as the splinters of glass. How had I ever thought I could squeeze her large and complicated life into my narrow, sentimental rhyming scheme? Her life was a *story*, a story that I immediately began to compose inside my head. "Fayella Henrietta Brown was born in Charleston, South Carolina . . ."

Mattie told Violet she absolutely couldn't wear her Headless Horseman costume during supper, which we were going to eat in the Steinhorns' kitchen. She was not even allowed to drink her milk through a straw pushed into one of the airholes in the oak tag. Violet said that she hated Mattie, right to her face, and Mattie said, "I hate you, too." Then she served us her special baked macaroni and cheese and buttered green beans.

By nightfall our decorous Riverdale neighborhood had undergone a metamorphosis. Jack-o'-lanterns leered from windows and doorsteps, like ill-behaved children of the moon that followed us faithfully from behind the trees. The more creative families on Morning Glory Drive had fashioned fluttering ghosts from bedsheets wrapped around lampposts, and the people at the house that was always so overdecorated at Christmas had installed sound effects for this holiday: owls hooting, chains clanking, and maniacal laughter.

On Magnolia Way, our class mother at Chapin came to the door dressed as a witch, and she cackled unconvincingly as she dropped Milky Ways and Mounds bars into our trick-or-treat sacks. Violet's costume was as big a hit as I'd feared it would be, and she tipped her father's hat over and over at every stop, to repeated acclaim and Mattie's and my disgust.

At home my mother emptied my sack onto the kitchen table and carefully examined my loot, on the lookout for razor blades embedded in caramel apples, or ant poison stirred into homemade treats. "What is this world coming to?" she said sadly to my father, who was helping himself to some M&M's in passing.

Faye was in her bedroom with the door shut. I could see the yellow light under it, flashing blue, and hear the murmur of her television set, interrupted by bursts of canned laughter. I can swear that time lurched forward at that moment, like a train that had been stalled between stations. But of course I couldn't have known then that someday I would keep a series of my own slaves, with exotic names like Grazyna and Olympia and Lupe and Esmeralda.

That Halloween night, my mother allowed me to have only one piece of candy, from a known source, before bedtime. I made my final choice after agonizing consideration—a hard, red, bite-sized square—and I sucked on it slowly, letting its sweetness last as long as I could.

7

On June 12, the day before my scheduled mammogram, I was awakened by the telephone. It was Marsha, the receptionist at the radiologist's office, calling to remind me that I was expected there at noon the following day. As if I could forget. She instructed me, as she does every year in that militant manner of hers, to be on time and not to use any deodorant or talcum powder. I listened to her groggily. I had been dreaming about work, about my old job at G&F. There were piles of manuscripts on my desk and I couldn't find my pencils. It was only a variation on the old examination dream, where I'm either late or unprepared, that I've had on and off since high school.

A few weeks after Everett and I got married, I had what I realized was the wedding version of the same dream: I'd forgotten to buy a bridal gown, my flowers were wilting and they were the wrong color, a truly violent purple. As I told Violet later, none of that made any sense, because we had eloped, and a formal dress and flowers were never even a consideration.

She immediately began to pontificate about purple as a symbol of mourning and that the wilted flowers might signify my fear of the marriage's failure, its *death*—maybe just in the sexual department.

"Oh, yeah?" I said, to cover the little ripple of panic she'd elicited. "And maybe it's just a dream about flowers and dresses. Didn't Freud himself say that sometimes a cigar is just a cigar?"

Violet gave me a pained look. "Our dreams are not merely transparent comments on our lives," she said sternly, "or we wouldn't bother having them."

Now I glanced at the bedside clock. It was only ten of eight—why did they have to round up their patients a day ahead of time, and at the crack of dawn? I could sense, without looking, that Ev was no longer beside me in the bed. I listened for the shower or for noises from the kitchen, but the apartment was silent. Of course; he'd told me the night before that he had to be at the plant in Hoboken first thing in the morning. "Yes, thanks, Marsha," I said into the phone, cranking my voice up from its usual low morning register, so she wouldn't think I was a late riser with nothing important to do. Then I was stuck with the day, a whole long day before my mammogram.

I've never met a woman who doesn't worry, at least a little, about her breasts. It starts in early adolescence, when you think you'll never get them, or, as in Violet's case, that the ones you've gotten are too sudden and disgustingly big. Sometimes they grow, as mine did, modestly, but at independent rates, like a pair of fraternal twins. My friends and I were spared some embarrassment by going to an all-girls school, although we were pretty critical of one another and of ourselves. And on an intramural outing in the park with some boys from Collegiate, we were wearing our regulation shorts and gym shirts with our names embroidered over the breast pocket, and a keyed-up fat boy yelled, "Hey, A. Brill! What's the name of the other one?"

I guess I was lucky. The first words most girls ever hear about their breasts are vulgar—*tits, jugs, boobs, hooters*—creating further humiliation in the bearer of such conspicuous accessories. But then men fall in love with them, and babies are nourished at them, and they sag a little or a lot from years of service, and you mourn the beauty you were late to recognize, and you start to think of cancer. Well, I did, anyway. There was history at work—my grandmother, my mother—putting me at high risk. So I'd always been meticulous about self-examinations and checkups.

Sitting in one of those little airless changing cubicles in a paper gown, waiting my turn at fate, I would pretend to read the withered, dated *Newsweek* in my hand, but all I could think of were the scary odds, and how much I *needed* deodorant or talcum powder. Once the exam was over, though, and I was given the all-clear, my relief was profound, as if the governor had just called the warden to grant me a one-year reprieve.

Later on the morning of the twelfth, I buried my concerns in work, first on my socialite's memoir, with all its thrilling gossip and fractured sentences, and then on the riveting issues of stem-cell research and euthanasia in the bioethics manuscript, which was slowly growing and becoming more accessible. Finally, I got to Michael's novel. I was always hungry for new pages from him, even when they were flawed, and I imagined how eagerly Dickens's readers must have looked forward to each installment of his serialized novels. Michael had developed a similar skill for finishing nearly every chapter on a note of emotional or narrative suspense that pulled you right into the next one.

In his latest pages Joe Packer was recalling the childhood he shared with his sister, Caitlin, a relationship far less easy than Holden and Phoebe Caulfield's. Joe was ambivalent about Caitlin, who had stepped on his heels, as he put it, by being born only sixteen months after he was. He had been much happier before her appearance, and she'd been a source of trouble all their lives, but he credits his sentimental education to his sister. Although she's younger, by mere months, she seems years older and wiser than he is, as if she had been born experienced.

During one retrospective passage, when the family is on vacation at a lakeside cabin, Caitlin dares Joe to go skinny-dipping late at night when everyone around them is asleep. They're ten and eleven years old, in transition between innocence and knowledge, and she leads the way into sexual curiosity, without any subsequent action. He compares her sleek, featureless body seen in moonlight with a flower caught in the freeze-frame of a movie he once saw in school that depicted, in slow motion, the flower's blossoming. He's ashamed, in an almost biblical way, and as delighted as he will be one day by the sight of the fully developed female form, that movie speeded up to its grand, voluptuous conclusion.

I was reminded of the satisfying neatness of my own body in childhood, before modesty and impatient desire kicked in, before the coming attractions of life became all that mattered. Violet and I, doing our sister act in the carriage, my small lolling self in the bathtub, under Faye's liquid gaze. And then I came back with a start to the body I was currently living in, and from there right to the next day's appointment.

If I had married Arthur Handler, as I'd once believed I would, the whole thing might have been resolved by now. Arthur had become a gynecologist; he'd have examined my breast right away and assured me that the thickening I'd felt was just normal tissue. When you're married to a writer, or just a writer at heart, all he can do in a medical crisis is succinctly articulate his own fears, which only confirm yours. So I'd decided not to tell Ev what was worrying me until I'd had the mammogram and my worries were over.

I was on the verge of becoming engaged to Arthur when my mother's chemotherapy stopped working. Arthur was in his final year of medical school at the University of Iowa and I was just across the river in the English-philosophy building, finishing my MFA. We'd met while jogging around the campus, so we were both sweaty and breathless before we'd even exchanged any words. I thought his opening gambit, "Do you run here often?" was kind of cute. It was the mid-1970s, when jogging was just becoming a national craze, and we earnestly compared our speed and stamina and the buoyancy of our sneakers. What else did we talk about? I'm not sure, but it must have been something pleasant and provocative because we arranged to meet for a drink later.

He was fair-skinned, with sandy blond hair, and by the end of the evening I'd had the shockingly inappropriate thought that our children would have to wear sunscreen. So I suppose there was an immediate physical attraction, and it was exciting to get to know someone outside the incestuous world of the workshop. Everything we did there revolved around our writing, around the worlds of our imaginations and ambitions. The fiction writers didn't even mingle that much with the poets and playwrights, as if there were a danger of cross-pollination.

Arthur's education was far more grueling and wide ranging and concrete than mine. He had memorized the Table of Elements and Newton's Laws of Physics, and he could name every bone in the human body, from the cranium to the metatarsals. I listened with rapt appreciation for the beauty and logic of the language. If my father had discussed the humerus or the scapula at dinner, I probably would have been bored to tears, but when Arthur did it, it became a kind of poetry.

I understood that part of my pleasure in him was an echo of my parents' pleasure. When my father heard that I was dating a medical student, he expressed his instant, enthusiastic approval. "Now your head's out of the clouds," he said, with an oblique reference to my previous boyfriend, a double major in meteorology and Victorian literature. And in a telephone call from my mother, when she was still feeling reasonably well, she asked if things were "getting serious" between Arthur and me and I said, "sort of," with complicit coyness. She sighed, with what I took to be contentment.

Arthur and I had already talked dreamily of a future together, like collaborators outlining a novel about our own lives. He would doctor and I would write; it sounded so sane and so safely familiar. Best of all, he loved my stories, which I read aloud to him in bed, our version of the postcoital cigarette. Looking back, his unconditional admiration seems unsurprising. He was still flushed with sexual happiness whenever I read to him, and I mostly wrote about us, in a thoroughly idealized fashion. Things didn't always end happily, but even tragedy, in my hands, had a kind of romantic appeal, at least for Arthur.

Everett Carroll, on the other hand, was my literary nemesis, and I, in turn, was his. The trouble with my stories, he pronounced in the workshop, was that too much happened in them, without any credible foundation for what he termed "all that *sturm und drang*." His own stories, usually written in the popular and annoying present tense, were so minimal they were barely there, and I observed that he was stingy with language, and much too reserved emotionally. Besides, *nothing* ever seemed to happen in his fiction.

In the middle of the wintry spring semester, I presented a story to the group only a day or two after Arthur had declared it sublime. Ev was the first one to comment in class, as usual, with almost a knee-jerk reaction. "What's missing for me," he began, with a surreptitious glance in my direction, "is true cause and effect. The guy only dies because the author *authorizes* it."

"And you don't believe in randomness," I said mockingly.

"Hold it, Alice," our instructor, Phil, said. "Let Everett finish."

"This is a *story*," Ev continued, as if there'd been no interruption. "It's supposed to give random events a meaningful *shape*." I couldn't stand the way he emphasized certain words, in that condescending tone some people use to talk to children or the elderly. What kind of phony name was "Everett," anyway? And "Ev" sounded like a woman, even if he was so blatantly masculine.

Someone else in our group tried to interject, citing Chekhov and siding with me, I think, but Ev cut him off. "Chekhov's characters *earn* their tragedy by their humanity. But there's no shock of recognition here. Not for me, anyway."

How could there be, when he was hardly human? "It's not about you!" I shouted.

"Exactly!" he shouted back.

We went on like that until Phil slammed a book on the table and yelled, "Bong!" to indicate the round was over. He'd given up on pushing his philosophy of noncompetition. Now he just wanted to keep us from killing each other.

That evening there was beer and pizza at somebody's house on South Gilbert Street. Arthur was cramming for exams, so I went to the party without him. It was the usual scene: loud music, blue lights, manic postworkshop chatter around the crowded room. Ev came up to me soon after I walked in. I was immediately aware of how aggressively big he was. Arthur was muscular, but compact, and we were almost the same height. At least we see things eye-to-eye, I thought at that moment, as if I'd been called upon to defend our relationship. Ev handed me a bottle of beer and grabbed another for himself. "Listen," he said. "I'm afraid I was a little hard on you this afternoon."

"Don't worry about it," I said, and turned to walk away.

He touched my arm. "I think you're really smart . . . ," he began.

"Thank you," I said stiffly, before he could continue. I wasn't in the mood for a belated handout from such a complacent bully.

"You just have to curb your passion a little."

I took a long swig of beer, wiped my mouth with the back of my hand, and plunked the bottle down on a table. "Oh?" I said. "And how would you know, since you don't seem to have any at all?"

He set his bottle down alongside mine. Then, without warning, he put his arms around me and kissed me hard on the mouth. I could feel the pressure of his teeth and taste the cold, beery breath we shared. I pulled away from him, enraged and intensely self-conscious. I glanced around, but to my amazement no one seemed to be looking at us. "What do you think you're doing?" I demanded.

"Demonstrating my passionate side," he said, flashing a sudden, unnerving smile.

"Save it for your writing," I told him, and I strode out of the room onto the front porch. It was snowing again. I had gotten a ride with friends, but I wasn't going to look for them now. I'd walk back to my place, even though it was very cold and I'd worn only a light denim jacket.

Ev came out a moment later, holding his hands up in a gesture of surrender. "Okay, okay," he said. "So I'm an idiot."

"At least we agree on something."

"Don't go, Alice," he said. "Please don't."

"Why not?" I wasn't fishing, I was genuinely curious. What did he want from me, anyway?

"Because I'll feel like hell if you do."

"That will be your problem, won't it?" I was shivering, shuffling my feet in a little get-warm dance.

"I'm trying to say that I'm sorry. Can I give you a ride, at least?" He was in shirtsleeves and shivering, too. He took a loose cigarette from his pocket. "Or a smoke?" He held it out to me and then lit up. "Or a brand-new Buick convertible?"

I laughed, attempting to sound sardonic. "You shouldn't smoke," I said with my father's imperious inflection. *And get a haircut,* I almost added; his dark curls were in a tumult around his attentive face.

He flicked the cigarette into the snow below the porch. "Okay," he said. "I won't."

"Good night," I told him, and made my way carefully down the icy steps. But this time he didn't come after me.

As Arthur and I became more deeply involved, the news from Riverdale grew more and more harrowing. Arthur was with me in my bed on Church Street when my father called and asked me to come home. "Daddy!" I cried. "What are you saying?"

Arthur gave me a questioning look, and I threw myself against him. He stroked my back and kissed my hair, while I finished my sobbing conversation with my father.

All they could offer my mother now was palliative treatment, something for the pain, something else for her spirits. It would probably be just weeks now, my father said in a weary, heartbroken voice, and she wanted to see me. Arthur offered to go, too, for the weekend, anyway, but I told him not to, that he needed to study. And I went home by myself.

I was shocked, not just by what had happened to my mother in my absence, but that I had been absent while it happened, and by what I had been doing during that time—writing my passionate little tales, and talking and talking about fiction, that inadequate imitation of life.

My father had referred all of his surgeries to colleagues, and he kept my mother at home, in a hospital bed in their bedroom. He hired nurses for two twelve-hour shifts each day, and he and Faye and I all took our own turns at her bedside. My mother had wanted to see me, but I wasn't supposed to see her. Don't look, sweetheart. Come back later, okay?

She had never let me see her scar, either, and I'd finally resorted to searching out post-op photos in one of my father's medical books, like a kid sneaking peeks at something pornographic behind her parents' backs. But the photos reminded me most of mug shots—the dispassionate faces, the defeated posture.

I wanted to ask my mother everything I had neglected to ask during those lost, languorous years. *Mother, were you happy? What did you really want? Have I disappointed you?* But she asked all the questions and they only skimmed the surface of things, as if this were an ordinary spring-break visit and we still had plenty of time to catch up. So I babbled about Arthur and school, and even about the weather, in that weatherproof room—a failed Scheherazade who couldn't keep anyone alive with her stories.

When the screaming began, only my father and one of the nurses stayed with her. I'd go to my old room, preserved like a shrine to my girl-hood, and shut the door. Sometimes I'd cover my ears and even hum, but I could still hear everything, even the pleading, mollifying woodwind of his voice under hers. And, as if we still shared a bloodstream, I always knew the very moment the morphine hit home, temporarily quelling the fire. I wept when I saw my father's face after those sessions, but I had murderous feelings toward him, as well, because he had let this happen, because he'd let it go on for so long. It took almost four weeks before it was finally over.

Arthur wasn't at the Cedar Rapids Airport when I arrived. I hadn't really expected him to be; although we'd spoken on the phone every day since I was gone, I'd never told him exactly when I was coming back. It was a very late flight—we were delayed by a snowstorm in Chicago—and the terminal was empty, except for a few people waiting to meet other passengers. I stood and watched as they embraced and departed. The ticket counters and the car rental places were closed, and there were no taxis on hand. By the time my suitcase came down the chute, only three or four stragglers were left, and soon they were gone, too. I wondered if I'd be able to get a taxi when I phoned, and knew belatedly that I should have asked someone for a ride before the terminal emptied.

Then the door swung open and Everett Carroll came through, stamping snow off his boots and calling my name. He was carrying a small paper sack. I was too surprised and grateful at that moment to ask how he knew when I was arriving. Much later he admitted that he'd done a little home-work, asking around and checking with the airline on a regular basis. But then he just grabbed my suitcase and handed me the paper sack.

In the parking lot, he curled his free hand around the back of my neck, laying his claim to me and offering consolation at once. My thighs trem-bled as we walked, from jet lag, I supposed, and the layover. From longing.

There were bagels in the sack, Iowa bagels, and they felt hard and cold through the paper. The heater in Ev's car was broken and I had to wipe the fogged-up windshield with my sleeve every time we spoke. We didn't speak all that much, though. When we got to my apartment, we warmed the bagels in the toaster oven and they were wonderful.

8

"Good morning, M! Alas, no e-mail from you today, just the usual unbeatable offers to refinance my mortgage and enlarge my penis. The new pages are simply splendid! I only have some semantic nitpicking, which I'll send on. Does Joe have a nickname for Caitlin? Please don't let it be Cat! Cheers, A."

Out of habit, I looked over my message to Michael with a critical eye, sharpening my mental red pencil as I read. Three exclamation points—I sounded like a teenager on speed, so I deleted the first two. Then the word *penis* looked startling on the screen, even in that ridiculous context, and why had I commented so plaintively about not hearing from him; he wasn't my pen pal, he wasn't *obliged* to write to me. I deleted that entire sentence, and the word *simply* from the next one. What was left had the economy of a telegram; the art of letter writing had clearly been sacrificed to the convenience of technology.

I remembered the letters my mother had received from that poetry editor in Massachusetts, and how effortless and friendly they'd seemed. Even his handwritten signature, his carelessly scrawled given name, imparted a sense of closeness between them. "Yours always, Tom." In comparison, "M" and "A," in neat, legible Courier 10 font, might have been distant relatives in a Russian novel, and "Cheers" came across as utterly phony and ironically cheerless. I moved the cursor back down to the closing of my message to Michael, deleted it, and typed in "Yours, Alice."

Ev came into the room, knotting his tie, and I shut my laptop so quickly I caught my fingers. "Ow," I said, shaking them.

"You okay?" he asked.

Yeah, I thought, except for this one-sided cyber affair I seem to be having, not to mention cancer in my breast and a sensation of disaster right next to it. But all I told Ev was that I was feeling a little achy, which wasn't completely untrue, and he offered to bring me some tea and Tylenol before he left for work. I waved him away, saying I'd be fine, that I just had to go back to bed and sleep it off.

As soon as I said it, it seemed like a good idea. It was early, not even nine yet, and my appointment at the radiologist's wasn't until noon. There was plenty of time. I hadn't mentioned the appointment to Ev, and he couldn't really be expected to remember on his own that another year of grace was up. The more casually I treated the whole business, the less spooked I felt by it.

But I couldn't fall asleep again, so I began rereading Michael's new pages in bed. During Joe's moonlight swim with Caitlin, she darts away from him in the water, appearing and disappearing like a silvery fish. Michael wrote, "When she truly vanished years later, I always imagined her in water, swimming just out of sight, out of my grasp, swimming for her life. What have I done?"

I think I dozed off for a moment or two, and then something strange happened: my mother came suddenly and urgently to mind, as if she were swimming alongside Caitlin, a couple of restless ghosts in search of . . . What? Justice? Retribution? Peace? I felt oddly excited and nervous. God, maybe the thing that was wrong with me was a *brain* tumor.

At ten o'clock I called Violet, with the idea of presenting all of this to her as an actual dream that required her expert interpretation. She relished those rare concessions I made to the role of the unconscious in my life. But after several rings her machine picked up, and I was treated to a few bars of hip-hop followed by Violet's throaty voice saying, "Hi, you've reached Nirvana. Well, actually you've missed me, so leave the usual details."

"Oh, grow up," I muttered after the beep. Then I called Scott, who worked the late shift at Tower on Fridays, and of course I woke him up. "Ma," he bleated. "God, what time is it?" He sounded as if he were being smothered with his pillow.

"Time to rise and shine, sunbeam," I sang, eliciting another, more protracted groan. He'd hated my saying that when he was a child, too, so why was I needling him after waking him up? Before I could stop myself, I added, breathlessly, "Scotty, Dad can't find one of his paperweights, the blue-and-white swirly one? You didn't happen to see it when you were here, did you?"

"What?" he said.

"Nothing. Go back to sleep. Forget it."

"God," he said again. "What is it, Friday?" And seconds later I could hear that unmistakable even, open-mouthed breathing. Well, at least he hadn't asked me for any more money.

I took a shower, remembering not to use talc or deodorant afterward. Then I sat down in my terry robe at the computer again. I logged onto the Internet and asked Google to search out *Thomas Roman* and *Leaves*. There were pages and pages of hits. Someone named Buddy **Thomas** was selling "genuine" Bible **leaves,** with authentication from the **Roman** Church; a college fraternity home page posted news: "**Roman leaves, Thomas** replaces him as Prez;" a literary site offered poems by **Thomas** Hardy, including "The **Roman** Road" and "During Wind and Rain," with the line "How the sick **leaves** reel down in throngs!" And so on. What did I expect to find, anyway? Some of Tom Roman's letters to my mother were written more than forty years ago; he might be dead by now, too, and I had no idea what I would do if I discovered he was still alive.

But I refined my search, typing in "Leaves Literary Magazine" and "Thomas Roman," carefully enclosing each phrase in quote marks, and came up with only one match, but a perfect one. Tom Roman—my mother's Tom Roman, I was certain of it—lived in Vergennes, Vermont, now, and sold back issues of *Leaves* from his home. I hoped that wasn't his sole means of support. I placed an order for all of the issues between 1961, the date of his earliest letter to her, and 1978, the year of her death, thinking, that should make his day. Then I opened the "contact us" link and began to compose an e-mail message. "Dear Thomas Roman, you don't know me, but I believe you were a friend of my mother's."

My fingers were still suspended over the keyboard, but I couldn't think of what to say next. Should I mention my mother's death? It would be a bizarrely belated announcement: "I'm sorry to inform you that Helen died twenty-seven years ago . . ." And maybe she had written to him about her illness and he'd figured the rest out for himself when he stopped hearing from her. Or maybe he'd seen a notice of her death.

"How is your back?" he'd once written to her, and he'd called her "love." Their exchanges were personal as well as professional, and there were so many letters from him in that folder. Could they have been more than just friends?

Where had *that* idea come from? From my own wild imagination, no doubt. Asking after someone's health was just plain courtesy, and *love* really a mild and not uncommon term of affection; my dentist's assistant called *everyone* that. And I hadn't read anything else that suggested a more intimate relationship between my mother and Tom Roman. But there might have been hidden messages, written between the lines, or other letters from him that she had destroyed. A little quiver ran up my spine as I envisioned those letters curling and melting in the flames of one of our Riverdale fireplaces, just as my father came into the room, carrying a Gibson and whistling Mozart.

I was acutely aware of my beating heart, which seemed to be keeping perfect time with the cursor flashing on the screen. Then the phone jangled, and I deleted what I'd just written, hastily, as if I were the one destroying incriminating evidence. "Hey," Violet said. "What's your problem?"

"Oh, you got my message. Sorry, I'm just overtired, I guess—I had such a weird dream. Listen, what are you doing today?"

"Working. Why?"

She was always working. I wanted to tell her that I was on the verge of some sort of psychological breakthrough. And I was going to say that I was frightened, and ask if she'd go to the radiologist's with me, but I found myself unable to say any of that. She would probably end up nagging me again about seeing a therapist, which she'd been doing fairly regularly since my little outburst at lunch. "I don't know," I said lamely. "I thought we'd play or something."

"Don't you have anything else to do?" Violet said, the ant scolding the grasshopper. "How are the books coming, Doctor?" The question was sardonic and sincere at the same time. Years ago, when I abandoned my own writing, Violet was dismayed, but when I took up editing, she'd deemed it a reasonably healthy defense mechanism.

"Stop calling me that," I said. "The books are coming along fine, I guess."

"You *guess*? Don't you know?"

"Yes, yes, I do. They're going swimmingly, they're going like gangbusters, like a house afire!"

"Jesus, Allie," Violet said. "Call me back when you're feeling civil again, okay?"

"Sorry," I said. "Sorry. It's probably only a little distemper. I haven't had my shots. And then there was this stupid dream . . ."

"All right then, you're forgiven," Violet told me. "I've got to go, anyway." And before I could say anything else, she hung up. The phone rang again immediately, and I picked it up and said, "Talk about *civil*." There was a significant pause before a man's resolutely cheerful voice said, "Good morning, ma'am! How are you doing today? I'm calling on behalf of your neighborhood Cancer Care drive—"

"Sorry, can't help you," I said, briskly. "I have cancer myself." Then I shut off the ringer on the phone and went back to the computer and wrote, "Dear Thomas Roman, I am writing a memoir about my mother, the late Helen Brill. You published some of her poems in your journal *Leaves* between the early 1960s and the late 1970s. I've just ordered back issues for that period, which might include work of hers that I'm not aware of. If you can offer any personal remembrances, anecdotes, etc. about her, they would be greatly appreciated. Thanks in advance. Yours, Alice Brill."

I was definitely getting better at this, at prevaricating and putting out bulletins from my fevered brain. To atone for the former, I picked up my journal and actually wrote a few brief lines about my mother—about her handwriting, the sound of her footsteps, her doubled self at the dressing table mirror—the stuff of a beginning workshop exercise, elements of character, that sort of thing. And I made notes on a couple of incidents: the broken glass on Halloween, a picnic in Chilmark made dramatic by a thunderstorm.

I remembered the only time I'd ever seen my mother angry with my father. She had been at her desk, working, and he called her name from another room. When she didn't answer right away, he called again, impatiently, and she yelled, "For God's sake, Sam, what do you *want*?" I think we were all astonished by her outburst.

I read back what I had written; it wasn't bad, and it wasn't really good, but I recognized the particular pleasure of having set something down. Then I yawned; what an exhausting morning it had been. I might have been doing manual labor instead of hanging around in my bathrobe, doodling and being rude on the phone and sending self-conscious e-mails to strangers, like a latter-day Herzog in drag. I stretched out across the bed and settled Ev's pillows and mine all around me in a makeshift nest. My eyes closed against the bars of slanted light coming in through the blinds. I told myself to just get up and get out of there, but it was like talking to Scott on a school-day morning, trying to force an inert object into action. Time to rise and shine, sunbeam. *Five more minutes, Ma*, he used to beg. *Five more minutes*, I agreed, and slid swiftly down the tunnel into sleep.

When I woke, the room was in shadow, and I could see the mute and frantic red pulse of the answering machine across the room. I was afraid to look at the clock and even more afraid of playing my messages. But I finally did both. It was almost four o'clock, and there were three messages. The first one was from Marsha at the doctor's office. "Ms. Brill," she said in the severest of tones. "It is twelve thirty, and you are now half an hour late for your appointment. Please call me *immediately*." The second message had come in twenty minutes later. "Hello. This is Mrs. Hernandez, the eighth-floor nursing supervisor at the Hebrew Home for the Aged. Please call me in reference to your father, Samuel Brill." The third call was a hang-up, the ensuing hum laden with ominous possibilities.

I had missed my mammogram, which was something like missing a plane that might have gone on to crash. I wondered what Mrs. Hernandez wanted. She seemed to be obligated by law or malpractice insurance to inform me of anything untoward in my father's life, from an ingrown toenail to his sudden death. Her voice was always the same—level and courteous—no matter what she was reporting, and I felt my heart swoop a little, the way it used to when the school nurse phoned about one of the kids.

Yet I called Marsha back first, and began offering excuses and apologies before she could uncoil and strike. "Marsha? It's Alice Brill. Gosh, I feel absolutely *terrible*. Believe me, I didn't forget my appointment. I just woke up this morning feeling so achy, I went right back to sleep. It was like a stupor, I must be running a fever." *Feel my head, I think I'm burning up.*

When I was a kid, it was just the sort of easy lie that was bound to bring on suitable punishment. If you cut school and explained that your grandmother had died, well, then, your perfectly healthy grandmother dropped dead in her kitchen the very next day. I put one hand to my cool forehead and then to each of my neglected breasts in an irreverent genuflection. And I listened, in the requisite docile silence, as Marsha reprimanded me, advising that I would have to pay a no-show fee and couldn't possibly be rescheduled for another three months. That heartless bitch; did she want a note from my mother?

If my father were alive, I thought, she'd fit me in a hell of a lot sooner. *If my father were alive.* Maybe I really was sick. I meant, of course, if he were still practicing, but that didn't make much sense, either. I'd never taken advantage of so-called professional courtesy, and even now I didn't make a plea for special dispensation by mentioning the thickening in my breast. I simply accepted another appointment—in mid-September, a different season—practically promising to engrave the date in my flesh.

Then I called Mrs. Hernandez back, trying to ready myself for anything she might have to tell me. On other occasions, she had called to report that my father's hearing aid was missing again or that he was developing a cold, but this was Friday the thirteenth, after all. It took a while to reach her, she wasn't at her desk, and when she picked up the phone at last, I blurted, "What's wrong?"

"Nothing, everything's fine," she said. I could hear assorted screams in the background that seemed to contradict her. "Your father asked me to call you."

"He *did*?" Although he'd claimed at times that he had been trying to reach me, that always proved to be delusional before this, some sort of ESP he imagined we shared. "What about?" I asked anxiously.

"He wanted you to bring him something when you visit. Let's see," she continued, rustling some papers. "I wrote this down someplace. Ah, here it is. Dr. Brill would like some decent notepaper. I offered him one of my pads, but he turned me down flat! That's the way he put it, by the way— '*decent*' notepaper." She chuckled, like a doting grandmother.

I was pleased and mystified. That sounded like his old authoritative self, but I couldn't imagine who he'd want to write to. "Are you sure it was my father?"

"Oh, it was *him*, all right, honey. You'd think he was in the operating room, asking for a sponge. Demanding it, I mean."

"Well, thanks, Mrs. Hernandez, thanks very much. And please tell him I'll bring him some stationery tomorrow."

It had been a day of letters, if not exactly a red-letter day. I went back to the computer to check my e-mail. There were two messages; both of them had come in while I slept. The first one was from Michael. "Dear Alice, Re: Caitlin's nickname, I was thinking of 'Cake,' because Joe couldn't say her name when he was a baby. Yours forever, Michael."

The other message was longer and more like a genuine letter. "Dear Alice Brill, You have given an old man a truly lovely surprise. I'm so glad you're writing about your mother, a dear friend and a fine poet, and I will think long and hard (a necessity these days, I'm afraid!) about your request for specific remembrances of her. In the meantime, thanks for your order of all those back issues of *Leaves*. It's always good to have a new reader. Sincerely yours, Tom Roman. P.S. I'll flag the copies with Helen's poems for you."

9

Ev said that my father probably wouldn't even remember asking for it, but the next morning I went shopping for what he might consider "decent" notepaper, with the proper weight and texture and color—white, of course, but the right *cast* of white. His request delighted me because it was specific and because it sounded so rational, although I still had no idea whom he intended to write to, if anyone at all.

When I was a child, my mother always helped me to choose birthday or Christmas gifts for my father. Left on my own, I would have selected some novelty-store item, a giant golf-ball pencil holder or a tie that lit up when you pressed its knot, but she steered me firmly toward more conventional and conservative alternatives at Saks or Brooks Brothers, like cashmere socks and rep-striped ties that didn't dare do anything unexpected.

Whenever my father received one of these gifts, he'd make the standard fuss, for which I was a pathetic foil. "My, my, what can this be?" he would begin. What could *possibly* have been in that flat little box besides a tie?

But I'd go along with the game by making him guess. And he would wink at my mother and say, "An umbrella? A pair of skis?" to which I'd say that he was getting either warmer or colder, or just dutifully shake my head and giggle. Then, uncovering the tie, he'd exclaim, "Aha! Well, this is very handsome, indeed. Thank you, Alice." And my mother and I would exchange satisfied smiles, although I'd imagine for a wistful moment what he might have said about the one that sparked and flickered like a swarm of fireflies.

I found the perfect notepaper at a small place on Madison Avenue, and I bought fifty sheets and twenty-five matching envelopes. It was very elegant and very expensive, which gave me a moment of perverse pleasure. He's *demented*, I reminded myself, even as I told the salesclerk that the paper was a present for my father, a retired surgeon, who lived in the country now. And I pictured what she must have been picturing: a dignified, tweedy gentleman, as curved as a comma but able and sound, tending his vegetable garden, or sitting in a book-lined den reading Trollope. I didn't know why I'd invented that more palatable image of my father for a casual stranger, or why I'd lied to Tom Roman in my e-mail, about writing a memoir of my mother. Maybe it was just convenient, or comforting. And it seemed like a harmless enough habit, not unlike writing fiction.

When I got to the nursing home, my father had other company. Violet's parents were sitting with him in the solarium, looking ancient and spiffy: Leo in his crested blazer, Marjorie dressed for the cocktail hour. I had been thinking of calling Marjorie, ever since I'd gone through my mother's folder, to see if she knew something significant that I didn't know about the poems or about my mother's private life. I still couldn't shake the sense that she was connected in some way I didn't yet understand to that bad feeling in my chest.

As soon as I walked into the solarium, Marjorie and Leo hauled themselves out of their seats, as if I were there to relieve them of guard duty and had arrived late. Leo even looked at his watch. "Hello and goodbye," he said.

They didn't leave right away, though, as I had hoped they would. "Alice, dear," Marjorie said in her confidential whisper, "don't you look lovely." She brushed my hair off my forehead, stared critically at me, and then let it drop back. *Hopeless*, her expression implied. "You're wearing it longer," she observed before turning her attention to my father in his chair. "And doesn't Dad look well?" The question was like a poke in the ribs; no wonder I'd put off calling her. And no wonder Violet needed all those years on the couch.

My father was wearing an unfamiliar and unlikely yellow plaid flannel shirt, with a conspicuous brown stain under the pocket; he could easily have been mistaken for a retired lumberjack. Someone had mixed up the laundry again. I noticed that his ears had sprouted fur, and there were sticky crumbs of sleep in the corners of his eyes. "Yes," I said, bending to kiss his cheek, "you look great," and certainly no one was hurt by this latest lie, least of all him.

Leo cleared his throat. "Let's get this show on the road," he told Marjorie, clasping her shoulder with one hand and patting my father on the back with the other. "Take care of yourself, sir," he boomed. "We'll see you in a couple of weeks, God willing."

"Goodbye, Sam darling, goodbye, Alice dear!" Marjorie called, blowing kisses to us as they walked toward the elevators, like a passenger on a cruise ship pulling out of the harbor. An old woman in a wheelchair a few feet away blew kisses back to her. My father hadn't made a sound.

I'd wanted the Steinhorns to leave, but once they were gone I felt strangely forsaken. And it was hard to distinguish between the usual anxiety this place brought on and that special misery I lugged everywhere lately. I took the package of stationery from my tote bag. "Daddy, I brought the notepaper you asked for." When he didn't respond, I tore the foolishly lavish wrapping paper off myself and opened the box. "Look," I said brightly. "Is this the kind you wanted?"

Everyone seems to have one parent whose approval we crave our entire lives and never fully receive. I remember how I longed for and dreaded his gaze upon me, that fierce searchlight of attention when I was being clever or annoying. Once again, I had that desperate impulse to please, as his eyes skittered across my face to the offering I held out and then to the room at large. He was like a child with ADD, wanting to escape the tedious demands of school. "Sam!" I said sharply, and he looked directly into my eyes for the first time. "Here is your notepaper. Do you want to write to someone?"

"Yes," he said, his rusty voice rising from the unused plumbing of his throat. It gave me a thrill, as if I'd taught an animal to speak.

"Who to?" I asked.

In the old days, he would have promptly corrected me. "It's *to whom*, Alice," he'd say, even after *whom* fell out of common usage, but this time he simply ignored my impertinent question. Resorting to sign language, he mimed holding a pen and writing in the air.

I dug a ballpoint out of my tote and arranged a sheet of the beautiful notepaper on top of the box. "Here," I said, handing him the pen and putting the rest on his lap. I realized that I was holding my breath and I let it out slowly as he sat there, frowning at those suspect implements of communication.

Just then the elevator doors slid open and Parksie came through them toward us, carrying a cake box by its string. She was in her mid-seventies now, plumped up in places, collapsed in others. Her eyes were still lined with smudged kohl, her hair that improbable shade of apricot. I jumped up to meet her and we hugged. She smelled of Jean Nate and baby powder, her bosom against mine as smothering and restful as a scented pillow.

"Alice, how are you? And how is your dear family?" she asked, speaking softly and with genuine interest. I was happy to see her, but fearful that she would break my father's fragile thread of concentration.

I needn't have worried. Years ago, I'd seen Parksie come to the threshold of his consultation room on her silent white shoes, and wait with remarkable patience while he finished examining a backlit X-ray or whatever he was reading at his desk, before she announced herself and the business that had brought her there. And he never acknowledged her solid, expectant presence in any way until he was good and ready. Now she stood a few feet from him in that same attitude, dangling the cake box from one pudgy finger. *Hers not to question why.* Dr. Brill was engaged and could not be disturbed.

We both waited, as if at a performance (the theater of the absurd, I couldn't help thinking), for the action to begin, and we were rewarded a minute or two later when my father began to write. He gripped the pen hard and wrote rapidly and with a characteristic flourish, line after line after line. He might have been trying to get it all down before he forgot what he wanted to say. His whole head trembled with the effort, but his hand was surprisingly steady.

Soon, he'd covered both sides of the paper, and I was about to offer him a fresh sheet when he retracted the ballpoint with a decisive click and held the pen out to me. He was done. I took the pen and the box with the filled page floating on top of it, and he put up no resistance. In fact, I felt dismissed, because he turned his attention to Parksie then, beckoning with one crooked finger—her old cue—and she approached him. They were in the blurry background of my vision, Parksie crouching at his wheelchair, my father pulling at the string on the cake box, as I stepped off to the side and stared at the piece of paper.

What he'd written with such furious intention was the word "Darling," in a surprisingly clear and graceful script, followed by streams of erratic peaks and declivities, like the electrocardiogram of a heart in crisis. The pen had bitten through the paper in several places, as if he'd meant to emphasize some indecipherable lines more than the others. There were no other recognizable words or symbols on either side of the page.

"Parksie," I said. "Could I speak to my father alone for a minute?"

She tilted her head inquiringly, but she didn't say anything as I helped her up. She just walked across the room to a sofa near the murmuring television set and sat down among strangers. *Hers but to do or die.*

I sat down, too, right next to my father. "Daddy," I said, and he deigned to look at me while his fingers caressed the cake box in his lap. I held the sheet of paper inches from his face. "Is this for me?" I asked, realizing as I said it that I used to ask my children that precise question whenever they'd finished another piece of refrigerator art. But then the question was merely rhetorical—all of their drawings were for me. Addressing a child's first creative efforts was a delicate process every young parent quickly learned. You never asked what a drawing represented; instead, like a canny, non-directive therapist, you said, "Do you want to tell me about it?"

I knew that I would have to approach my father the same way in his hideous new childhood. "Is this for me?" I asked again, waving the paper at him, and he snatched it from my hand and said, "No!" How had this monosyllabic statue of my father ever conveyed his wish for notepaper to Mrs. Hernandez? Maybe I was the only one he wasn't talking to.

"Do you want to tell me about it?" I said, and my tears rose up and spilled over. He didn't seem to notice, and he didn't answer. His expression wasn't blank, though; it was bold, almost rebellious.

"Is it for Mother?" I persisted. "Sam, is it for Helen? My heart was banging to get out, while he held those hieroglyphics hostage in his fist. A surge of anger came on like a speeding car. I wanted to hit him. "Tell me," I demanded. *"Tell me!"* And I imagined him standing up and shouting, *Alice, go to your room!*

People were glancing at us. I could see Parksie on the other side of the solarium, pretending to watch the game show on the television screen, but her face reflected my shocking impropriety. I was making a scene. I was bullying a helpless, senile old man in front of witnesses.

"Daddy," I said in a more subdued voice. "Who is the letter for? Don't you want me to deliver it for you?" They were the magic words, or he'd simply given up the fight, because his hand unclenched and the paper fell soundlessly at my feet. "Thank you," I said, bending to pick it up. "Now, to *whom* should I give your letter? Won't you please tell me?"

Again he didn't answer, and his eyes had become unfocused and as flat as pennies. When I snapped my fingers, he barely blinked, and I slumped in defeat.

Somehow, Parksie knew that it was time to come back across the room. "Is everything all right?" she asked.

"Sure," I said. "We're fine." And suddenly I remembered how she'd looked long ago in her pristinely white, starched uniform, like the bride of the god of suffering, with that dove of a hat poised on the back of her head, ready to fly off. *Then the goose ate that feathery thing and flew away.* "Parksie," I said. "Something is bothering me."

"What is it?" she asked with concern.

"That's the problem, I don't actually know. It's just that I feel bad, or guilty, about something."

Her eyes glistened with sympathy. "Everyone feels that way when their parents fail," she said. "We always think we haven't done enough." For the first time I wondered who her parents were, and if she believed she had failed them. Like Faye, she seemed to have come to my family without personal history, without her own needs and desires, as if we'd invented her. Her real name was Eleanor. Had anyone ever called her Ellie? She was the unmarried aunt in the family, the governess in Victorian literature whose story turns out to be at the center of everything.

"It's not that," I said, "or at least not only that. Although I think it has something to do with my mother." I felt as if I were feeling my way blindly along the edge of a cliff.

"Oh, but you never let her down, Alice," Parksie assured me. "She absolutely adored you. Why, you were her life."

"But there was Daddy, too," I said, "and her poetry." *My jealous sibling,* was my unbidden thought.

"You came first," she insisted, and a swell of gladness flooded that rough place in my chest. How intuitively kind Parksie was.

"Did she ever talk to you about her work?" I asked.

"Do you mean her poems? No, she never did."

Of course she hadn't. And she would never have spoken to Marjorie Steinhorn, either, about her poems or anything else essential to her, or private. They weren't friends, exactly; they were simply two women who happened to serve on the same committee, a committee dedicated to the success of their husbands' careers. My mother had nobody like Violet in her life. I went on, anyway. "Did she ever happen to mention anyone she corresponded with about her poetry, anyone called . . . Tom?" I made it sound as if I had just plucked his name from a hat.

"I don't think so," Parksie said. "Who is he?"

"No one, really. It's not important." I thought fleetingly of asking her about the thickening in my breast. She was a well-trained surgical nurse, and her opinion could be trusted, but I'd remembered someone else I could approach about that. I decided to just leave and let Parksie and my father share the angel food cake or the *babka* she'd brought—why did elderly people have such a craving for sweets? She would probably try to soothe away the turmoil I'd caused him. Then she'd go back to Roosevelt Island, to the high-rise apartment she'd moved into after she retired.

Esmeralda was putting the vacuum cleaner away when I came home. The coins from Ev's pockets that she'd retrieved from under the sofa cushions were piled up on the kitchen counter as irrevocable proof of her honesty. But she seemed to have forgiven me for asking her about Ev's missing Clichy, as she cheerfully offered a rundown of current domestic events. Mr. Carroll was in the park, taking a walk. The phone had rung many times during the day, but, as instructed, she hadn't answered it. We needed Windex and Lemon Pledge and Mr. Clean. Scott had come by that afternoon to get some stuff from his old closet. I'd just missed him—such a cute boy.

I still stored various things for all of the children—from high school yearbooks to baseball card collections—although I periodically threatened to throw everything out if they didn't come to claim it. I briefly wondered what Scott had repossessed and why he didn't wait to see us. Then I went to the park.

Ev was sitting, asleep, on a bench near the river, with his face turned up, and I sat next to him and kissed him on the lips. He kissed me back before he even opened his eyes. That evening in Iowa City, when he first kissed me, a few people around us *had* noticed, and for some reason I was perceived as the aggressor. One woman with an overzealous imagination thought that I had *bitten* him, and after that we were sometimes referred to, with mocking envy, as Sylvia and Ted. Maybe they were also thinking about the fireworks between us in the workshop.

Now Ev said, "Did your father like the notepaper? Did he know who you are?"

"He loved it," I told him. "And it doesn't matter who I am."

"Yes, it does," he declared, and to hide my immoderate pleasure, I ducked my head into the curve of his neck and said, "So how was tennis?" Ev played every Saturday morning with two men from his office, on the indoor courts on 89th Street.

"Good. We got three sets in, and I beat Bradley's ass."

He was competitive, that was all. Even as a kid he'd always tried to catch up to his older brother, in school and in sports. It was just his nature; it really had nothing to do with me.

"Did you see Scotty today?" I asked.

"Where?"

I hesitated. "Anywhere," I said slyly.

Ev laughed. "Are you drunk, Al?"

"No. Maybe. I don't know."

We walked home holding hands. The apartment smelled of disinfectant and the last of the Lemon Pledge. I inhaled deeply, as if I needed that chemically pungent air in order to live. Then I rummaged in the refrigerator for the components that would become our supper. Lettuce, eggs, butter, cheese. Ev scooped up the coins on the counter and put them back into his pocket. Later, he would lie down on the sofa and they would fall out again. I decided that I would show him my father's inscrutable note when we were in bed that night. Maybe I'd even finally admit that something intangible was troubling me. If Ev was naturally competitive, it was also in his nature to empathize and want to help when someone he loved was in distress. I would just keep my notebook jottings to myself.

So this is happiness, I thought, seconds before I noticed Ev's blue-and-white paperweight behind the sheer curtain on the kitchen windowsill, catching the last glints of western light.

10

"Hey! Look what's here," Ev said. He had come to the door of the kitchen just as I noticed the Clichy, and he went right to the windowsill and picked it up. "It wasn't here this morning, was it?" He seemed to be talking to himself and to me at the same time.

We had eaten breakfast together that morning in the kitchen; one of us would have noticed it if it had been there. "No, of course not," I said, ripping lettuce into the salad bowl, and groping for a benign and reasonable explanation for the paperweight's reappearance.

Ev polished it, like an apple, on his T-shirt, looking happy but perplexed. "So where did you find it?" he asked.

I contemplated saying that Esmeralda was the one who'd discovered it, on the rug under the side table in the living room, when she was vacuuming. He knew that she had been at the apartment that day, which would have made it a credible lie. But I recalled how offended she'd become when I asked her if she'd seen it, and what if Ev decided to thank her? The two of them were so damned cozy. I might have told him the truth, that I really didn't know where the paperweight had been all this time, and that its recovery was as much a mystery to me as it was to him. But that would have been merely a legal truth. Beneath all the layers of denial, I *did* know; it was just that my usual maternal instincts had kicked in, along with my new talent and propensity for deceit.

"Under the side table in the living room," I said. "It must have gotten knocked off somehow." I took a tomato from a bowl on the counter and chopped it with the celerity of a TV chef. I wouldn't have been all that surprised to find a few fingers in the bloody pulp on the cutting board.

"No scratches, no chips," Ev marveled, holding his treasure up to the light.

"Well, it landed on the rug," I said. "Lucky." My face was torrid, my heart was cold.

Ev put the Clichy back on the windowsill. "I like it there," he said. "Don't you?"

"Yes," I said. And that was that, or at least I thought it was.

The next day I made two phone calls, the first one to Scott, informing his recorded self that I was coming down to his place at six that evening, that it was important and he had better be there. Ev was going to be working late, so I didn't have to make up yet another story to tell him.

The second call was to Jeannette Joie, my mother's oncologist. I was relieved to find her in a recent telephone directory, still alive and still in practice—she was in her early forties when I knew her—although she'd moved from Mount Sinai to NYU. I didn't reach her, either, but I left my name and number with her service, explaining that I was the daughter of a former patient, and that I would like to speak to her.

She called me back in less than an hour. I remembered then that she had limited her practice in order to always be able to return phone calls from patients, and to give them time for real conversation during their office visits. My mother and she had been on a first-name basis. "If not now, when?" Dr. Joie used to say, and my mother once referred to her, without irony, as "my new best friend."

"I'm Helen Brill's daughter," I said on the phone. "She died so many years ago, I don't really expect you to remember . . ."

"But I do," she said, after the briefest pause. "She was a poet, wasn't she? And you were a little redhead."

"That's amazing," I said. It was as if a mentalist had just performed an uncanny feat of perception.

"How is your father?" Dr. Joie asked. "I imagine he must be retired by now."

"Yes, from surgery and from the world in general. He's in a nursing home, with senile dementia."

"Oh, that's too bad."

"But I'm really happy that you're still practicing, although I have to confess that's partly for selfish reasons."

"What's the matter?" she asked.

I told her about the change in my breast, how I had managed to screw up my appointment for the mammogram, and that I was sorry now and frightened. She asked me to hold on for a minute, and when she got back on the line she said that she could see me in her office the next day, at five o'clock, after her last scheduled patient of the afternoon.

That evening I went downtown on the subway to Scott's apartment. He was there, and so were his two roommates, Amy Lowe and Jeffrey Greenberg. At the beginning of their shared tenancy in that tiny space, I speculated about various possible sexual arrangements among them, including a ménage à trois, but all of my conjectures turned out to be wrong. Amy was gay, and both she and Jeffrey had girlfriends living elsewhere. Scott was straight and currently unattached.

Everyone was in the living room—which doubles as Jeffrey's sleeping quarters—when I got there. You would think I'd been invited to a social gathering. The usual clutter was gone—no soda cans, shoes, loose CDs, or remnants of meals. Jeffrey's sofa bed had been folded and covered with a brown-and-orange afghan his grandmother must have crocheted. The three of them were lined up on it, as expectant as heirs to a will, leaving the place of honor, the shaggy, bear-like black velvet chair they'd found at a thrift shop, for me. There was a plate of Pepperidge Farm cookies on the coffee table. The doors to the two minuscule bedrooms, where I was sure the debris had been hurriedly stored, were prudently closed.

I was impressed by the tidy domestic scene they'd managed to effect in

the few minutes since they'd all come home from work, and annoyed that
Scott hadn't figured out from my message that I wanted to speak to him
alone. Or maybe he *had* figured it out and having his roommates around
was his line of defense. I ate a cookie, declined a drink, and stood up.
"Let's take a walk, Scott," I told him. When he stood, too, I saw that his
T-shirt said SUPPORT MENTAL HEALTH OR I'LL KILL YOU.

His seedy street was becoming gentrified, with interesting little restaurants every few doors, it seemed. Scott tried to use my glancing interest as
a delaying tactic. "The neighborhood's really picking up," he said, conver-
sationally, "isn't it?"

I stopped dead and he almost went past me. Then he did a goofy little
double take and shuffled to my side, but I didn't smile. "Scott," I said. "Listen to me. I'm very upset and I think you know why."

He looked miserable, I was glad to see, pale and slack-jawed. "Ma," he
said, "it was stupid."

"Yes, it was. Are you doing drugs, Scott? Tell me the truth."

"No. No, not really. I mean me and Jeff and Amy do a little pot now
and then, but that's all."

"So why did you take the paperweight?"

"I don't know," he said. "I told you, it was stupid."

"But what were you thinking? Were you planning on selling it?"

He appeared shocked. "No!" he protested.

"Well, was it because you were angry with Dad? I'm really trying to understand this."

"Listen, Ma," he said. "I wasn't thinking about anything. I just saw it
there on the table, and it was like there was a light inside it, sort of blinking at me? And . . . and I put it in my pocket."

"Scotty, you're nineteen now, not twelve. You don't just act on every
crazy impulse. And that wasn't some candy bar or key chain you took; it
was your father's precious possession. It was in our *home*." I thought of
Ev's innocent joy in finding his missing paperweight, and how the home
I'd mentioned with such solemnity had changed. The lies I'd told the
night before had disqualified me from confiding my secrets to Ev, of receiving his understanding in return. Some of that, anyway, was Scott's
fault.

And he looked guilty. "I know, I know," he said, pacing around me. "I feel like shit. I'm really sorry."

I felt like shit, too. Scott's eyelashes were spiky and damp, and his pallor had turned to an agitated pink. But I didn't have the familiar urge to patch things up, to make him feel better at any cost. "I'm not covering for you anymore," I said, grabbing his arm roughly to make him stand still. "Do you hear me?" Both of us were close to tears.

"Yeah," he said in a muffled voice. "I hear you."

"Okay, then. I'm going home now." And I hailed a cab and ran to it, without kissing him first, without even saying goodbye.

The following afternoon I went downtown again, to Dr. Joie's office at NYU. I would never have recognized her out of a medical context; she was Ingrid Bergman playing Golda Meir. Her nurse was gone for the day, she told me, and she sent me right to a dressing cubicle to put on a gown.

When I came out, she was waiting for me. "Let's take a look at you," she said. "We can talk later."

Then she led me into the sonogram room and told me to lie on the table. She examined my breasts quickly and lightly with long, cool fingers. I was reminded of touch typing. I sat up, I lay down again, I raised my arms and lowered them, and she made a few little X's on both of my breasts with a black marker. "Do you drink much coffee?" she asked. "Do you like chocolate?"

"Yes," I said. "Yes. Do you feel something?" A dumb question with all those tattooed X's circling my nipples.

"Lots of things, nothing in particular. Now show me what you felt." And I took her hand and guided it to the thickening on my left breast. She closed her eyes as she explored the area, as if to visualize what she was feeling. "Let's skip the mammogram and go right to the sonogram," she said.

"Do not pass Go," I said, inanely. "Do not collect two hundred dollars." Why hadn't I told Ev about this, at least? He would have been here with me.

"This will be cold," Dr. Joie said as she squeezed jelly onto my breast. She pushed the probe around the right breast and then the left, and I watched on the bedside screen as the shadowy images changed, and something that sounded like a paparazzo's camera clicked and clicked.

"Look at this," she said, holding the probe still and painfully deep on the outer rim of my left breast, and I saw a cluster of darkness that made my breath catch. "These are only cysts. All that caffeine, I'll bet. You don't have cancer."

"Really?" I said, as she wiped my breasts briskly with a paper cloth. The cold jelly felt oddly like the cooling fluids of sex, and that moment held something like the bitter sweetness of postcoital tristesse.

"Get dressed," Dr. Joie said, patting my shoulder, "and we'll talk."

This wasn't the room in which she'd talked to my mother, but that other one couldn't have been very different: the family photographs, the medical books, diplomas and licenses from Montreal and Chicago and New York. My mother's news had been bad, and mine was good. The relief of it filled me like helium, and I expected my voice to be high and silly. "Thank you," I said, sounding surprisingly normal and inadequately grateful.

I was waiting to be dismissed with some standard reminders about the caffeine and a follow-up visit, but Dr. Joie leaned back in her chair and said, "You were in school when your mother became ill, weren't you?"

For the first time I could see vestiges of the doctor's younger self in her eyes, in their open, frank expression. "Yes," I said. "I was at Swarthmore. When she died I was in graduate school."

"What did you study?" she asked.

"Writing. I was going to be a writer."

"And?"

"And I wasn't good enough."

"That must have been hard," she said. "What did you end up doing?"

I hesitated. Book doctor, that sly title I'd taken, seemed especially frivolous and fraudulent in that setting. "I became an editor," I said at last. "As close to the kingdom as I could get. And I have a family."

She smiled, and I remembered a phone call from my mother when she was recuperating from her mastectomy. "I have a wonderful new doctor," she'd said.

"What's so wonderful about him?" I asked, disdaining my mother's thrall to the princes of medicine.

"*Her*," my mother said. "Do you know the first thing she asked me, Alice? 'What do you want to do with the rest of your life?'"

I didn't see anything so remarkable about that, but sitting in Dr. Joie's office, I realized how atypically friendly and nonclinical her question was, and that by asking it she had given my mother hope of *having* more life.

"My mother really liked you," I said.

"I was fond of her, too."

"Then, how do you do what you do?" I asked. "I mean, when people die."

"Helping people to die is in the job description." She paused, and then she said, "You know, your father and I disagreed at the end about your mother's care." I sat forward a little. "He let her go on too long."

"Yes," I said. "Why do you think he did that?"

She shrugged. "His training, maybe, you know, life *über alles*. But lots of things motivate people to hang on beyond reason—the complications of love, of guilt, or just an inability to let go."

"Did you ever read my mother's work?"

"Yes, I did. She gave me a couple of journals with her poems in them. I liked them." My eyes grazed the bookshelves behind her, and she said, "They're in my library, at home."

"Dr. Joie, did you happen to read a poem of hers about feeding the ducks and geese in Central Park? I think it was also meant to be about losing hope."

She was thoughtful, and then she shook her head. "I'm sorry," she said. "It was a long time ago."

"I know. Of course."

"She never spoke directly about giving up, you know. I think she was afraid of disappointing your father. But maybe she did put it into a poem."

"Maybe," I said. "And you never raised the subject with her?"

"That's a dance where I always let the patient lead."

"I have one more question, if you don't mind." She nodded, and I said, "Do you remember telling my mother to listen to her body, that sometimes it knows something is wrong, even before there are any symptoms?"

"That sounds like me. Why?"

I took a shaky breath. "I've had this peculiar feeling, since April." I put my hand to my chest. "In here. It's a sort of hollow aching, as if something is really wrong. I thought it might be breast cancer—an atypical symptom—because of my mother, my family history—and now I know it isn't. But it wasn't just the *fear* of having cancer, either, because the feeling's still there." And it was, adamantly there, even as I spoke.

"What do you think it might be?" she asked.

"I was hoping you could tell me."

"Ah, but it's your feeling," she said.

My mother did have someone like Violet in her life.

11

In mid-July Michael lost his job at GM and acquired an apparent writer's block. He had extra time on his hands now, he said, and enough unemployment insurance and some savings to subsist for a while. I kept receiving genial and entertaining e-mails from him, but no new manuscript pages and no explanation for their absence. It was as if the final pages of a published book I was avidly reading had fallen out, and I might never get to know what happened next.

Of course I wanted to find out where Caitlin was; Michael had made that part of the narrative terrifically suspenseful, and Caitlin herself, Joe's beloved Cake, an intriguing figure. Why did she always choose such selfish and unstable men? And what did the three small tattoos on her body—the blue circle on her ankle, the white bracelet around her wrist, and the yellow half-moon on her back—represent? But more than anything else, I wanted to know why Joe felt so responsible for Caitlin's disappearance.

When other writers I'd edited developed blocks, I would carefully feel my way around the problem. It never seemed like a good idea to just ask if they were stuck; someone superstitious might take that as the laying-on of a curse. Until most writers are forced to admit they're blocked, it simply isn't true. It's merely a lull in the creative process, a time for dreaming and gestation. And who's to say that isn't so? To paraphrase Dr. Joie, it's one dance where I always let the writer lead.

So I wrote chatty, cheerful notes back to Michael, without even mentioning his manuscript, the elephant in the room. And I resisted a startling temptation to bring up that other pressing, but much too personal matter, the steadfast worried feeling in my chest. So instead I spoke of the humid weather in Manhattan; the arrest of another prominent athlete on assault charges; and a couple of interesting pieces I'd read in *The New Yorker*, one on the patenting of ideas, and the other on St. Petersburg.

Perhaps because I had more time to myself now, too, I was writing more often in my notebook—nothing shapely enough to be considered a story yet, but the cast of characters had grown. A fictional version of Dr. Joie, and an amalgam of Michael, Joe Packer, and Tom Roman had been added to that someone who now was and wasn't my mother. And all of their lives were loosely connected by certain details. I'd forgotten how pleasurable it was to unroll the ribbon of language onto the page, especially when there was no pressure to do so, and no one to cast a negative opinion about what was written. My notebook had become a place to retreat, which I badly needed since the big blowup with Ev a couple of weeks before.

He'd come home from work one night, slamming the door hard behind him. His footsteps were heavy, and he didn't call out to me as he usually did. I was sitting up in bed, writing, and I quickly closed my notebook and shoved it into the night table drawer. I didn't call to him, either. When I came out of the bedroom, he was standing in the hallway, yanking off his tie. "Oh, so you're home," he said flatly, and I could hear the scarcely controlled anger in his voice.

"What's the matter?" I asked, knowing the answer already, and wanting and dreading to have it said and over with.

"Your son paid me a visit at the office today. To *apologize*. I guess he figured you'd busted him."

Your son. "He's your son, too," I said, sullenly. I wasn't even going to attempt to deny the charges.

"Yeah," Ev said. "A little detail you seem to have forgotten."

"I don't know what you're talking about."

"I'm talking about the way you shut me out, Alice, and the way you've lied to me."

"Listen," I said, "I'm sorry that I lied to you about the Clichy. It was really stupid." Wasn't that what Scott had said about taking it?

"What else have you lied about?" he asked.

I thought immediately of Violet asking that day in the diner if I was having an affair. "What? Nothing!" I told Ev in an outraged squeal, although I felt strangely guilty, and probably looked as if I needed to be hosed down. "And I didn't even know for sure where the Clichy was until it turned up on the windowsill that day."

"But you didn't bother sharing it with me, then, either, did you? And you make me out to be some kind of monster to my own children."

"No, I don't."

"Yes, you do! You feel as if you have to protect Scott from me. What have I ever done to him?"

"You're exaggerating, as usual," I said. "But you are harder on Scott than on the other two."

"That's because Suzy and Jer don't break my balls the way Scotty does."

"*There,*" I said. "It's just that kind of hostility and crude language I'm trying to spare him."

"Is that because of his royal blood?"

"What?"

"Like yours. They may have sheltered you from 'bad' words back at the palace, but the rest of us have to live in the real world."

As he spoke I envisioned the house in Riverdale, the gated gardens where men were bent over hoeing weeds, the windows of my room with the white curtains billowing. He was right, he was wrong! "Fuck you," I said, shocking both of us. I had never said anything like that to Ev before, and it seemed to turn every loving act between us right onto its head.

"Ha!" he countered. "And *I'm* the one who's crude."

"Crude and cruel," I said. "You *pick* on Scott. He's your little scape-goat, isn't he?"

"Get off it, Al. That's bullshit and you know it. I'm just reacting to his con-man behavior. You're always covering for that kid, and believe me, you aren't doing him any favors."

"And you're always so critical of him."

"Because he screws up all the time, that's why! We gave him an expensive education and what has he done with it? He's not even going to college."

"Not everybody is college material."

"So is he going to work in the stockroom at Tower the rest of his life?"

"There are worse things," I said, although I couldn't think of any at that moment.

"Jesus, you've got an answer for everything, don't you?"

"No, I don't understand why you hate your own child." That was untrue and unfair. The moment I said it, I saw Ev holding Scotty's forehead over the toilet when he was little and throwing up. I couldn't do it because I'd always begin to retch myself. But I was still reeling from what he'd said about me, as if Scott and I were a couple of helpless siblings against a brutal parent, and I wouldn't take it back.

"How can you say that?" Ev shouted. "I love him! That's why I want him to grow up and take some responsibility for his own actions."

"You're just jealous of his freedom," I said.

"What the hell are you talking about?"

"He's young and he can still do anything he wants to with his life, that's what you can't stand. And what have you done with your expensive education?" I added, because I couldn't stop myself. "Where is *your* brilliant career?" Even before I saw the stricken expression on Ev's face, I knew that I'd just had the final, fatal word in our argument.

We hardly spoke to each other after that. And then Ev, too, began to appear in my notebook, but only as a minor character, a cynical dentist named Earl whom the other characters visit. He causes them pain, and stuffs their mouths with cotton and clamps, so that they can't speak or even cry out. His office becomes a masochist's mecca for his patients, who think deeply about their own troubled lives as he works torturously on their teeth. Across the top of the first page of my notebook, I scrawled "The Dentist's Chair." Now I had a villain of sorts, and a title, even if I didn't have an actual plot.

But venting myself on the page didn't make me feel much better about Ev and me. Our life together didn't seem authentic anymore, and I couldn't help comparing our marriage to my parents'. When you grow up in Eden, everything elsewhere can seem pretty flawed. And Ev and I had both become really miserable. He was still furious with me, he'd implied I wasn't trustworthy, and he'd taken to sleeping in our sons' old bedroom, which served as a guest room now. I noted that he'd chosen Scott's bed, and sometimes I wandered around the apartment at night with my pillow and a book, looking for another place to lie down that wasn't the lonely, mine-strewn field of our own king-sized bed.

One night I could hear Ev moaning in his sleep as I passed the boys' room, and I almost went inside to wake him and try to talk about everything. But I couldn't bring myself to do it. My own anger was still alive under all that despair, and I guess I was afraid of intensifying his. Besides, it was our style to wait things out, to let them blow over by themselves, and then just go on.

When I told Violet what was happening at home, leaving out the final awful thing I'd said to Ev, she still took his side. "Well, you did lie to him," she said. "That wasn't exactly a vote of confidence."

"I was in a lousy position," I argued. "And I had to give Scotty the benefit of the doubt."

"Why? You knew in your heart what had happened."

She was so exasperatingly rational. Maybe she didn't get it because she had no children of her own, but I wouldn't give her the free pass I'd so wantonly handed Scotty. I was angry with Violet, too, now, and feeling even more isolated.

A few days later Suzy came to see me after work—a rare occurrence in her busy life. I knew I couldn't burden her with my marital problems, but it was oddly soothing just to see her there, to be reminded of previous domestic happiness. When she was in the first grade, Suzy had made Ev and me raise our right hands and solemnly promise that we'd never divorce, like the parents of so many of her schoolmates. Were we still bound by that oath?

I suddenly decided to give her some things of mine that she'd liked and coveted since childhood, when she used to try on my clothes and jewelry as if she were auditioning for the future. We went into the bedroom and I began to open drawers and closets. "Why are you doing this, Mom?" Suzy asked, surreptitiously eyeing my red Bakelite snake bracelet. "You're not sick or anything, are you?"

"No, no, honey," I assured her. "It's just that I have too much stuff, it's time to thin it out. And you'd look better in most of it, anyway." I handed over the Bakelite bracelet, which was still one of my favorites. She slid it onto her slender, tanned wrist and I said, after struggling a moment with the opposing tugs of possessiveness and generosity, "That's yours."

"Are you sure? Maybe I could just borrow it for a while."

"I'll borrow it from you sometime."

Even when she was dying, my mother never spoke about the disposition of her worldly goods. Of course she had a will, in which I was bequeathed a sizable trust, and Faye a cash gift, but it didn't specifically mention any items of sentimental value. Maybe she thought it wasn't necessary, that it was clear the only heirs to everything she owned were my father and myself. Or maybe it was because she was still in denial, right up to the final moments of her life. I remembered reading about a young actress with terminal cancer who put her jewelry into individual sandwich bags, labeled with the names of her relatives and friends, and it seemed like such a civilized and courageous act.

Still wearing the bracelet, Suzy turned the key on the Lucien Lelong bottle. The dancers started to slowly move in their intimate dance, and the tinkling music spilled out. The defining sound of my childhood, and of hers. As the mechanism wound down, Suzy gazed at a framed photograph on the dresser of my parents taken only a few years before my mother's death. "They look so happy together," she said.

"They made it seem easy . . ." Had they done it with mirrors? I was suddenly, uncomfortably conscious of that feeling in my chest.

"It's not?" Suzy asked mockingly. Then she looked sharply at me. "What?"

I hesitated. "Nothing," I said. "I just miss them, that's all."

She appraised me for another moment before turning her attention back to the photograph. "Grandma was really beautiful, wasn't she?" Suzy said.

I was thrilled by her reference to "Grandma," a title my mother had never known. "Yeah, she was. I always wished that I looked like her."

"Me, too," Suzy said.

"Maybe you do, a little."

"No, I don't." She peered into the mirror above the dresser and made a series of grimaces that distorted her pretty face. "I look like Dad."

"You could have done worse," I told her. "You could have looked like me."

"Mom," she said. "You know I've always loved your hair." She picked up my brush and began to slowly pull it through my flyaway hair, from the roots to the tips.

I hadn't been touched by anyone for weeks, and the drag of the brush against my scalp was a staggeringly lovely sensation. I sank down onto the bed, thinking that I could have fallen asleep right then, sitting up. "But my *freckles*," I moaned.

"They're cute."

"Cute?" I said. "Do you mean like Howdy Doody?" But I was thinking of an unusually tender short story Ev wrote shortly after we were married, about a woman whose skin appears to have flecks of trapped sunlight under it.

Suzy continued to brush my hair, which had risen in veils around my face and was sizzling with static by then, and she said, "Mom, I've met somebody." The brush paused for just an instant before it began its mesmerizing work again. But I was fully alert now. So this was the reason for her visit.

"Who is he?" I asked, wondering why this news made me feel so unpleasantly peculiar. Suzy had never wanted for boyfriends, and her popularity had always been a source of pride and even vicarious pleasure for me.

"His name is George, George Levinson. He joined the firm a few months ago."

"Isn't there an unwritten rule against that at Stubbs? About mixing business and pleasure?"

"Yes," she said. "So we have to be really careful."

I looked up and saw that she was smiling dreamily. The danger factor probably only helped to charge the eroticism of her relationship. I could certainly appreciate that feeling. When I was still keeping Ev a secret from my father, I was very nervous about his finding out about us, and sexually reckless at the same time, one sensation seeming to feed the other.

"Tell me about him," I said.

She sat down beside me, and I took the brush from her lax grip and began to pull it through her dark, springy curls. "Well," she said, "he's very smart and funny. And idealistic."

"An idealistic corporate *lawyer*?" I teased, but I was already envisioning a Hepburn–Tracy movie romance, with the exciting added edge of competition between them. Like Ev and I used to be, I thought, and I understood then that I was envious of my own child, just starting out. The very sin I'd accused Ev of committing.

"*Mother*," Suzy scolded, bringing me back.

"Is he handsome?" I asked.

"Very, but not in the conventional sense. He looks a little like a gangster."

"They all do. So, is this serious?"

She leaned against me, with the same absolute trust she'd displayed when she was very young, and I could feel her solid grown-up weight and the heat of her flushed skin. "Yes, I think so," she said.

"Darling, that's wonderful," I said, relieved to realize that I truly meant it. "I can't wait to meet him."

When Ev and I got married, I was newly pregnant with Suzy. It wasn't exactly a shotgun wedding—we had already decided to marry, only not right away. We were going to give our writing careers, our calling, a chance to develop first. But now this unknown baby became the abiding idea and the chief character in my imagination, while Ev was hustled into a suit and tie and his family's printing business.

My father will die, I kept thinking, my father will kill me. He was still

in deep mourning, and I'd never dared to mention Ev to him, or ever
really told him that Arthur was no longer in my life. My mother was the
one I needed to tell. I was sure that she would have approved, and that she
would have been the buffer between my father and myself.

I called Violet and she immediately volunteered to come to Iowa to be
our witness. She and Eli were still living in New Haven, because Eli had
a teaching fellowship in the philosophy department at Yale. Their own
young marriage was in trouble by then, although I don't think Violet knew
that yet.

She tried to dispel my worries about my father. "He'll get over it," she
said with a shrug when I picked her up at the airport. "Those old birds are
tougher than you think." My father wasn't that much older then than we
were now. "And you're making him a grandfather, besides. Maybe you
ought to give him the good news first."

We had both grown up overhearing every medical "bad news, good
news" joke in the book, and we thought some of them were pretty funny,
but I was afraid there would be nothing amusing about my father's reaction to the news of my marriage to Ev.

I'd decided to do it in person. My father's aversion to the telephone
might influence his response, and how could he resist the irresistible presence of my delightful new husband? But even Ev's good looks and witty
charm, and our obvious love for each other, didn't win my father over. He
seemed to rise up out of his grief to attain a fresh level of disapproval of me.
The worst part, he said, was that I had done this behind his back, and I had
to acknowledge that there was some truth in that. I might have been a
teenage girl again, caught smoking in the schoolyard. But I'd only held off
his displeasure in order to hang on to my own bliss a little longer. All love
affairs are private, anyway; they're always behind someone else's back.

In retrospect, I realize that I probably should have broken everything to
my father in slow, easy stages, even if the chronological order was off: the
split with Arthur, Ev's courtship, our wedding, my pregnancy. Or maybe
Violet was right, and I should have leavened the rest of it by giving him the
"good news" first. I don't think any of that finally mattered, though. With
my mother's death, he'd lost control of his neatly ordered world, and this
was only another blow, another challenge to his autocracy.

After Suzy left, I waited impatiently for Ev to come home from work, and I told him about Suzy and George as soon as he walked in, as if I were giving him a conciliatory, homemade gift. "Guess what!" I said. "Suzy's in love."

"Oh, yeah?" he said coolly. "That's good." Nothing else.

I don't know what I expected—that Suzy's love affair would somehow rekindle ours? No, of course not. Only maybe that he would be reminded of us, of the powerful connection we'd had that led to our having Suzy, and that eventually led her into the thrilling, risky business of giving yourself to someone else.

Later, I heard him talking to her on the telephone in the boys' bedroom, his voice full of the affection and enthusiasm he'd withheld from me. I went into our bedroom and shut the door. Then I sat down at my computer and sent an e-mail to Michael. "What's going on?" I wrote.

12

The next morning the doorman buzzed me on the intercom to say I had a
delivery, and did I want the package man to bring it up. My first foolish
thought was that Ev had sent me flowers as a peace offering, although
I knew that wasn't his style. My father, on the other hand, had been a
florist's dream customer. He seemed to have had whole formal gardens
decimated for my mother's pleasure, his exotic offerings arriving regularly
in a white van. Any flowers I'd ever received from Ev were delivered in person, clutched in his fist, and they had been bought from a street vendor on
the impulse of love, or the onset of spring, or for no apparent reason at all.
Daffodils and daisies, usually, that looked as if they'd just been plucked
from a meadow.

When he wanted to apologize—a pretty rare event—or to make up
after an argument, he was more likely to ambush me with an embrace at
the kitchen sink, or bridge the distance between us in bed with his entire

body. "Let's stop this, okay?" whispered huskily into my hair or my neck was the closest Ev ever came to an act of contrition.

The delivery turned out to be a large carton filled with the back issues of *Leaves* I'd ordered. There was no note enclosed, only a standard packing slip buried under those Styrofoam peanuts that cling weightlessly to everything, especially your fingers. The journals themselves were so crisp, they might have come right off the press, except for a slight yellowing of the covers and the edges of the pages. *Sunning*, I think rare-book dealers call it, a cheerful word for the ravages of age.

As he'd promised, Tom Roman had flagged those issues containing my mother's poems, with yellow Post-its affixed to the pale gray covers. There were a number of them, and my hands trembled as I opened the earliest issue. Her poem, called "Minor Surgery," about slicing radishes, was short and delicate, until the last line. I tried to imagine how she must have felt, seeing her name in print, and those broad, clean margins around the poem, like breathing space. I could almost hear her voice in my head saying the lines with me as I read them aloud. When I reached up to dab at my eyes, a packing peanut drifted silently out of my hair onto the page, like a comical sign from beyond.

My mother's contributor's note in the back of the magazine said, "Helen Brill lives in Riverdale, New York, with her husband and daughter." It was typical of new writers in those days—women, anyway—to identify themselves by their domestic arrangements.

I scanned the other contributors' notes for recognizable names and there were a few, including Phil Santo, our workshop leader in Iowa, and a poet whose single collection came out quietly, almost stealthily, from G&F in the 1980s. One or two writers were said to be have finished novels or volumes of poetry, but I guess they were never published. So much for fame and fortune, I thought, surprised that the bitter ache of rejection was still so easily revived.

My mother's poems in the other issues of *Leaves* were all familiar to me; there had been drafts of them in her accordion folder. I observed the way her contributor's note had evolved over the years. For the issue with her third poem in it, she'd written, "Helen Brill lives in New York with her husband and daughter"—deftly discarding unhip, suburban Riverdale—and from then on, "Helen Brill's work has appeared in previous issues of *Leaves* and other journals," disposing just as neatly of my father and me. I also noted, on the copyright page, that *Leaves* had been published in Menemsha, Massachusetts. Wasn't that on Martha's Vineyard, right next door to Chilmark?

That afternoon there was a letter from Thomas Roman in the regular mail delivery. He said that he had been thinking about my request for anecdotes about my mother. "I wonder if the following might be useful for your memoir." I had almost forgotten that particular lie. "In one of her early letters, Helen told me that you'd contracted chicken pox, and how difficult it was to keep you from scratching at the rash. 'My poor little Alice,' she wrote. 'It comes over her in a frenzy, and I have to hold her hands and sing to distract her. Songs like "Row, Row, Row Your Boat" and "Ninety-nine Bottles of Beer on the Wall" seem to work best, although by the third or fourth round, I'm usually starting to itch, myself. Thank goodness she bites her nails!'"

This excerpt from my mother's chatty letter gratified and disappointed me at once. I realized how eager I was for anecdotes about my early days that I could no longer hear from my parents, and I was pleased that she had chosen to write about me to a literary friend. But at the same time I felt strangely let down by the bland familial content of the letter. I was still looking for passionate secrets, the parts of her life I didn't know about. Maybe Tom Roman had kept the more significant letters to himself.

I could vividly recall having chicken pox, the violent itching, those unsightly spots. I'd caught it from Violet, like all the other childhood diseases, and despite my mother's best efforts to keep me from tearing at my own flesh I still bear two faint scars, one on my chin and the other just under my hairline. The mention of my bitten nails reminded me of what a ticky child I was—the way I twirled one particular strand of hair until it finally fell out, and that blinking I did in my tenth year.

What was it I hadn't wanted to see? So many things, starting with my own scowling, pale face in the mirror, those nearly invisible eyelashes and eyebrows. I looked something like Pinky, the pet rabbit in my classroom at

Chapin. I practiced wrinkling my nose the way he did, but that, at least, was one tic I didn't acquire.

"It wouldn't kill you to smile, Alice," my father used to say, unsmilingly. And, "Watch out, or your face will freeze that way." I took him literally, of course, believing that my sour expression might be forever fixed, especially in winter, when everything was frozen into place. Blink, blink, and he would be gone, along with his ominous predictions. But there was another unsavory sight that refused to rise to the surface, that dove under the skin of memory and made my chest tighten whenever I tried to think of it. Why couldn't I remember what that was?

When the phone rang, I found myself hoping that it would be Ev, even if he'd only called on the pretext of some household matter. I still felt alienated from him, but I also missed him, perversely enough, and nothing had been resolved between us. Or maybe it was Scott; I'd hardly spoken to him since that painful conversation on his street. Despite Ev's cynicism, I'd tried to assign purer motives to Scott's unexpected visit to Carroll Graphics than merely copping a plea, and I had put in a call to him the night before, leaving a message on his tape. "Hi, Scotty, it's Mom. I just wanted to say hello, and that I'm really happy you went to see Dad the other day."

It was only Violet on the phone, but I was even glad to hear from her— I guess I couldn't stand being at odds with everybody at once. She didn't apologize for siding with Ev and criticizing me; she just resumed talking to me as if nothing had ever been wrong between us. And I didn't really mind. As Violet herself once remarked, too much time and energy are wasted on the social graces.

"Violet," I said. "Do you remember when you gave me the chicken pox?"

"You never forget a favor, do you?"

"No, listen. I got a letter from this man my mother used to know, Thomas Roman. He was the editor of a small literary magazine about a million years ago. It was called *Leaves*."

"How come he wrote to you?"

"It's a long story. Actually, I wrote to him first. He published several of my mother's poems. Anyway, I don't know why, but I think she may have had an affair with him." Was that something I *wished* had happened?

"My God," Violet said. Then, "But what does that have to do with the chicken pox?"

"Nothing, really. But you know that something has been bothering me, right?"

"Duh, yes."

"Well, maybe this is it."

"What are you talking about?" she said. "You've completely lost me now."

"Do you remember when we were ten, and I started blinking and my parents took me to that awful Dr. Pinch?"

"Am I on *This Is Your Life?*"

"Violet, wait. That bad feeling I've been having? I think it has to do with that, with my blinking, with my father and mother, and something I couldn't stand to look at."

"I thought it was just a midlife crisis."

"Well, maybe that, too," I conceded.

"So what couldn't you stand to look at?"

"That's the thing," I said, feeling the air go out of my elation. "I don't really know."

"Then why don't you try finding out?" Violet said, gently for her.

"You mean, go to see someone?" I asked, beset by a sudden wave of panic. "I'm liable to start blinking again."

"It doesn't have to be a Dr. Pinch. How about that psychologist you saw after you lost your job?"

"Andrea Stern," I said, and I remembered sobbing in her office as she studied me with contemplative sympathy. I was surprised and pleased that Violet had brought her up, since she hadn't found her for me. Lucy Seo, my friend at G&F, had recommended Dr. Stern as "literate and compassionate." "I did like her," I told Violet. "And at least that was short-term therapy."

"Alice, you *quit.*"

"I suppose so. But why go digging up things that might not even be true? And I hate all that recovered-memory crap. Do you remember the travesty in that nursery school in California? What am I supposed to find out, anyway—that my father abused me?"

Violet's silence, fraught with everything unsaid—*You brought this up, you know. Don't you want to feel better? What are you afraid of?*—was finally, mercifully, interrupted by the beep of my call waiting, and I said, "I have to take that. It might be Ev."

But this time it was Scott, returning my call. "Thanks for the message, Ma," he said, "but I don't think Dad was all that thrilled to see me the other day."

"Well, I guess he's still a little mad at you."

"Way more than a little."

"Yes, maybe," I conceded. "But you know that he loves you. He even made a point of telling me that, right after you came to see him. He just wants you to behave more responsibly. Me, too, of course," I added. I realized that Ev and I were acting in concert, for once, even if he wasn't actually aware of it, and even if we were working Scotty over like the proverbial good cop and bad cop.

It seemed to be effective, though, because Scott sighed and said, with seeming sincerity, "I'm really trying."

"Good, dear. That's all we ask of you."

That night, alone in bed again, I browsed through my new library of *Leaves*, the way I used to scour other literary magazines, on the lookout for new talent. That was a long time ago, when I was still a real editor at a real publishing house and profit mattered, but it wasn't *all* that mattered. A couple of the stories were truly promising—Tom Roman had had a good ear and a responsive heart.

I could hear Ev padding down the hallway to the kids' bathroom, brushing his teeth, flushing the toilet. He'd come home late; his secretary had called during the afternoon to say he wouldn't be here in time for dinner, that he'd get something downtown. I'd eaten my dinner alone, choosing undemanding nursery foods—poached eggs on buttered toast—with the TV on for company. And now I was listening like a nocturnal animal for further sounds from his end of the apartment. But I didn't hear anything else, and soon the bar of light under my door went out.

Scott's narrow single bed had to be confining for Ev; he was such a

turbulent, sprawling sleeper. I squeezed my eyes shut and sent him a tele-
pathic message, the way Violet and I used to beam messages to each other
over the rooftops of Riverdale, when we were seven or eight and convinced
that we had special powers of communication. *Ev,* I signaled, with fierce
concentration, *come back to bed. Come back to me.* I lay very still in the
waiting silence, but of course nothing happened. So I shut off my light,
too, and tried to prepare myself for sleep.

And then the phone rang, with that jarring shrillness it always seems to
have late at night. I glanced at the clock—it was almost midnight—before
I grabbed the receiver. "Hello," I said, and I could hear Ev breathing into
the extension in the boys' bedroom. A man said, "Alice?" and Ev abruptly
hung up.

"Who is this?" I demanded, identifying the voice on the phone in the
same instant. "Michael?" Had the message I'd tried to send to Ev gone that
far astray? I switched on the lamp. "What's the matter?"

"Oh, Jesus," he said. "It's late, isn't it? Did I wake you up?" I could hear
background noises now: other voices; music; laughter in little bursts, like
gunfire. He was probably in a bar, but he sounded sober, in every sense of
the word.

"No, it's all right, I was reading. Are you okay?" I realized that I had slid
down under the covers with the phone, and I was whispering, the way I did
when I was a teenager and a boy called.

"Yes. No." He gave a dry little laugh. "I guess I'm having some sort of a
crisis."

"With the writing, you mean?"

"Yes. It seems to have stopped."

I heard Ev's footsteps again, going past my door this time, heading for
the kitchen. The water ran and then stopped with its customary little shriek.
"You've been really prolific," I said into the phone. "This might only be a
normal pause, you know, to catch your breath, collect your thoughts."

"You think?"

"I do, Michael," I said. "I really do."

Ev went by once more right then, in the other direction. Had he hesitated for just a moment? I couldn't be sure, and soon I heard the door to
the boys' room close.

"Maybe," Michael said, doubtfully.

"Some people, some writers, have a fear of closure," I told him, thinking, with a start, fear of *dis*closure. When he didn't respond, I said, "Do you know how the book ends? Have you done an outline?" These were questions I usually asked much earlier in a project, but the pages had been coming steadily, so I'd simply assumed his answers—that he did know the whole story, and that a formal outline would have been stultifying.

"No outline," he said. "And I thought I knew the ending, but I'm not so sure anymore."

"That's all right," I said. "That happens." I felt oddly like an actual doctor as I rummaged in my head for something else to say, something professional and practical. I remembered the chirpy advice given in writing manuals for overcoming a block, everything from not writing a word to forcing yourself to work for at least one hour every day. "Listen, Michael," I said. "Writing is like sleeping or breathing, those things you do naturally, and you're a natural writer. But if you fixate on it, it might become harder and harder to do. You know, the way you get insomnia when you try to sleep, or start to hyperventilate when you think about your breathing." I was scrambling now, saying anything that came to mind.

"So you think I shouldn't try to go on?"

Was that what I'd said? "No. No, I just think you shouldn't become too anxious about it." Oh, great. Relax, why don't you, just breathe normally, go to sleep this minute, stop blinking. "But if you want to talk it over, or try things out on me, I'm here."

"That's good to know. I probably will want to. Soon. But I'll let you go to bed now. Sweet dreams, Alice."

"You, too," I said, although he seemed to be hours away from sleeping.

Of course, I couldn't fall asleep after that, either. I wondered why I'd tiptoed so carefully around Michael's problem, why I wasn't more direct. Hadn't I learned anything from Violet? I might have asked him to tell me the ending he'd planned, and why he wasn't sure about it anymore. Or I could have simply asked what he was afraid of.

And why hadn't I apologized to Ev? I knew that his feelings were terribly hurt. I'd accused him of being a bad father and reminded him of being a failed writer, all in one argument. But he'd attacked me, too, blaming me for having had a pampered childhood, and he hardly ever apologized for anything. He should have discerned, somehow, that I was struggling with something else, that peculiar burden I couldn't seem to name or set aside.

The room was dark—I had turned off my lamp again—but the silhouettes of our bedroom furniture were becoming visible, that known landscape I always gazed at just before sleep. Ev was probably out cold by now; he was able to escape that way no matter how troubled he was. I took his pillow and punched it a few times before clutching it to my breast, trying to smother whatever was still smoldering there.

Suzy must have been entwined in sleep with her lover; it gave me a pang of wistful pleasure to imagine them. And down in Philadelphia, Jeremy and Celia were surely sleeping, too, the music in their heads stilled for the night. Scotty, I hoped, with a rush of meanness, was tossing and turning in Alphabet City.

I thought of my father in his crib at the home, with light and voices filtering in from the nurses' station. Was he restored to his former, sentient self in his dreams? Then, languorously, I conjured up my mother, reading to me in bed. But it wasn't a children's story she read; it was her poem in *Leaves*, the one in which "the blade cuts through that maiden blush / to the bloodless radish heart."

13

Help was on the way or, more accurately, I was on my way to getting help. Andrea Stern had called back to say that indeed she remembered me, as well as her offer to resume treatment whenever I was ready. The only problem was that she was going to be away for all of August, the month New Yorkers had better not be in emotional crisis. She could fit me in for one session before she left, though, giving us a chance to re-connect; and then, in September, we'd be able to pick up where we had left off. Or she could try to find someone else for me who'd be more avail-able.

It was like the condition set before the hero in a fairy tale: you may have only one session, one wish. Dr. Stern's voice was instantly recognizable, even after all this time, like an old friend's from school or from work. I thought of her brownstone office with its two worn leather chairs, where we sat facing each other at a civil distance, and the way the blinds were slanted at the tall windows to let in just enough light, and I made an appointment to see her the following Wednesday at noon.

Wednesday turned out to be the kind of day we so rarely had that summer, without either oppressive heat or drowning rains. The office was in the 60s on the West Side, and I decided to walk there, going through Central Park at 66th Street. Everything was green and abundant, fulfilling the promise of that April morning when my sense of something wrong had begun. I'd given myself lots of time to get to Dr. Stern's, and to think about what I was going to say once I got there.

As I walked along, I went over the issues that concerned me, in chronological order, beginning with that sensation behind my breastbone and ending with my estrangement from Ev. My father's voice might have been in my head, warning, as he so often had, "Why don't you *think* before you speak, Alice." I was sure that Violet would have objected to my careful preparations for therapy. Free association, she'd often told me, was the best way to get to the crux of things. But I felt that my father was right, for once. I'd been guilty too often in the past of blurting out whatever was on my mind. That's what had escalated the recent hostilities between Ev and me, and I was afraid of what might fly out of my mouth at Dr. Stern's if I didn't have a good idea first of what I wanted to say.

It was the middle of a workday, but the park was crowded with people who had abandoned their offices and shops to collapse on the fragrant grass for an alfresco lunch, or to run or bicycle on the paths. Lovers, families, friends. For a while I followed a group of day campers and their counselors on a nature hike, feeling as if I had been away for a long time, but was back now in the current of life. The children, in green camp T-shirts, walked in orderly pairs, holding hands, while their counselors acted as sheepdogs, herding them along. Real dogs ran about the lawns off their leashes, against the law, but true to their own nature.

I crossed the path to lean against a tree and scribble something in my notebook about the scene and about the conflict between rules and desire. Then I skipped a few pages and started to write down the list of concerns I was bringing to Dr. Stern. Was I becoming too compulsive? But it was only going to be a fifty-minute hour, and I wanted to be sure to raise the things that bothered me the most. I had to mention the business of Scott and the paperweight because that was so closely related to my troubles with Ev. But I would feel as if I were playing favorites if I left the other children out, especially Suzy and her new love affair. And I probably had to fill Dr. Stern in briefly on the freelance work I was doing, and, of course, there was my father's continuing deterioration.

In the middle of the park I veered north for a while, so I could walk alongside the lake where my mother and I used to feed the ducks and geese. Sometimes, after school, instead of boarding the bus, I would wait near the reception desk inside the main entrance for her to fetch me, and we would take a taxi to Rumpelmayer's for ice cream or hot chocolate before walking into the park. Later, we might go shopping or to the Met, and then up to Mount Sinai Hospital to meet my father, who would drive us home in his Lincoln. Parksie or Miss Snow usually gave me paper and some colored pencils to draw with in the back of the car, and I chose safe little suburban scenes from memory—house, trees, flowers, child—rather than the hard-edged city landscape I glimpsed as it raced by the windows.

It may have been cloudy or chilly on a few of those excursions, but memory is a benevolent editor; all I could envision now were golden afternoons like this one, under a flawless blue sky. Occasionally my mother took Violet along, too, but my sharpest recollections were of just the two of us, strolling hand in hand in the park, like the little day campers I'd just followed.

I sat down on a bench—maybe the same bench where my mother and I had once sat—and swigged some water, while new generations of birds pecked around my feet, looking for the bread crumbs I hadn't brought. I opened my notebook again and pondered mentioning my "writing" to Dr. Stern. It was still such a tentative, self-conscious endeavor, nothing more than dabbling, really, and I couldn't bring it up without filling her in about my time at Iowa, the competition with Ev, and our forsaken ambition.

I remembered Phil Santo saying that all experience is useful to a writer—a mild consolation then for every painful or pointless act I'd ever committed—and I could easily imagine Violet's paraphrase about an analysand. But my efforts weren't significant in the context of my crowded life, and the little bit of time I had to convey it, so I didn't add writing and not writing to my list.

I had cried my eyes out during the few previous sessions I'd had with Andrea Stern, with the loss of my job as the ostensible focus of my misery. But she'd suggested that there were probably other, buried grievances causing my tears, and that it was important to try to uncover them. That, of course, was when I balked, when I left. Now I was determined not to waste my time and money by crying that way again, or by refusing to face up to things. Yet another reason to be prepared. There wasn't anything or anyone on my list, even Ev, I couldn't talk about now without breaking down.

When I was almost out of the park, I became aware of a couple lying on the lawn to my left, kissing and writhing with passion. The man straddled the woman, who was wearing a hiked-up sundress. The sun highlighted them with an almost theatrical brilliance. It was such a deliberately public act—they hadn't even bothered to retreat behind a nearby stand of trees—but I felt unaccountably like a trespasser. Everything around them seemed to have gone still and the grass was too green, the sky almost piercingly blue. The whole scene had the surreal, spooky quality of a dreamscape, something in a painting by Magritte or Dalí.

I turned away abruptly and began to run. And I kept on running until I was out of the park, breathing hard and with my heart drumming. By the time I came to 68th and Amsterdam, close to Dr. Stern's office, my pulse had slowed, and everything around me was reassuringly ordinary again: buildings, traffic, strangers going about their business. It was as if I'd just witnessed a crime I had no intention of reporting.

I rang the doorbell at the brownstone, and after a long beat I was buzzed in. Another patient, a woman about my own age, left as soon as I entered. We were like the husband and wife in a Swiss weather clock, and we didn't make eye contact as our bodies skimmed past each other. I caught a whiff of a citrusy scent. In the waiting room, I saw the *Time* magazine she must have been reading before she was called in to her session. It was on the coffee table in front of the sofa, set apart from the neat, fanned display of other periodicals, and it was open to an article on the occupation of Iraq.

What could I tell about that unknown woman from these meager clues? That she'd chosen to look at *Time* over ARTnews or *People*. A middlebrow, then, with an interest in the larger world, or apprehension about it. And a sentimentalist, who clung to the season with that summery cologne. I sniffed my own arm, which smelled a little like laundry starch and bread. What did that say about me? Out-of-season hausfrau. My hand came up and twirled a strand of hair, and I sniffed at that, too.

Dr. Stern had come quietly to the doorway, and when she said my name I jumped up, poking and patting my hair back into place. She was younger than I remembered, only thirty-eight or forty, and shorter, too. If I wasn't exactly old enough to be her mother, I might have once been her babysitter. I had a moment of misgiving as I went past her into the office and took my assigned seat.

The room, at least, was the same. Grass cloth on the walls, the green sofa in the background, that Hockney print of irises, instead of the typical swimming pool. As soon as we were facing each other again, I thought of my last visit here, that awful, abject weeping, and of being released, finally, like a homesick child let out of school. I thought, too, of Portnoy and his long complaint. *Now vee may perhaps to begin.* Dr. Stern was looking at me, waiting, and I felt inexplicably shy. "I'm not sure I know how to do this," I said.

"There's no particular way," she said. "What are you thinking about?"

"Your last patient, actually."

"Why does she interest you?"

"She doesn't. I mean, I was just trying to figure out who she was. Not her name or anything, just . . . No, that's not true. I was really thinking about myself—who else?"

"That's why you're here."

I glanced at my watch and saw the second hand flit past the hour. "Is it normal," I asked, "for a fifty-one-year-old woman to be obsessed with her mother, who's been dead for many years?"

"Most of us are concerned with our parents all of our lives."

"Then maybe we should choose them more carefully," I said, winning a faint smile. And I remembered Dr. Pinch asking if I'd ever imagined I didn't live with my "real" parents, and that I would be claimed by them someday. Years later, I found out that Freud referred to this fantasy as a "family romance." But to me the true family romance was the one I lived, as the beloved child of a happy marriage, an essential part of the perfect triumvirate.

I realized that Dr. Stern was waiting for me to say something else. "Do you have a mother?" I asked, quickly adding, "I'm not supposed to ask questions like that, am I?"

"You may ask anything you like," she said. "I do have a mother. But you really are here to talk about yourself."

"I had this all planned, what I was going to say. I was afraid to leave it to chance."

"What did you think might happen if you did 'leave it to chance,' as you say?"

I shrugged. "That's the thing—I didn't know, but it seemed dangerous, like opening Pandora's box."

"You'd release some evils?"

"Yeah, I guess so. Or bore you to death. The last time, I just bawled, remember? I was determined not to do that again, to just stay with the script. And then something happened on my way here." I sat forward in my chair. "I saw a couple making out in the park." She waited. "Big deal, I know," I said, "but it seemed so weird, this time, like a sequence in a dream."

"How did that make you feel?"

"Kind of helpless, the way you do in dreams. And like an intruder."

"Helpless and intrusive. Something like a child?"

I nodded and paused, but it was apparently still my turn to speak. I cleared my throat and hastily switched gears. "I've been working a little since I was here last. Not a real job. I'm just sort of a freelance book doctor now." As soon as I said it, it sounded absurd. Physician, heal thyself! I thought, and then I changed the subject again.

The fifty minutes went whizzing by, and I'd barely touched on most of the things on my agenda. Being in therapy, it seemed, was something like writing a book, a novel; you simply made it up as you went along. And there was a plot and a theme, distinct from each other, yet entangled. I'd tell Andrea Stern my story and together we would try to figure out the theme. That would make her sort of the editor of my life. But it was such a convenient and smug correlation. Would a plumber in therapy envision his angst as just a clog of hair and shit in the pipes, something to be snaked out so that the truth could come gushing through?

Later, I waited for the crosstown bus at the corner of 65th Street, suddenly too tired to walk anymore. I hadn't cried at all during my session, which was a modest triumph, but now I felt close to tears, although I wasn't sure why. I'd finally gotten around to talking about Ev and me and the children, of the push and clutch of our marriage, and of how lucky we were, really, despite the setbacks we were having, that everyone was healthy, and functioning pretty well in society.

I know I didn't convey how awful things actually were at home, or even mention that persistent sensation in my chest, the catalyst for my going back into therapy in the first place. Had I come there merely to gloat, or to comfort myself? No, certainly not, and my mind flitted off my family so quickly, they might have been only minor characters in my narrative. I began to tell Dr. Stern about my work with Michael instead, but that seemed like just a subplot of my life, irrelevant to the real matters that had brought me there.

I sat quietly for several seconds before I felt a desperate impulse to break the silence again. "I've been writing a little, myself," I said. I could feel the heat rise in my neck and my face. It was like a great, guilty confession. I opened my bag and took my notebook out and held it up, as validation of my claim, I suppose, although I didn't open it. "I was going to be a writer once. Like my mother." Mother!

Then I put my hand to my breast, where the feeling had been patiently crouching, and it leapt at my touch, clamoring to be announced. And I would have done so, but of course my time was up then, in the middle of a thought, of what I belatedly knew should have been my first thought. Another patient rang the doorbell, and Dr. Stern stood and so did I.

"Why don't we pick up there when you come back?" she said. We shook hands and made another appointment for the first Wednesday after Labor Day. When I stepped outside, the sunlight, the whole busy world, was as astonishing as it is when you leave a darkened movie theater and the story of someone else's life.

14

It was August and I was on my own, feeling as warily independent and lonesome as a latchkey child. Dr. Stern had said she'd be reachable by e-mail or by phone. From the area code I knew that she was on the eastern end of Long Island, and in a fit of pseudo-nostalgia I envisioned a damp, cozy little cottage, the creak and twang of a screen door as happy children ran in and out. It was a silly, wishful fantasy—I didn't even know if Dr. Stern had any children, happy or otherwise. Her invitation to intrude on her vacation was sincere, but nothing had radically changed in my life since I'd seen her, and I prided myself on my lack of neediness, my ability to wait until our appointment in September.

In the meantime, I kept that disturbance in my chest in careful check, like a leashed but potentially dangerous pet. And I tried to muddle through things at home, where Ev and I were still sleeping apart and still on pointedly civil speaking terms, in what I thought of as a shaky cease-fire. (The metaphors of the embattled Middle East were always so apt and handy.) We had no summer vacation plans ourselves, having decided earlier in the year to go to Europe in late autumn, to southern Italy or Provence. Of course, everything was on hold now. Traveling together in our current state would be impossible, especially with the forced intimacy of shared hotel rooms in foreign places; it hardly seemed as if we still spoke the same language. In our apartment, at least, we could retreat to separate, silent corners, and take some of our meals apart. And we could both seek relief in work and in the company of our respective friends.

I made a lunch date with Lucy, but when I arrived at G&F to pick her up, she was in the middle of a production crisis and couldn't leave. The familiar chaos there, the much ado about something—an endangered book—revived my longing to be a part of it all. *Come on, kids, let's put on a show!*

In the street again, I called Violet on her cell phone and found her at her studio. She sounded distracted, but she agreed to meet me for a quick lunch if I'd come downtown. Violet was going to be in a group show again in early December, called Women at Work. She'd already started to spend most of her spare time in the studio, or in meetings with the other female members of her co-op gallery. I was frankly jealous of her excitement, of the unwavering attention she paid to her painting, so I suppose I was less than tactful when I told her, at a crowded Soho sushi bar, that I thought the show's title was kitschy, and the accompanying logo, of a highway construction sign, tacky and dated.

Apparently I'd tapped into Violet's own submerged doubts, because she immediately said, "What would you call it?"

I was caught off guard, and I had to think for several frantic moments before I said I wasn't sure, but that I would organize the show around common concerns rather than gender, and perhaps mention gender in the catalog as one of the reasons for the artists having common concerns. I was just blathering to cover my mean-spiritedness, but Violet nodded thoughtfully and said she'd bring it up at the next artists' co-op meeting.

A few days later she called and asked if I'd like to help the group rename the show and then write the copy for the catalog, which should briefly describe each artist's work, and then expound on their collective mission. I quickly demurred: I couldn't, it wasn't my field, I didn't really have the time, but Violet cut right through my sputtering objections. "That's a load of crap, Allie," she said. "Just do it. If you can't visit everybody's studio, you can look at slides. And I'll give you one of my paintings for your trouble." Just what I needed. But I finally said that I would try.

And I told myself that I would try to do something about the situation between Ev and me, too. When he came home that evening, I was wearing a gauzy lilac-colored dress he liked, and I had dinner all prepared. It was mostly comprised of the unhealthy foods Ev favored, including rare roast beef, buttered potatoes, and a rich chocolate tart—not exactly light summer fare. This will either seduce him or kill him, I thought when he walked in looking so handsome and hateful that either scenario seemed reasonable.

But the dinner only succeeded in making him sleepy; he kept yawning during dessert and he declined the espresso I offered with a little wave of his hand, as if I were merely an overly solicitous waiter. Being the wronged party had imbued him with a kind of magisterial power. I couldn't even rouse his interest in Violet's new project, and I didn't bother mentioning my part in it. My hands were shaking as I started to clear the table.

When he was shuffling out of the kitchen, heading for the boys' bedroom, I flung a plate into the sink, smashing it, and shouted at his back, "This is so damn *stupid*, Ev!" I felt sick to my stomach, bloated with animal fat and anger and sadness. "Either really live with me or don't at all!"

He turned and looked at me in my wilted lilac splendor for a long moment before he said, coldly, "You're right, I am pretty stupid, to hang around here and take this crap. It's time I found another place."

His words went through me like a spray of bullets, but I said "Yes!" as if I'd just had the same bright idea myself. "I really wish you would."

"Don't worry, I'll be out of here tomorrow," he said, and of course I came right back with "Good!"

This conversation, or something very much like it, was probably taking place in kitchens and bedrooms all over the country, maybe the world—you only had to look at the divorce rates—but that knowledge didn't alleviate the horror of it taking place between us, in our kitchen, with the nesting spongeware bowls we'd received as a wedding gift all those years ago, and Ev's blue-and-white paperweight winking innocently at us from the windowsill.

How impossible marriage was; it had to be a matter of sadomasochism or just plain lethargy when it lasted. Ev never really listened to me; no wonder he'd always misread my stories. It was our *quarrel* I'd meant was stupid; how could he not have understood that? And what I'd said after that may have sounded like an ultimatum, but it was meant to be an invitation—*come live with me and be my love*. The man I had been prepared to take back to my bed, to my shredded heart, seemed repulsive to me now. We were so conspicuously different from each other we might have been members of separate species. Look at the foods he preferred—if it weren't for Ev's carnivorous appetites, and my own occasional meat hunger, I might have been a vegetarian by now. And didn't he once admit that he found *To the Lighthouse* "too political"?

Even our metabolisms were out of sync; I turned the heat up, he turned it down. All the emotional injuries I'd ever endured at his hands, from the workshop insults to the arguments over Scott, were instantly, blisteringly recalled. Most of all, it shamed me to think that his darkly bristled jaw, his hairy otherness, had once been a source of such arousal in me. Lumbering from the room now, he most resembled a bear leaving a campsite he had just plundered. Good riddance, I thought, go to hell, die.

When the phone rang the next morning, I almost didn't answer it. It was after ten, but I was still in bed, dazed by the Valium I'd finally washed down with a little vodka after midnight, and swamped with misery. Now there was something concretely wrong in my life, alongside the other, unaccounted-for something. I remembered hurting my own foot in a temper tantrum when I was about three or four, and my father saying, as he rubbed away the pain, "Well, now you really have something to cry about."

I'd heard Ev leave hours before, without a word. What was left for us to say, anyway? But when I finally picked up the phone, it was Michael, not Ev, on the line. "Is this a good time?" he asked, and I had to contain a hysterical urge to laugh. He seemed to be a genius of bad timing.

"Sure," I said, shutting my eyes against the light seeping poisonously through the blinds. Another day. "How are things going?" It was actually a relief to have my concentration jerked away from my own troubles like that.

"Not so hot," he said. "I was wondering if I could see you."

"What? When?" I opened my eyes and sat up. My heart began chugging, like a reluctant motor that had unexpectedly turned over.

"Whenever it's convenient."

"Michael," I said, "where are you?"

"Well, the airport, actually."

"*What* airport?"

"La Guardia."

"You're in New York," I said inanely. "Then why don't you just grab a cab and come here." And I gave him the address. Alice, think before you speak!

Then I was completely, urgently awake, throwing off the covers and rushing into the shower, where the water, too hot at first and then too cold, lashed at my defenseless skin until I howled a little, and felt better.

I had had little daydreams about Michael for weeks, about how he'd look, and how I would look to him. Mostly, I simply saw him as Joe Packer, that rawboned hero whose melancholy was modulated by a killer smile, but at other times, when I was feeling guilty or preposterous, I pictured Oliver Hardy, jammed into a squeaky desk chair, eating éclairs and writing a novel about a sexy, rawboned hero. As for myself, I seemed to be able to revamp my looks at will, becoming younger and more supple and vibrant each time—they were my own daydreams, after all.

But when I looked in the mirror after my shower, squinting to soften my view of a faded, menopausal redhead, there was clear confirmation of my decline: the gray strands, the persistent gravitational pull (even when I sucked everything in), the freckles that might just as easily be seen as age spots. And only recently, I'd had to get reading glasses. Maybe I'd gone downhill since the defection of the man who once swore he "loved the sorrows of [my] changing face." I thought grimly that I would need cataracts to do a real job of revision, and I'd probably have those pretty soon, too.

"Michael is here," the doorman told me in jovial tones half an hour later, as if he were announcing the arrival of an old, mutual friend. I watched through the peephole until the elevator door opened at the other end of the hallway, releasing a block of silvery light, like a spotlight on a stage, onto which the small, distant figure of a man, wearing jeans and a backpack, stepped.

If he'd begun to recite a soliloquy then, or burst into song, I wouldn't have been all that surprised. But he only paused for a moment before setting out in the direction of my apartment, growing larger and larger as he silently, inexorably approached. No Oliver Hardy, I was relieved to see, but no Joe Packer, either. Someone in between those impossible brackets of comic miscreant and romantic idol. Someone ordinary and oddly familiar. Had I ever seen him before?

Soon we were inches apart, almost eye-to-eye, with only the thickness of the door between us, and I watched as he grabbed a comb from his pocket and ran it through his thick, close-cropped hair. Then he licked his lips, the way I always do before my photograph is taken. He had a nice, curly mouth that seemed primed to register amusement.

When he rang the bell, I dropped the flap of the peephole as if it were hot, and waited for several beats before I opened the door. After the briefest pause, I put my hand out to shake his, but he'd already begun to embrace me, and I ended up poking him in the midsection, which made him let out a little "Oof!" and then laugh.

"So this is you," he said after putting his backpack down in the entrance. His expression was uncritical, even admiring. At least he didn't seem to be counting the rings in my neck to assess my age.

And *you*, I thought, but I only said, "In the flesh," and then worried because that sounded so provocative. "Come on in," I added hastily, gesturing toward the living room.

"This is great," Michael said, meaning the apartment. He went to the west-facing windows and looked out at the city. When he whistled in appreciation, I felt proud, as if I had erected the skyline myself moments ago, just for his appreciation. But I might have constructed him, too. "It sure beats my view," he said.

"Oh? What do you see?"

He shrugged. "A couple of scruffy trees, my neighbor's chain-link fence—with her pit bulls behind it—a shutdown GM plant in the distance. The same one I was laid off from."

Other people's lives. Exactly what had made me want to write fiction in the first place, so I could get inside someone else's psyche, someone else's experience, even if I had to seek them out in my imagination. It was the same reason I read fiction; curiosity and desire and fear made one measly life seem not nearly enough. I acknowledged the many privileges of my own, though, and wondered how I still managed to be so unhappy.

Michael looked unhappy, too, behind all his polite enthusiasm about me and my surroundings, and I reminded myself why he was here. "Let's have something to eat," I said, leading him into the kitchen. Somehow I still clung to the notion that it was easiest to talk across the common ground of a table spread with food and drink.

Michael's worry over his halted novel didn't seem to have affected his appetite. He ate the way my teenage sons used to, as if they were frantically refueling their racing engines. I remembered that they seemed to undergo a growth spurt after almost every meal. But Michael was a fully grown man.

For the first time, I allowed myself to really look at him, to observe the breadth of his shoulders in the black T-shirt he wore, and the smooth, hypnotic way his Adam's apple moved when he swallowed. I'd made coffee for both of us, serving him the leftovers, the wreckage, of last night's disastrous dinner with Ev, and he polished everything off.

When he was finished, he sighed his contentment and reached into his pocket for what I realized must have been cigarettes. But then he appeared to think better of it, and put his hands on the table, one on each side of his empty plate. He had long, restless spatulate fingers with close-bitten nails, as ravaged as mine were as a girl's. And he appeared to have more than one of the bad, impulsive habits I used to have — maybe that's why he'd seemed so familiar. "That was really delicious. Thank you," he said, the way he'd probably been taught to say it as a child. The only thing missing was the word *ma'am*. Still, it was a lot more than I'd gotten from Ev in return for the same offering.

I cleared the dishes, refilled our mugs, and sat down across from Michael again. "Do you want to smoke?" I asked him, and he looked shocked, as if I'd read his mind. "It's okay, go ahead," I said, and I even smiled in encouragement. But I was actually pretty shocked, myself. I was my father's daughter, in some ways, at least, and I didn't usually allow anyone to smoke in our apartment. I had to suppress the urge to jump up and throw open the window.

As he reached into his pocket once more, I felt blindly around the counter behind me for something that could serve as an ashtray, and came up with the sunny yellow bowl that Ev and I used for household odds and ends, like loose pennies, the screw whose source we couldn't figure out, and the collar button I kept meaning to sew back onto one of his shirts. I dumped the contents onto the counter, ignoring whatever had rolled onto the floor and under the stove, and presented the bowl to Michael.

"Would you like one?" he asked, extending the pack of cigarettes, Marlboros, of course.

I stared at the red-and-white box. It might have been made of plastic or fabric, an Oldenburg sculpture meant to comment on our stupid social mores. I hadn't had a cigarette in . . . I did the arithmetic in my head . . . God, it was thirty-six years. I didn't even know how much they cost these days. *Michael* was thirty-six; maybe I was taking my final puff the very moment he slid screaming into the world.

He tapped the cigarette pack and two of them popped up, one just a little higher than the other. I recalled the way it felt to do that particular trick: the heft of the pack in my hand, the silkiness of the cellophane, the precise amount of pressure in the tap. Voilà! And everything else about smoking that I'd loved came back in a flash: all the gestures and poses (I thought of Bacall and Bogart, Paul Henreid lighting up for two); the spark and stink of sulfur when the match was struck; the first gasp, followed by that little nicotine rush; and then the release of breath in a vaporous cloud, like an empty thought balloon floating around my head.

I hadn't actively thought about smoking in years, except in a forbidding, negative way—warning my own children about its dangers, feeling pious about all the idiots who still ignored the surgeon general's warning, and in a rage over the mendacity of the tobacco companies. But now this sweet young man, this writer of charm and talent and mystery, was holding out his precious pack of Marlboros to me, and I reached out my own hand to take one from him. Moses touching God, was my irreverent thought.

My fingers remembered how to hold it. How insubstantial it seemed, how purely white and perfectly cylindrical. I hoped he had a carton of them in his backpack, and for the briefest moment my father's irate voice was in my head—"What the hell do you think you're doing!" Then Michael flicked his lighter too close to my hair—there was actually a little sizzle—and I pulled it back from my face impatiently and put the cigarette between my lips, sucking in those delectable toxins the way I did at fifteen.

As soon as I inhaled, I felt woozy. "My," I said, putting my fingertips to my forehead, and Michael leaned forward companionably and said, "What?"

I could see his clean, crooked part, and the comb lines in his hair, which I realized was the same nut-brown color and texture as the coat of a Lab mix named Corky I'd had as a child. And Michael's head seemed almost irresistibly pettable to me then. Good boy, I thought, in a kind of delirium, but fortunately I had something else to do with my hands, another reason that I'd liked to smoke as a teenager.

Well, so Ev was a menacing bear and Michael a friendly puppy; ergo, all men are animals. And I remained supremely, irresistibly human, like Fay Wray. I might have been smoking pot, I felt so relaxed and witty. I think I even laughed out loud.

"What?" Michael said again, his pretty mouth, his whole expectant doggy being, poised to share the joke.

"Nothing," I told him, composing myself, flicking my cigarette at the yellow bowl, and then looking with regret at the ashes settling at the bottom of it. What if Ev walked in at that moment? What if he never walked in again? "Nothing at all," I said, after I took another, more satisfying drag. "So, tell me about Joe and Caitlin."

15

Ev found a place to stay, a Midtown sublet, so quickly he couldn't have had much of a chance to change his mind. I learned much later that the vacancy had been conveniently posted on the bulletin board at work the day he left, and he'd moved right in. That afternoon, after I'd directed Michael to the West Side Y, I went to the park for a while to try to sort out my feelings. But all I really did was stare at the mesmerizing movement of the river and wish things unsaid, undone.

When I came home I realized that Ev had been there in my absence. I'm not sure exactly how I knew it, but I did, as soon as I entered the apartment. I can only say that there was a disturbance in the air around me. It felt as if the place had been robbed, although I didn't notice anything missing right away. Then I put my purse down on the kitchen counter and took in the space on the windowsill where Ev's paperweight had been.

It was like that chilling moment in a thriller when the victim realizes she's not alone, that her murderer is somewhere in the house. Except that the very opposite was true; my murderer had been here and was gone. In the bedroom, the door of Ev's closet was ajar, and I could see the abandoned hangers dangling there.

I looked for a note from him in all the usual places—the bathroom mirror, the refrigerator door, my pillow—but all I found was a blue Post-it stuck to the cover of my computer, with his new address and phone number printed on it. I held the little square of paper up to the light, as if I hoped to find a hidden message, like the ones Jeremy used to write with the invisible ink in his junior spy kit, and that he'd probably cribbed from the Hardy Boys: "The treasure map is under the body." "Watch out, Jim, the girl has a gun!"

The only invisible subtext on the Post-it was *In case of emergency only*. There was a slight depression at the edge of the bed, on my side, where he may have sat for a moment or two before he left again. I put my hand on it and it felt cool, but I lay down there anyway, where he'd so recently been. Now, as my father would say, I really had something to cry about. And I had plenty to tell Andrea Stern, too, if psychotherapy was, as I tended to believe, something like the oral installments of a serialized novel.

"Well," Violet grudgingly conceded, "it's *something* like that." We were on a subway platform on Canal Street, waiting for a train to take us to Williamsburg and the live-in studio of one of her fellow co-op artists. "But with plenty of flashbacks," she said. "And CliffsNotes," she added.

I'd told Violet that Ev and I were having very serious problems, but not that he'd actually left. I suppose I felt ashamed, and afraid of hearing her opinion. And I still hadn't called or written to Dr. Stern, but my reticence there was inspired more by hopelessness now than by pride. When Violet asked, as we boarded the train, if I'd been in touch with her, I said, "What can she possibly say to make things better?"

"She's not supposed to make things better," Violet said with her usual annoyance. "She's not a trauma doctor, for God's sake. She can only help you to interpret your own responses to what's happening."

"Ah, the CliffsNotes," I said. And we rode all the way to Brooklyn in silence. Violet sketched the sleeping man sitting opposite her as we rattled across the bridge, while I kept glancing at and away from the other passengers in our car, most of whom looked, to my alarm and sorrow, either like would-be terrorists or the potential victims of terrorists. And no one wanted to make eye contact any more than I did.

Long ago, when we were all more innocent, and when I still thought of myself as a writer, the strangers on subways and buses seemed to hold the key to existence itself in their infinitely complex inner lives. Each one was a possible lover or friend, and worthy of being the hero or heroine of a least one short story.

As Violet and I walked down the steps from the elevated tracks on Broadway, in Brooklyn, I took out my cell phone to check for messages, which I did compulsively these days. I felt her questioning gaze on me—she could always smell my troubles—but she didn't say anything. There had been three calls.

The first was from Suzy, who lately often sounded as if she were still under the covers in bed, drowsing and warm, even when she phoned from her desk at the office. It was surely dangerous to be so conspicuously, complacently happy in such a miserable world, like flashing a wad of bills around in a bad neighborhood.

I hadn't said anything to the children about Ev and me—that was his job, *he* was the one who'd left. But he probably hadn't said anything, either, because none of them mentioned him when we spoke, except for the usual, casual "How's Dad?"—which I answered with my usual, offhand "Fine" before changing the subject. Now Suzy wanted to know if she could bring her George around to the apartment to meet us. Could that be construed as an emergency?

The second message was from Michael, who had taken a room at the Y. He phoned at least once every day, even when I had seen him only hours before, and he seemed surprised and let down whenever he reached my recorded voice. "Hello? Alice, are you there?" he'd ask. "Can you pick up?" Sometimes I was actually at home, screening my calls like other paranoid New Yorkers, taking only every other one or so from him. And when we met it was in what I thought of as safe, neutral places, like the park or a coffee shop, to defuse whatever I had sensed was happening between us that first morning in my apartment.

"Hey, Alice," he said this time. "I guess you're not there. Anyway, I've been thinking about what you said, and it feels right to me. So, thanks."

Then he simply breathed for a while, like a crank caller, before he said, abruptly, "Okay. Later."

I wasn't sure what he was referring to; I had said lots of things to him about his stalled manuscript in the week he'd been here. Sometimes I offered the examples of other blocked writers I had worked with, who'd managed to find their way through the impasse. Once, I'd quoted Kurt Vonnegut, who's supposed to have said, "God lets you write; he also lets you not write." And I talked about Joe and Caitlin as if they were old friends we'd both lost touch with, but had remained curious about. Mostly, I tried to draw him out about what he thought had happened, to both his characters and his creative flow, but I still wasn't asking any direct questions. And he didn't offer any insights of his own.

Michael had left his pack of Marlboros at the apartment the day of his arrival, and I'd smoked one every evening since then in what had become a kind of secret ritual, after which I gargled with mouthwash, showered thoroughly, and aired the place out. You would think it was out of consideration for someone else who lived there.

The final phone call was a hang-up, which came through as several rings followed by that irritating recorded announcement: "If you'd like to make a call, please hang up and try again." Coward, I nearly said aloud, meaning Ev, of course, who might or might not have been my third caller. Either way, the epithet fit.

Imogene Donnell, the artist we were visiting, and her girlfriend, Patty Berger, a textile designer, lived on Mezzarole Street, in a railroad flat above a bodega. Years ago, Violet told me, there'd been a pharmacy on that very corner that belonged to one of her father's cousins and his wife, who were known in the neighborhood as Doc and Mrs. Doc. They had retired in their sixties and moved to Florida, where they both died a few years later. The store window, which bore a large banner announcing TENEMOS CERVEZA! backed up by a pyramid of beer cans, had once been filled with blue and yellow apothecary jars, and the dusty objects of those seemingly simpler times: rubber shower caps and metal curlers, trusses and glass baby bottles.

"Cousin Edgar removed cinders from people's eyes, and offered second medical opinions, gratis," Violet said dreamily. "And he and Rose sold cough medicine laced with alcohol and codeine, right over the counter. Nobody sued anybody and they were all happy."

"I'll bet," I said.

Imogene was a small, shy woman who made enormous sculptures that crowded all the rooms of the apartment. Some of them almost grazed the high ceilings. I couldn't imagine how she'd gotten the raw material—mostly rough, gray slabs of what looked like granite—up the narrow staircase, or how she would ever get the finished pieces out. They most resembled tombstones, and at first I felt like a child in a cemetery, awed and oppressed by such incontrovertible evidence of mortality. Imogene had even chiseled some words and figures onto her sculptures, although I was relieved to see on closer inspection that they weren't epitaphs.

Her inscriptions were more like graffiti, the stuff that kids spray-paint on every available surface of the city. There were the nicknames of the living—Nicki, Chino, Mike, Kooby—not the permanent names and dates of the dead. And the drawings, of skateboarders and taxicabs, pigeons and bicyclists, were kinetic and cartoon-like, as opposed to the somber, stilled life, the carved angels and crosses, of genuine monuments.

She owed a clear debt to the action figures and urban slogans of Keith Haring. But there was something newer, and more ancient, about Imogene's work, too. I was reminded of cave drawings. The raw texture of the stone and her primitive style contributed to that idea, but so did a sense of recorded history, a groping toward a common language that would withstand time and change. *I was here,* they seemed to say, just like the grunting cavemen and, later, the more evolved artists with their paintings on canvas of perishable fruit and people. The ghosts of Violet's father's cousins, the white-coated pharmacists, paced beneath us as an Afro-Cuban number beat its way up through the floorboards.

If I'd been there under any other auspices, I don't think I would have been so generous in my assessment of Imogene's sculpture. All those years of editing had hardened my critical eye, and these pieces were both undeniably derivative and determinedly odd. Typical of Violet's nutty, artsy little circle.

I wondered fleetingly what it was like to be a lesbian. And where the hell did Imogene and Patty sleep? How did they find their way to the bathroom at night without breaking their toes? But because I had to write about this second-story graveyard for the co-op's catalog, I was forced to try to understand, rather than to simply judge it. I scribbled into the notebook I'd grudgingly bought just for this unsolicited project. "Hieroglyphics in the age of terror," I wrote. "Bigger than life." But I quickly crossed out "life," and put in "death" instead. I asked Imogene why she made art, hoping for something I could quote in the piece, and she just shrugged and said, "It doesn't make much sense, does it, given the way things are. But I do it anyway."

Then there were footsteps on the stairway, and Patty, a tall, leggy blonde, came in, breathless and bearing grocery bags. She and Imogene embraced, and their domestic happiness was obvious and disquieting. The bags were emptied of milk and eggs and butter and a net sack of golden oranges. I wouldn't have been completely surprised if they pulled out a chain of knotted silk scarves, and a live rabbit, too. For the first time I noticed the sculpture-sized refrigerator that Imogene had opened to receive all that bounty. And soon I saw the bed, with its rumpled Indian-print throw and inviting pile of jewel-colored pillows, behind a row of sculptures that served as a stonework screen. I wanted to wail. I wanted a cigarette.

When I came home, there was a new message flashing on my machine. Michael again. He wanted to talk some more about something I'd told him in the coffee shop the day before, while he shredded a little mountain of paper napkins on the table between us. "Maybe Joe doesn't want to find Caitlin," I'd said. "Maybe he feels guilty about something related to her." It was only a stab in the dark—there was that almost incestuous scene in their childhood, and all the abusive men she chose ever afterward—and Michael had merely looked thoughtful when I said it.

Perhaps I had managed to spark a breakthrough, after all, but I didn't feel like calling him back right then and reentering his novel's dark, parallel life. For once, my own lousy life seemed to be all I could handle. Instead I grazed in the cool light of the open refrigerator—bits of cheese and fruit and pickle chips—and then I took my mother's folder from my desk and got into bed with it.

I reread the letters from Tom Roman and the one from that editor at *The New Yorker*. And I went through the poem about feeding the ducks and geese in Central Park once more. When I shut my eyes the scene was instantly revived: the gritty feel of the bread crumbs as I sprinkled them at our feet, the beating of wings when the birds finally took off, and the shadows they cast across our faces. What was the invisible message here? And why did it seem so connected to that enduring burden behind my breastbone?

On an impulse I set the poem aside on my night table. Then I put the folder back into my desk drawer and went into the kitchen to call Suzy, with a glass of Merlot in one hand and a lit Marlboro in the other. "So, you want George to discover your aristocratic roots," I said. "Should I prepare myself for an announcement?"

There was muffled whispering and laughter at the other end, and then Suzy said, into the receiver, "Maybe, maybe not. Did you tell Dad that we want to come over?"

"No," I said. "I mean, not yet."

"Can I talk to him?"

"He's not here," I told her. "He's working late." Under other circumstances, I might have teased her about the vow she'd made when she was four to marry Ev, her "big sweetheart," someday. "But Daddy's already married," I told her then, and she patted my arm consolingly and said, "Don't worry. You can get another husband."

"He's working late *again*?" she said now. "Well, tell him to call me when he gets in, okay?"

"Okay," I agreed. Damn him, I thought. Now he's making me lie to my own child. I'd finished the glass of wine, too quickly, and smoked the cigarette almost down to the filter.

"Is next Friday all right?" Suzy asked. "For dinner?" When I didn't answer right away, she said, "So, is it all right? Mom?"

I walked to the sink and tossed the butt in, where it sparked and sputtered out, like a dud firecracker. "Sure," I said. I sniffed my hands, and they smelled as if I'd been in a bar for about a week. "Well, I think so, anyway. Let me check with Dad." *And by the way, if you still want him, he's all yours.*

After Suzy and I hung up, I went to my computer to retrieve the Post-it that clung to its cover like a strip of toilet paper to the bottom of a shoe.

Then I poured a little more wine into my glass and lit another cigarette to stall for time and to give me courage. Still, I had to walk around the apartment with the phone in my hand for a few minutes before I worked up the nerve to dial the unfamiliar number that I immediately committed to memory.

He didn't answer for several rings—maybe he'd forgotten where the phone was in his new place—and then he picked it up and said, "Yes?" cautiously, as if I might be a telemarketer. Or maybe he was more afraid that it would be me.

"It's Alice," I said. I heard his sudden intake of breath—had he taken up smoking again, too? No, he just wasn't prepared to hear my voice, and that was something like a home-team advantage. "We have a problem," I told him, and I paused just long enough to let him imagine the worst, before I went on. "Suzy called. She wants to bring her sweetheart here to meet us." That appellation, I knew, wasn't idly chosen.

"What did you tell her?" Ev asked.

"Nothing," I said. "Just that I would inform you. She wants you to call her tonight, by the way."

"You didn't say anything about us?"

"No," I said, and I blew some smoke rings at the ceiling. "I think that's your responsibility, don't you?" Normal people, I thought bitterly, would be saying, "Should we use the good china? What do you think about veal? Or would the chicken with prunes and olives be more festive?"

"Al," he said plaintively, and I wondered how my name tasted in his mouth. I couldn't bring myself to utter his.

"What?"

"This is really awkward," Ev said. "I mean it's such a bad way for Suzy to start out with this guy."

"Yes, I suppose it is," I said, and then I waited, not filling in the silence nervously as I was ordinarily inclined to do. When he still didn't say anything else, I finally gave in and said, "They want to come here next Friday night."

"Oh, shit," he muttered.

"Do you have other plans?" I asked in that mock-pleasant tone he hated more than sincere anger. "Or didn't you intend to ever tell the children?"

"Eventually," he said. "Soon. You can tell her Friday's okay. That's if it's all right with you."

His careful courtesy infuriated me. "You can tell her yourself," I said, and I hung up. Then I counted the cigarettes left in the pack, like a miser totting up his gold. There were only six of them, so I picked up the phone again and called my supplier.

16

Michael wanted to see me the next day to discuss his manuscript and whatever I had said to help liberate his writing, but I'd made plans to have lunch with Lucy Seo, and to visit my father after that. "I have an idea," I told Michael. "How would you like to go to a nursing home with me?"

"Gee, already?" He laughed, and I smiled in response, even though he couldn't see me. How easy it was to cheer him up.

"I meant just to browse," I said. "The thing is, I have to visit my father there, and I wouldn't mind some company." And maybe a witness, I thought, not knowing exactly what I meant by that. "You just have to remember that *all* experience is useful to a writer." That old workshop chestnut again; it's a good thing he wasn't paying me by the hour.

"Yes, ma'am," Michael said.

"And we can have coffee somewhere afterward and talk about the book."

"Sure," he said, and we arranged to meet in Midtown right after my lunch with Lucy.

Those plans were still in my head as Lucy and I read the menus at Gillie's, the big, brightly lit deli I'd chosen because we wouldn't run into any of the literary lights who frequented the more elegant restaurants nearby, like the Union Square Café and Gramercy Tavern. And I had a contrary craving for the school-cafeteria ruckus of this place, the blood-clogging daily specials, the aging, sardonic waiters in their dated tuxedos. It was like the old days, cramming lunch in during a frantic day at the office, and Lucy was, as always, slightly, comfortably overweight and very wound up, but willing and able to unwind for our brief respite.

I didn't mention that I was meeting Michael later, but as we leaned toward each other across a bowl of pickles, I talked about his book. Lucy seemed to be infected by my excitement and, like me, she loved the title *Walking to Europe*. I told her that I hoped to show the manuscript to someone at G&F when it was ready, instead of just giving Michael the names of some agents and editors, my usual method when the writer has no connections of his own. Together Lucy and I sketched possible jacket designs on paper napkins—footprints traversing a globe, a cubist rendering of Caitlin's three tattoos—like teenagers trying out the name of some newly beloved in a loose-leaf binder. Then we shared a massive corned beef sandwich, dripping with mustard and Russian dressing.

Over coffee, I told Lucy that Ev and I were having a marital crisis, without offering any details, and she grabbed my hands and expressed her sympathy. Unlike Violet, she didn't ask too many questions or offer unsolicited advice, and she was in a happy marriage herself. My friendship with safe, lenient Lucy was much more casual and occasional than the intensity Violet and I shared. But maybe I needed that extra challenge, as I'd seemed to need it in my marriage, an edge that often threatened to become a precipice you could throw yourself from when the going became too difficult.

"I'm seeing that shrink again," I told Lucy.

"Well, good," she said.

"Not just for that, though."

She looked inquiringly at me, and I said, "Something's really been bothering me."

"What is it?"

"That's what I hope to find out."

"You're not sick, Alice, are you?"

"No, no. It's just an uncomfortable feeling I've been having, a little, you know, *angst.*" Another deficient description of that thing in my chest, and I began to feel uncomfortable just talking about it, so I said briskly, "Enough about that. I'll work it out. Tell me what's new in the literary world." And she finally dropped her searching glance and began to fill me in on all the publishing gossip, which I still stubbornly, voraciously wanted to hear—about the latest firings and hirings, and the hot new books. But I listened without the usual yearning this time.

When Lucy saw Michael waiting eagerly outside Gillie's for me, she appeared startled, then thoughtful. He was supposed to have met me at the subway entrance on the next corner, but I'd mentioned the name of the restaurant, and he'd taken his chances and waited there. His hair seemed wet, as if he'd rushed over after a shower, and the idiot had brought flowers, a bunch of heavy-headed magenta dahlias that I tried to ignore. I quickly introduced him to Lucy as that writer whose novel she'd probably be designing before long.

I felt myself going rashy red, though, as if I'd made that up on the spot, and I saw that Lucy took critical note of my unease and of the way Michael gazed at me. Our earlier, easy mood seemed to have completely dissipated. But she shook Michael's hand politely and told him that she looked forward to working with his book. Then she turned to me and said, purposefully and as if we were quite alone, "Alice, I really hope everything works out."

"Well, thanks," I replied breezily. "I'm sure it will."

As soon as she was gone, Michael asked, "Are you okay?"

"Of course," I told him, in the same dismissive tone I'd used with Lucy. "Why shouldn't I be?" And I stepped to the curb and hailed a cab to take us to Riverdale.

My father had no other visitors that day, but he didn't seem very pleased to see me. I had warned Michael about his senility and his mood swings, that he might not even know who I was. But my father, who was at his usual station in the wheelchair next to his bed, said, "Oh, it's you," sourly, almost accusingly, as soon as I walked into the room, with Michael trailing a few feet behind me, still carrying the bouquet of dahlias.

"Daddy, how are you?" I said, bending to kiss his cheek, and then I tugged Michael forward a little, feeling the weight of his reluctance. "This is my friend Michael Doyle—he's brought you these lovely flowers. Michael's writing a wonderful book that I'm editing." Again, that sounded like a convenient lie, and my father's face was as skeptical as Lucy's had been. "Michael," I resolutely continued, "this is my father, Dr. Samuel Brill."

Michael's extended hand was conspicuously ignored, and my father stared up at him with undisguised contempt. "So this is the fellow," he said. *Now* what? "You have some nerve showing your face around here, mister."

"Daddy, stop that," I said.

"Maybe I ought to wait outside for you," Michael murmured, and I touched his arm and said, "No, stay, please." I turned to my father again. "What are you talking about?" I asked.

"Maybe this isn't—" Michael began, but I stopped him again, and his bicep rippled nervously under my fingers.

"Why do you bring that filth, your . . . paramour in here!" my father demanded. "Are you getting even?"

My heart thrummed, but I answered him boldly. "For what?"

"Oh, don't play dumb with me," my father said. "I know your game."

"Sam," I said softly. "There's no game. You know I would never hurt you."

He put his face into his hands then and began to make odd, gulping noises that I realized, after a perplexed moment, were the spasms of dry sobbing.

"Jesus," Michael murmured. He sounded prayerful rather than blasphemous, but he was riveted now, and instinctively protective. His hand gripped my shoulder, and all the heat in my body seemed to go to that juncture.

"He thinks I'm my mother," I whispered to Michael, and to myself. It was like translating the dialogue of a foreign film without titles.

"Oh," he said.

I knelt at my father's chair and pried his hands away from his face. "It's me, Daddy, it's *Alice*," I said firmly, and I saw the comprehension slowly take shape in his eyes—a clearing between clouds—and I watched his jaw relax. I opened my purse and took out my mother's untitled poem, rattling it a little to hold his attention. "Daddy, listen. Do you remember Mother's . . . do you remember Helen's poems?"

"Yes. Of course I do." His old, edgy hauteur was restored. "My wife is a poetess," he said, addressing Michael, who looked searchingly at me, uncertain of his next lines.

"I especially like this one," I said, still kneeling, forcing my father's roaming gaze. Then I began to read the poem aloud. The room was still, and I could see the shadow of a figure standing in the doorway, listening. When I finished, someone began clapping, slowly and deliberately. I looked up, slightly disoriented, almost expecting to see the old crowd in my parents' living room at one of my little poetry "recitals." But it was only the person in the doorway, a wraith-like inmate in baggy sweats. For a few seconds I didn't know whether it was a man or a woman. A woman, I decided as she wandered away, and I saw the long white hair escaping from a kid's pink plastic barrette.

"Jesus," Michael said again and he sat down on the edge of my father's bed.

I took my father's mottled hand. It was the same lizard-like temperature as my own. "Did you like that, Daddy?" I asked. "It's about Central Park, where Mother and I used to feed the birds. We'd come up and meet you at the hospital afterward. Do you remember?" I could summon up those events clearly, myself, and with all my senses: my mother's fragrance giving way to the antiseptic odors of the hospital; the sound of Miss Snow's heels as she led us into the inner sanctum of my father's consultation room; the way he always stood up to greet us, dwarfing the plaster models of the heart and brain behind him, making him look taller than he actually was; the plush, majestic Lincoln bearing us home through the fading day.

"Not bad. For an amateur," my father said.

But she wasn't! I wanted to shout. Instead I took my hand back and calmly said, "Well, maybe it's not her best. I'm not sure I even understand it. I mean, who do you suppose the goose in the poem is?"

"Why, it's you," he said promptly.

"Me?"

"Certainly." And only his mouth smiled. "Goosey girl."

I sank down on the bed next to Michael. "My God," I said.

"What is it?" Michael asked. "Alice, what's this all about?"

I was going to say it was nothing, that my father was crazy, that's all, and not responsible for the things he said. But I could only wave my hand weakly at Michael until he took it between the twin furnaces of his own.

Later, in a diner on Broadway, I told him everything: about my mother's death and my father's decline, about the loss of my job and how I'd become a book doctor, about the feeling in my chest that I'd been harboring since April, even about the Grimms' Goose Girl, and all the letters and poems in my mother's folder. The only thing, the only one I left out of my story was Ev.

But Michael wanted all of the pieces or, at least for him, the most essential one. "You're married, aren't you?" he asked.

"Yes," I said. "Sort of, anyway. We're separated," I added, and the impact of my own words was so acute, I might have been reporting a disaster that had happened only moments before. I should have changed the subject then—talked about the weather, the bitter coffee cooling before us, the city scurrying past outside the windows—anything at all would have done. Neither of us had even mentioned his manuscript, the reason we were meeting in the first place. But I seemed to have lost the desire or the ability to speak.

He kept looking at me with his dark, unguarded eyes until I had to glance away. Then he picked up my hand again, turning it over as if he were going to tell my fortune, and pressed his mouth against it. An electric thrill went directly from my palm through all the circuits in my body down to my curling toes. "Oh, Alice," he said. Exactly what I was thinking.

There was so much time for the spell to lift, for the sequence of events to falter and stop, like a torn strip of film. Michael dropped a few bills on the table and led me outside to another cab, which took long minutes to find. And there was the usual late-day crosstown traffic; we didn't fly through the park to the East Side. We moved slowly through a sunlit aspic all the way to my building, where we went right past Luis, my favorite doorman, and up the nineteen flights in the stately, sluggish elevator.

Then I had to find my key ring in the usual morass at the bottom of my purse, and isolate the right keys, and fit them into the proper keyholes, and open the door. All such nerveless, astonishing feats of skill. He shoved me up against the wall as soon as we were inside, and I shoved back, but not in resistance. When he kissed me, my head banged a little, but even that didn't bring me to my senses. What if Ev had come home before us? But of course he hadn't; the apartment was empty and waiting.

I could smell furniture polish, the moth sachets in the closets, our mingled, intoxicated breath. *What is this?* I thought, as if I didn't know, and *help me,* and *please,* and even *alas, queen's daughter.* The word *paramour* blazed up like a migraine aura on the velvet screen behind my eyes. All that before my knees folded like paper and fell open.

17

Everything in the world seemed to be sexually charged after that. I found myself flushing and blanching the way I had in the perpetual embarrassment of adolescence. And like Joe Packer, in Michael's book, I kept thinking: what have I done? But somehow I managed to forestall the question and banish most of the heated images from my head while I planned and prepared the dinner for Suzy and George.

The white peaches I'd found at the Vinegar Factory were especially sweet—it was the heart of their season—and Faye's flan recipe was precise and surprisingly easy to follow. When I inverted each little ramekin, its silken contents fell out with a delicate plop and then quivered for a moment, as if it had just had a narrow escape. Esmeralda, who'd come to help me serve and clean up, had prepared the receiving plates with dabs of gingered syrup, to make it possible to center the flan, and I scribbled gibberish in raspberry sauce with a pastry tube around the rim of the plates. The results were so beautiful, I quivered a little myself as I looked at them and contemplated the evening ahead.

Having ordinary dinner guests during ordinary times had always been a particular pleasure. Maybe that's because my parents let me sit in on their dinner parties when I was a child, and they had always seemed like such natural, cheerful events. It made perfect sense to me to break bread with friends and family, to share our common needs for sustenance and company at the same time. And why not add the enhancements of candlelight and flowers, the seductive tones of Schubert or Shearing?

But this was hardly an ordinary occasion. Suzy was bringing the man she loved to dinner at her parents' home, without knowing that her father didn't live there anymore, or that her mother, in a state of opaque fear and sheer anguish, had recently taken a young lover, too. None of the children knew anything. With Suzy's consent, I'd invited Scott and Jeremy and Celia to join us. "Okay, let's just get it all over with," was the way she put it, sighing heavily, as if she were facing serious surgery with a certain grim bravado.

I dreaded the whole elaborate charade myself, but once things had been set into motion, it seemed impossible to stop them. And here I was, admiring the flan, worrying over the sole and the sautéed greens. It was a little like thinking about death before going on with our lives, a curiously brief panic from which we can be so easily seduced by the very worldly goods we're going to lose.

Ev was the first to arrive, at least twenty minutes early. When everyone else got there, I realized, he would be smoothly in place, as if he'd never left—what a sly trick. He rang the bell rather than use his keys. He might have been afraid that I had changed the locks and he would have to fumble outside the apartment in growing humiliation and anger before I let him in, or perhaps he was simply presenting himself anew to me, a stranger without our long history of love and its recent dissolution. I was sure that it was Ev who had rung the bell, even before I looked through the peephole. The four-to-midnight doorman, someone new enough not to really know the children, hadn't announced anyone, and I could sense Ev's nervous, waiting presence just beyond the door.

I had told Esmeralda that I would let everyone in that evening, and I walked slowly down the long foyer, the way overeager brides stroll down the aisle when they become conscious of having to pace themselves. That foyer, the very wall where Michael and I had fallen so avidly upon each other, was innocent of afterimages, except in my own mind, and I blinked several times in an effort to erase them. But when I saw Ev through the peephole, I remembered seeing Michael framed that way for the first time, the way he'd combed his hair and licked his lips—*the better to kiss you with, my dear!* I felt that old, low ache in my belly as I opened the door to Ev, and unreasonable fury with him for my own unfaithfulness.

"Hi," he said, standing there a little slumped, a door-to-door salesman who'd had a discouraging day. He was freshly shaven, though, and wore his creamy linen jacket, and I was reminded of a time long ago when I would have bought just about anything he pitched. There were no flowers tonight, no attempt at a kiss or even a friendly embrace. Just as well, because I had instinctively taken a step backward, as if to avoid the germs of someone with a bad cold.

"Hi," I said lamely in return. If it wasn't such balmy summer weather, if he'd had an overcoat or an umbrella, I might have taken it from him, a conveniently mundane gesture to interrupt the terrible tension between us. Instead I foolishly waved him inside. One would think he didn't know his own way.

Esmeralda came out of the kitchen to greet her *"Señor Guapo."* She had always openly favored Ev over me, despite what I considered my domestic bond with her—we sometimes tackled big jobs, like the closets, together; consulted on household or beauty products; and I offered sympathetic glances when she quarreled with her own husband on our telephone. Well, so much for sisterhood. Of course, I was the one who occasionally suggested (but never demanded) that it was time to wipe out the refrigerator or vacuum behind the furniture. But I was also the one who considerately tidied the apartment before she came to clean it. She'd picked up cheerfully after slovenly Ev, though, and the incident of the Clichy—my merely having asked her if she'd seen it—had only added to my villainy, while he remained, as always, pure and guiltless.

I was certain Esmeralda knew that he had moved out. She had access to our closets and drawers, to the depressions we left in our pillows and our mattress, even to our trash, all intimate clues to the occupancy of the apartment, the state of our marriage. I wondered with a chill if Michael had left clues of himself here, too, if Esmeralda had that much power of knowledge over me. I had meticulously disposed of all the cigarette stubs and sprayed one of those scented air fresheners I hate everywhere after Michael left, to cover the damning odors of smoke and sex, but she still sniffed suspiciously whenever she entered the apartment. And I imagined her in her yellow rubber gloves, dusting for fingerprints and dropping evidence against me into ziplock plastic bags, like a vice-squad detective. Ev had a kiss for *her*, I noticed, an affectionate little peck on the cheek that almost caused me to snort in indignation, and they exchanged a few bantering words in Spanish. Without the benefit of foresight, I had taken useless French in school.

Ev went into the dining area and surveyed the table. Among his former responsibilities, when we had dinner guests, was to take the chest of good silverware down from the hall closet, put the extra leaves into the table, and unfurl the tablecloth down its extended length. As he could plainly see, all of this had been done without him tonight, and I wondered if he was brooding over his easy expendability. It would have pleased him greatly, I thought, to watch me drag the step stool to the closet before handing the silver chest down to Esmeralda, and to know that it took the two of us to maneuver the heavy table leaves.

Jeremy and Celia arrived next, and I quickly detected a rare estrangement between them. They'd always displayed a patent oneness that was sexual, social, and musical. Violet had once wryly referred to them as "Adam and his rib." And they'd often made me think of the pair of cardinals—the red male and the brown female—that once lived in my parents' garden, and were always seen in tandem. But Jeremy and Celia headed in different directions as soon as they walked in, as if they'd just been demagnetized. Was it something familial? Was it catching? Jeremy, who could never hide his feelings, seemed miserable as he handed me a bottle of the awful Algerian red they drank. His eyes were pink-rimmed and his cheeks were dappled with contained emotion. I believed that if I said the wrong thing to him, he would have started bawling. At the opposite end of the living room, Celia was merely defiant, with her arms folded across her flat chest, her pointy little chin lifted. Ev glanced questioningly at me, but I turned away. Somehow, this was his fault, too.

Scott, life's sleepwalker, came in a few minutes later, waved casually to everyone, and went straight to the cashews and the cheese board. He was wearing a Hawaiian sport shirt with his jeans, rather than the tattered T-shirts he favored, and he looked flashy, but also a little blank without some name or slogan spanning his narrow chest. I had told him he could bring someone if he liked, that it would even out the table, but I really only wanted him to feel comfortable, not to be the only one without a dinner partner. He'd arrived alone, anyway, and it didn't matter very much, since no one else in the room appeared to still be coupled. We needed Suzy and George desperately by then, for romantic relief. They were late, of course, which only made them more keenly anticipated, and when they finally made their entrance, they received all of our ardent attention.

George was the one bearing flowers, a sumptuous summer bouquet he presented so grandly, I might have just won a beauty contest. He was the beauty, though, unconventionally so, just as Suzy had said; kind of a cross between Lenny Bruce and the young Marlon Brando. I especially liked the openness of his expression, and I was moved by the tiny razor nick on his upper lip; he had worried over meeting us, too. As I greeted him, Suzy was on the edge of my vision, looking peach-skinned and ripe in a skimpy black eyelet shift. What gorgeous children they'll have, was my precipitate thought. "Hello, Suzy's mom," George said, beaming at me as he bestowed my new world title. My father would have been delighted—a lawyer, the next best thing to a doctor, and a diplomat to boot. Suzy's pride in George, her intemperate happiness, was so dazzling, I had to avert my eyes for a moment. Oh, my lucky girl! My poor girl.

I watched the rest of the action around the room as if it were a ballet, something modern, but with traditional origins. Ev stepped up from behind me to greet his daughter and his replacement in her affections with what I grudgingly allowed was good sportsmanship. The men shook hands gravely, sealing an unspoken bargain, and Ev draped his arm across Suzy's shoulders for a few seconds before he seemed to nudge her in George's direction. He was already, reluctantly, giving her away.

Scotty approached next, tossing cashews quickly into his mouth and wiping his palms on his jeans so he could shake hands, too. "Hey, whassup?" he mumbled to his sister, accidentally bumping heads with her when she presented her cheek for a kiss. His oddball, abbreviated way of saying hello, I suppose, of offering his blessings. And for once, no one seemed to mind. Suzy rubbed her head and smiled indulgently at her baby brother, the erstwhile scourge of her existence, and George lightly punched him on the shoulder and called him "man," just when Scotty seemed to me most obviously a boy.

As Scott wandered off, Celia and Jeremy came warily from their opposite corners, almost, but not quite, converging. I found myself trying to measure the pulsing space between them, willing it vainly to close. There were sisterly kisses and more manly handshakes, followed soon by cocktails and appetizers. Ev played host, and Esmeralda wove in and out among the guests with the precision of a flamenco dancer, balancing a tray of miniature crab cakes and flirting with all the men before rushing back to the kitchen. I rushed in after her, transferring all of my anxieties at the last minute to the food.

And then we were seated around the table in the flattering flicker of candlelight. I silently thanked Faye for her recipes as the minted pea soup and the delicate sole were each lauded in turn. For some reason, things weren't that awkward; we might have been any family sharing a special, festive dinner. Ev did more than his share to contribute to the illusion, attentively pouring the Chardonnay and starting a lively conversation with George about things we'd never discussed between ourselves, like legal advocacy for the homeless and the intricacies of city planning.

Jeremy and Celia wrenched themselves out of their private misery long enough to join in a little, and even Scott awakened from his usual fugue state to offer opinions. They were decidedly offbeat, of course, even absurd—some of the homeless should be given accelerated law degrees, for example, and parts of Central Park turned into farmland for homesteaders.

I had a flash of name-calling and food fights, of Suzy or Jeremy leaving the table in tears. There was passionate argument this time, and a little jeering, but nobody really attacked Scott or laughed directly at him. "Maybe you should go to law school," George told him in a not-completely-ironic tone. Scott coolly took it as his due, and Suzy even said, "Why not?" I wondered if she was drunk, and when they had all become so mature, so incredibly tolerant of one another. I hardly even cared that Ev said, "Brava!" to Esmeralda as she cleared the soup plates, or that she bowed slightly in acceptance of his praise, as if she'd done more than just shell the peas and ladle out the soup.

When the phone rang, I didn't recognize the sound at first. It might have been the oven timer or a car alarm going off down in the street. I even hoped, rather hopelessly, that it was someone else's cell phone, but the ring was too familiar, too persistent. And when I heard Esmeralda say "The Carroll residence" in her stagy company voice into the sudden quiet, I knew immediately who it was. Even before she came into the room and said "Mrs.?" in that knowing and insinuating way, I'd risen from my seat, blazing, letting my fork clatter onto my plate and my napkin drop to the floor.

I had a rapid and dizzying run of disconnected thoughts. Why isn't she ever on my side? Did he have to call now? Why couldn't Faye have lived with her son? Why was the door to my father's office locked? "Excuse me," I said to the table at large, to George in particular, and then hurried down the hallway to pick up the master bedroom extension. "I have it," I said firmly to Esmeralda's expectant breath in my ear, and after hearing that definitive click, "Hello?"

"Alice," Michael said. "Wow, I'm so glad you're there."

"This really isn't a good time. I have dinner guests," I told him, thinking what a handy euphemism that was for my nuclear family.

"Ah," he said, his disappointment as evident as a child's. "When can we talk, then?"

"Later. Tomorrow, maybe."

"All right," he said. And after a pause, "Listen, I think I love you."

"This isn't a good time," I said again, and I hung up. I sat on the bed, trembling, and possessed by that thought: what have I done?

Except that I knew exactly what I had done. I'd yanked off my clothes, as if they were the things on fire, instead of all those secret, inflamed pink parts of me: tongue, nipples, labia. I thought of them deliberately by their clinical, erotic names; they might have just appeared before me in a medical manual or a pornographic film. Our kisses were like an eating contest. And at the same time, I put my hands over Michael's crazy hands, to hurry him up, to slow him down. I wasn't sure what I wanted, but it didn't matter, the whole point was the wanting itself. By the time he'd lifted me, so that my legs were around his waist, I was laughing out loud, or he was— every barrier between us had broken down by then, had melted. Michael, who smelled as shockingly new as the first boy I'd ever kissed, was beautiful and completely erect, a toy on a spring I jammed inside me, while we were still kissing, with what I can only call savage happiness. We moved as steadily, as urgently as blood, as marathon runners, and when that whole frenzy of lovemaking, begun in the foyer and ending on one of the living room sofas, was over, I didn't feel anything resembling remorse, anything at all that wasn't physical and colored by triumph.

Even much later that night, after cigarettes and food and sleep, when Michael finally began to talk about his book, about the amazing breakthrough he'd had because of me, I had to force myself to listen. He said that I'd zapped him out of his block with my question about Joe's guilt over Caitlin's disappearance; it was like an electrical charge that had jump-started his brain. I began to think that the sex had rendered mine useless.

"She's probably dead, though," he said, and he seemed stricken by his own insight.

I came to, then, startled and leery. "What do you mean? He didn't kill her, did he? You're not turning the book into a murder mystery, are you?"

Michael smiled at my rush of worried questions. "No, no," he assured me. "There's no mystery, at least not in the genre sense. It's more psychological. You'll see."

"Okay," I told him. "Just write it, though. Don't talk it out, or you might lose it." My favorite literary cliché.

His face became intensely serious. "Let's not talk at all," he said, and his mouth and hands began to move over me again.

I had missed the grand entrance of the flan. No doubt Esmeralda had taken credit for that, too, in my absence. Hadn't I heard something like a ruffle of applause while I was on the phone with Michael? As I took my place at the table, feeling drained and weak-kneed, they all picked up their spoons, and Ev said, "Who was that, Al?" as if he had every right to ask.

"Nobody. A friend," I muttered, and my face grew hot. With all of the lying I'd done recently, I still hadn't learned how to do it with ease or grace. I could imagine Esmeralda smiling to herself in the kitchen, and I thought that Suzy gave me a brief but penetrating glance.

Ev was digging into the flan. "This is terrific," he said, raising a whole new chorus of acclaim.

Then George stood up, clutching his napkin in his fist. He held his other hand out to Suzy, who stood, shimmering, beside him. Everyone around the table grew still. "We have an announcement," George said.

At the end of "The Goose Girl," in my childhood volume of Grimms' fairy tales, when the princess and her prince were finally wed, "the whole kingdom rang with merriment," which always seemed much better to me than the traditional translation, with just the two of them living happily ever after. And that phrase echoed in my head when George spoke, declaring his love for Suzy and proclaiming their engagement. He had a ring to give her, an immodest blue-white solitaire that had been his late mother's, and I noticed that Suzy's hand was steadier than his as he slipped it on. The little kingdom around our table rang with merriment, except maybe for Celia and Jeremy, whose responses were courteous but subdued.

There were congratulations and toasts, and then people wandered back into the living room and down the hallway to the bathrooms. Ev came around the table before I could leave, too. "That was really something, wasn't it?" he said. "Thank you." Did he mean for the dinner, for the children, for allowing the impression, tonight, that our household was intact? "You're welcome," I said, a generic answer that covered everything, and then I moved quickly ahead of him out of the room.

Suzy was standing alone in my bedroom when I got there. I shut the door behind me. "Honey," I said, going toward her, smiling. "I can't believe it."

"I'm the one having trouble believing things," she answered.

"What do you mean?" But I already knew what she meant. I could see the master bathroom just beyond her, where the door to the medicine cabinet was ajar. And Ev's closet door was open, too, revealing the emptiness inside, a mute reproach to Ev's and my whole performance.

"Were you looking for something?" I asked, just to buy myself a little more time, but Suzy ignored that pathetic ruse.

"Where are Dad's things?" she demanded, as if she thought I'd hidden or stolen them.

"Suzy, let's not spoil everything . . ."

"It's too late for that, Mom," she said. Her eyes and her new diamond glittered with a similar glacial light. "Everything's spoiled already. Why didn't you *tell* me about this?"

"It's complicated," I said, somewhat ashamed of using that old, evasive saw. At least I didn't say "Mind your own happiness," which had also occurred to me, but would have sounded more like a rebuke than maternal caution.

"So are you getting a divorce?" She wore the same alarmed and bossy face she'd worn as a child when she'd made us swear never to do precisely that.

"We're just living apart right now. We're both angry about things, so it's hard to be together."

"Do you have somebody else?" she said.

Why did she only ask this about me? It probably wasn't that she saw me as being more desirable than her father, but only as more treacherous. For the first time, I felt a throb of jealous curiosity about Ev. "No," I said, because that really wasn't any of her business. "Listen," I continued, "I know our timing isn't great. And maybe it was naïve, but we wanted you and George to have a perfect evening. It's the first thing your Dad and I have agreed about for a while."

That earned me a small, bitter smile. "It's your life, I guess," she said at last, and then her arms came around me in an assault of angry love.

Celia and Jeremy, who were staying overnight with friends, downtown, were the first to leave, taking their troubles with them. Then Suzy, fully composed now, took George away. He would comfort her, I knew; that was *his* role now. A few minutes later Scotty looked around him pensively and left, too, empty-handed.

When Esmeralda came out of the clean kitchen, shutting off the lights, Ev said, "Come on, *chica*, I'll put you in a cab."

I stayed up for a couple of hours after that, but he didn't return.

18

Summer was finally over, and Dr. Stern was coming back. By Labor Day, every Duane Reade in the neighborhood featured notebooks and lunch boxes in its windows, replacing the water wings and the stacks of sunblock and mosquito repellent. Children went by with balloons from shoe stores and the beaten look of savages being forced into civilized society. All of the little greengrocers on York Avenue reflected the changing seasons, too: the resolute beauty of their final plums and nectarines proved to be only skin-deep, and pomegranates and pumpkins began to appear, a few of the latter grinning in early anticipation of Halloween. How we hustle into the holidays, I thought, how we hurry our entire lives away.

I chided myself for being so maudlin, but I'd always felt a little melancholy at this time of year. When I was a child it meant the end of summer's freedom and the beginning of a new school term, with all the daunting things I didn't yet know, scholastically and socially. There was always the fear of never being able to catch up. And for many of my adult years, the calendar was neatly divided into the seasonal lists at Grace & Findlay. In early September the beach books were already heading for the remainder tables or the shredders, and the fate of those fall and winter contenders for serious reviews and literary prizes pretty much foretold. The manic or depressed moods of my authors seemed valid then, and highly contagious.

So much had happened since I'd fallen out of Andrea Stern's protective aura. Although I still hadn't figured out the essential thing plaguing me, I had all this other news to report—about Ev, Michael, and Suzy—as if I'd deliberately jazzed up my life for fear of boring her when she returned. Not that I had kept everything to myself in the meantime. I'd finally told Violet about Ev leaving, but not about Michael and me. In my convoluted logic, it seemed *disloyal* to Ev for anyone else to know about my affair when he didn't.

Violet admitted that Ev had called to tell her about our separation a while ago, but that she had guessed as much, anyway. "He really sounds like shit," she commented. "I think he's having trouble sleeping." Which was actually welcome news, delivered in more neutral tones than usual. Why should Ev be able to sleep when I was having so much trouble, myself?

I would carry my pillow from bed to bed in the apartment, like a graying Goldilocks still trying to find a place that was just right. Sometimes one of my writers would complain about the insomnia brought on by characters waking him to listen to their stories. That had always sounded suspect to me, and more than a bit affected. Perhaps I was only jealous of such round-the-clock inspiration, but Michael's claim that his own writing tended to *put* him to sleep seemed much more honest.

When I woke in the middle of the night, it was because of heartache or maybe heartburn—it was sometimes hard to tell the difference, to identify exactly what was disturbing me. It might have even been simple hunger, and occasionally I'd get up and nibble some crackers and cheese. When Ev was still there, he would often sense my wakefulness and join me in the kitchen for a late, late snack. Or I wouldn't get up at all; I would simply lie there with my face pressed against the warm loaf of his back, as if we were about to go off on a wild motorcycle ride instead of an uneventful journey into sleep. Maybe loneliness was what woke everyone up, and writers just try to fill that hollow space with imaginary friends. If it kept happening to me, I was going to ask the doctor for some sleeping pills.

Despite all of these concerns, I'd managed to write a good part of the essay for the art show catalog, after Violet took me to a couple of the other artists' studios. Greta Gordon's paper collages were vividly bright, abstract miniatures. I thought of them as antidotes to Violet's muddied, looming canvases, a bell-like chorus of hope against the darkness. Greta herself, who made her art in the kitchen of the Murray Hill apartment she shared with her husband and two children, referred to the collages as night lights. I considered using that as the title for the entire show, but it didn't suit everyone's work, and it would have been downright contradictory about Violet's.

After we left Greta's place, we visited a photographer on Chambers Street who went only by the name of India, although the plate above the doorbell of her loft said RIZZUTO/MOSCOWITZ. I was dismissive of her one-name pretension, but Violet defended it as an assertion of originality, of self-generation. "It helped to set Cher apart, didn't it?" she said. "Not to mention Madonna, and Sting."

"Yeah, right," I said, "and let's not forget Leonardo."

India's photographs won me over, though, with their utter weirdness and self-deprecation. As with Imogene Donnell's work, there were obvious influences. Looking at India's array of self-portraits, Cindy Sherman and Lucas Samaras came easily to mind. There wasn't much role-playing, though, and, to my relief, no visible genitalia. India depended mostly on popular references to hunger and self-denial. She was a fat woman whose untouched, patently unflattering photos of herself were related to food in one way or another.

Sometimes she was seen in close-up, the camera catching her at the very moment she bit into something juicy, like a hamburger or a ripe piece of fruit, and she was often posed nude at a Formica table, with a plate of something set before her and a napkin opened discreetly over her lap.

In a series of other photographs, printed in strips like single frames of a film, she stood off to one side and stared wistfully at the items laid out on a tray—a pear and a slab of cheese and a dead pheasant—in a send-up of a classical still life. When you looked closely, you could see tooth marks in the pear, and a fork with a chunk of white meat impaled on it almost hidden on a shadowed corner of the table. The pheasant wore a defeated expression and a few singed tail feathers.

I noticed a calendar on the wall in the background, and, using a magnifying glass, I saw that it was dated 1945, about twenty-five years before India was born. Violet explained later that India had found the calendar at a yard sale, and that it represented the year her grandparents had been liberated from Bergen-Belsen.

I spoke to the other two artists in the show on the phone and looked at slides of their paintings and drawings, which seemed sufficient for my purpose, and I made copious notes before I began the actual text of the essay. The thrust of it, which I discovered as I wrote, was that all of them, like Violet, had kept on going, right over history and the news of the day, the fickle fashions of the art world, and any received opinion about their own efforts. The first paragraphs flowed out, as if I had known all along what I'd intended to say, and just needed to get it down. I imagined telling Andrea Stern about the essay as substantiation of my mental health, my worth. *See*, it would say, *I may have failed at marriage and motherhood, and I may be involved in an unseemly affair, but I'm not all bad.* Something like showing off my reading skills to a new teacher, one who could still see directly into my evil, uneasy heart.

But all the little fits and starts in my notebook of what I'd thought of as my *real* writing, that stuff of my poor, stingy imagination, had simply fizzled out. My inner critic had spoken, I guess, loudly and clearly. So why couldn't I just give it up, the way I gave up my summery, succulent youth, with regret, surely, but without histrionics or resorting to plastic surgery? Something else to talk about in therapy.

The Wednesday I went back, I took the bus across town, and I looked out at the trees in the park with a feeling akin to homesickness. Maybe that's because some of those trees were actually the same ones that had gone by the windows of my father's car all those years ago. The bus windows were tinted, too, giving the whole moving scene a strange but not unpleasant reality, like early Technicolor.

The patient whose hour preceded mine skimmed past again with hummingbird speed, and I was safely inside the shelter of the waiting room, and then in the office itself. Dr. Stern had a tan, and she looked rested, although there were threads of silver in her hair I didn't remember seeing a month before. Was that possible?

"How are you?" she asked after we were seated. It was not a rhetorical question, and my throat was brimming with answers, about my family and Michael, the essay I was writing and the books I was editing—all the vicissitudes of my shaky, stupid life; she would be stunned by how much had gone on since I was last here, in this room as oddly familiar as any of my own. I felt almost exultant about having all that accelerated history to spill like gold coins between us. But when I opened my mouth only a high-pitched, abbreviated wail came out—something like a dolphin's squeak—and then I burst into tears, just as I'd done the very first time I'd faced her. Dr. Stern waited quietly, as she'd done then, while I gulped and sobbed and blew my nose noisily into one of the proffered Kleenex.

When I was calm again, I gave her a condensed version of recent events, as if I were reading tabloid headlines aloud. WOMAN HARBORS MYSTERIOUS DEMON. HUSBAND LEAVES. WOMAN TAKES LOVER. DAUGHTER BECOMES ENGAGED. And I tried to summarize how I felt about everything, but words like *guilty* and *confused* and even *happy* and *unhappy* had the trite, impersonal sound of psycho-speak.

The questions Andrea Stern asked were straightforward and sensible, the equivalent of the questions a policeman might ask at the scene of an accident, to determine the extent of someone's injuries. No, I hadn't figured out what had been plaguing me all these months, although I suspected that it had something to do with my mother. Yes, I still had feelings for Ev, some of them rather harsh, some of them confused by longing, and yes, I was still going to bed with Michael, although I understood, at least intellectually, that it was a bad idea. "It's pretty visceral," I said. "I don't really think a lot about it first." I thought about it a lot afterward, though, especially when I caught an unexpected glimpse of my glowing, rejuvenated face in a mirror. The only thing missing was a big scarlet "A" plastered across my breast.

I didn't tell Dr. Stern that Michael had moved out of the Y into an apartment share in Long Island City, and that he'd taken a job as a machinist in a dental tool factory there. Or that both of these changes made him seem like less of a transient in my life. And I didn't mention his blurted declaration of love on the telephone; that would have only been hearsay in this court of emotional justice. When Michael had repeated it later, in the throes of a sexual spasm, I'd said, "No, you don't," the way you'd correct an outspoken child, and he hadn't really argued the point, or demanded a reciprocal declaration. Just as well, since I couldn't have even faked such a thing. It *was* all visceral, just as I'd said, as if the mind and the body were completely independent entities. Dr. Stern seemed neither approving nor disapproving—I could see that that sort of moral judgment would be left entirely up to me.

When I spoke about the engagement dinner, I felt buoyant until I came to the place in the story where Michael called and I rose from the table, having that peculiar string of disparate thoughts. "Where did that all come from?" I asked. And then I answered myself, dubiously. "Maybe I just stood up too quickly and all the blood went to my feet." She made no comment, so I went on. "Of course, some of it makes sense, in a way. I mean, thinking about Esmeralda, and then, seconds later, about Faye."

"They were both your family's housekeepers," Dr. Stern said.

"Uh-huh. But Esmeralda is a day worker and Faye lived in." Her lamplit room. The slosh of bathwater, the rough caress of the towel. I sighed. "So Faye couldn't live with her son because she lived with me."

"You feel responsible for that, for their separation?"

"Yeah, I think I do. But I didn't hire her, you know, I was just a kid." A *junior* slaveholder. What I didn't say was that I'd had trouble ever since then with anyone doing my dirty work. It had to do with issues of race and class, of power and subjection, but it never stopped me from having household help. My consciousness of all this was my real sin, and it was my punishment, too.

"And I was an only child," I said, "so I've always been spared all that sibling rivalry my own kids went through. But I had an invisible sibling all along, an absent brother." I fumbled through memory and found the photograph on Faye's dresser, his dark face squinting in sunlight, the green, shingled house behind him. Roger.

"Is that how you think of him?"

"Now I do, anyway."

"And what about Esmeralda?"

"Well," I said immediately, self-righteously. "She's *always* favored Ev." As soon as I said it, I saw the adolescent Suzy spring up from the dinner table, jostling Scotty's arm in the process, and his fork falling with a clang, the way mine did that other night. And I remembered Suzy yelling, "You *always* take his side!"

"Wow," I said, sinking back in my seat. "Ev, too? I've suddenly got all these brothers, all this competition." I looked at my watch then, aware of the elapsing minutes, and that I badly wanted to talk about something else before it was too late. "I've had this disturbing notion," I said, "that my father may have sabotaged my mother's career."

"How?"

"Oh, very subtly. For one thing, he referred to her—he *still* refers to her as a 'poetess.'"

"Couldn't that be mere semantics, a generational thing?"

"He used to call her his *very own* poetess laureate. That would have really limited her audience, wouldn't it?"

"Did she take offense?"

"My mother? She must have, but she never expressed it. She once got fifty dollars for a poem, and he told her not to spend it all in one place. She just laughed."

"It doesn't sound as if she was traumatized by it. Yet you think he broke her spirit."

"It was a slow, erosive process," I said. "In a letter he wrote when I was away at college, he mentioned that she was still 'scribbling away.' But she was publishing in decent little places by then. Now it seems like a put-down to me."

"Why do you think he'd want to do that?"

"I honestly don't know. I mean he had such a fabulous career, himself. Wasn't that enough for him? Couldn't she succeed, too?"

"We can speculate," Dr. Stern said, "but only your father really could have answered that."

"And now he never will." I felt rudely shut out of knowledge, excluded, as if the grown-ups were talking over my head. After a moment, I said,

"The last of those crazy thoughts I had at the dinner party—about my father's locked office door—that was more of an image, really."

"Something from memory?" she asked.

"Maybe. I don't know. It could have just been a dream, couldn't it?" Whatever it was, the picture was fixed inside my head: the solid oak door with its embossed brass knob; his name above, spelled out in gold.

"Was the door usually locked when you were there?"

"Well, closed at least, anyway, if there was a patient inside. And I was taught to knock."

"So this was from when you were a child," she said.

"I guess so. Yes. I knocked, and when he didn't answer, I jiggled the doorknob and it was locked." I looked around uneasily. Was the door behind me now, the one to the waiting room, locked?

"What are you thinking?" Dr. Stern asked.

"Do you lock that door?"

"No. Are you concerned that someone might interrupt us?"

"Not really," I said. But I *was* concerned, even though I knew there was no one out there, and that she would have to buzz the next patient in. The trouble was, I didn't want her to have a next patient. What I wanted then was to be an only child again.

19

My father was lying in bed in the middle of the afternoon, something he had never permitted me to do when I lived under his roof, except when I was sick enough to run a fever. And whenever he'd succumbed to a nap in this place, it was in his wheelchair. He would refuse to get into bed, insisting that he hadn't been sleeping at all; he had merely shut his eyes for a minute.

He certainly wasn't sleeping now; his head swiveled toward me like a sentry's as soon as I entered his room. "Daddy," I said, "what's going on? Don't you feel well?" He didn't answer, but he looked all right, only a little disheveled, and no one had called me to report a problem. I pulled a chair up to his bedside. "What are you doing in bed at this hour?" I asked, taking his hand in mine. As if time really mattered here.

"Thank God," he said, gripping my hand so hard it hurt. "You've come."

"What is it?" I asked. I wriggled free of his grasp and put my hand firmly on top of his. It made me think of that game Violet and I used to play, one of our hands quickly topping the other's in a struggle for dominance, until we were weakly slapping at the air, yelling with laughter. "Is something wrong?"

"They were here again," he said.

"Who? Who was here?"

"The police, of course. Who did you think?"

I relaxed; it was only the dementia, banal and familiar now. In the beginning, I'd argue with him, try to point him in the direction of reason and sanity. *But Mother died, don't you remember? No, there are no patients waiting for you. It's all right, you don't need your keys.* All the grief those uttered truths brought on. And his grieving was justified—it's an abysmal thing to suffer such losses, to no longer need keys to anything. "Don't worry," I assured him. "I'll take care of it." This had become my stock answer to every paranoid delusion he could dream up, and it worked more often than not.

I'd mostly given up trying to conduct ordinary conversations with him, so he was spared the terrible news of the larger world, and deprived of personal news, like Suzy's engagement, which would have made him very happy if he could have comprehended it. When I tried to tell him about her and George, he merely looked quizzical. And I think he would have been sorry to learn about Ev and me, after all these years. There was so much that I was keeping to myself—experiences, feelings, ideas— especially now that Ev wasn't home anymore.

My infrequent telephone exchanges with Ev were fairly formal and safe, about everyone's health or something that had come in the mail for him. I didn't tell him that I'd called Jeremy one day, and that Celia had answered the phone, sounding tearful. Yet she assured me things were better between them. They'd had a petty argument the night of the dinner party, and now she was just being emotional. Then she cried, "Why does it always have to be such a power struggle?" I might have said something about Jeremy being a middle child, and how he'd had to fight sometimes, against the battling bookends of his brother and sister, for attention and justice. But I didn't really think that was the answer. I didn't have any answer at all.

I went out to the nurses' station to ask why my father was in bed, and was told that he'd become especially agitated at lunch, and that the doctor had prescribed additional sedation. He'd been sleeping on and off since then, and he seemed much calmer.

"Did anything happen to set him off?" I asked.

The nurse smiled. "Well, in his own mind, maybe," she said, not unkindly, and I knew she'd had some version of this conversation many times before. I was in typical denial, still trying to make sense of my father's insensibility. But his loss was mine, too, because he was my only link now to certain aspects of the past. True memories often require collaboration, or at least confirmation by another witness, preferably one in his right mind.

I went back to his room and this time he was asleep, his hands open at his sides. I studied him in that undefended posture, searching for his old, irretrievable self, the one who would never have let himself be looked at this way, like a specimen under the lens of a microscope. Some molecules of that person were still intact, though, because his eyes swung open, as if he had felt my impudent gaze.

"You dozed off," I said consolingly. "It's that kind of day." In fact, it wasn't that kind of drowsy day at all. It was a crisply beautiful and sunny autumn afternoon. There were gently swaying treetops outside his window and I looked toward them as symbols of my own thrilling freedom, my ability to simply walk out of there into their lovely, dappled shade. "Do you want to get up now?" I asked him, pulling his wheelchair closer to the bed.

He was weaker, I noticed, and very unsteady, though that could have been just a side effect of the sedatives, but he was still able to cooperate, to move himself from bed to chair with my assistance. When he was settled, I murmured, "Oh, that's much better, Daddy, isn't it?" and accepted his angry glare as just. To make up for my condescension, I said, "Would you like to get out of here for a while?" and he nodded his assent.

I'd taken him outside on other occasions, just for a change of scenery, and to put him back into the traffic of life, in touch again with the weather and the seasons. As usual, there were other people—relatives and aides— pushing other wheelchairs on the grounds of the home. I remembered pushing a stroller down a busy street with one of my children inside, and how my toddler would stare with avid interest at the mirror image of another toddler going by in her stroller. Suzy used to even reach out her hand, in greeting, maybe, or just to grab the other kid's toy. But most of these adults, borne along in their oversized prams, strapped and tucked in like toddlers, shrank from one another's glances, as if to avoid being recognized as someone reduced to this, someone so completely stripped of autonomy.

I took my father to a secluded area close to the high, black, wrought-iron fence that surrounded the property, where ordinary pedestrians and cars passed once in a while, just to remind him that the moving world hadn't stopped in his absence. I sat down on a bench, arranging his chair to face me. He looked around him in an alert manner, and then up at the parasol of trees above us, with their pale, feathery leaves. "Acacia," he pronounced, and I felt inordinately pleased, as if my child had said his first precocious word.

"Yes," I said, eagerly. "Do you remember that we had a pair of them in the garden at home? They would get yellow flowers every spring." *Do you remember?* would be my theme, my refrain for the entire afternoon.

"Helen liked them," he said. Past tense, I noted, and he seemed reflective but not terribly sad.

"She did," I agreed. After a moment, I said, "Daddy, I've been thinking a lot about the old days lately." He returned my gaze, but he didn't answer, so I went on. "I've been thinking about those trips into the city that Mother and I took when I was little. Do you remember—we would come to your office to meet you? And those wonderful dinners we had."

"Barbetta," he said promptly. His favorite theater district restaurant, where everyone knew him by name, and the maître d' always kissed my mother's hand and then mine. "The Russian Tea Room," my father continued, squinting into the past. We were favored guests there, too, who never had to sit upstairs in what was disparagingly referred to as "Siberia." And the waiter would bring a plate of pierogi to our table before we'd even looked at the menus. I saw myself in a dress of jewel-colored velvet, ruby or amethyst, and patent-leather shoes that reflected the omnipresent Christmas ornaments.

"And everywhere we went, your patients came out of the woodwork to adore you," I said. He couldn't keep himself from smiling at that. He was still in there. "You were a very good doctor," I added, trying out the past tense, leavened by praise, in direct reference to him, to his self-image. He didn't seem offended or dismayed, so I went on. "You saved so many lives." And of course he only sniffed haughtily at that; he didn't need verification of his bona fides from me. A laboratory at Mount Sinai had been named in his honor, and I still have the letters I rescued from his discarded files, sent by some of the men and women whose days on earth he'd extended— oh, just a few more moments of happiness! Sunlight winked at us between the moving fronds of the acacia. In the distance a woman's voice called, "Tony! Tony!" over and over again, as if to summon someone back from the dead.

The first person you saw when you entered the reception room to my father's medical suite was his secretary, Miss Snow. My mother called her "the dragon lady," because she was so fiercely protective of my father's privacy and his time, although she was soft-spoken and pretty. Miss Snow reminded me of those secretaries in the movies, after they'd removed their spectacles and unpinned their hair. If I could have looked like anybody, besides my mother, I would have picked Miss Snow. She was usually seated at her desk when we arrived, but sometimes she was in my father's consultation room, taking dictation. Parksie's smaller office was right next door to his, and the examining rooms were on either side of a long corridor off to the left.

There were plaster models of various human organs in the consultation room that opened on hinges to show the intricate network of their interiors, the arteries and veins depicted in soothing nursery colors of pink and beige and blue. My father used the models to explain surgical procedures to his patients, and after extracting my promise to be careful, he'd let me handle them when I visited. This was probably done more to trigger my interest in science than to entertain his bored child. But I *was* entertained, and horrified at once. He would put my hands on my own body, on the places that held those hidden parts—the kidneys like twin toilets discreetly flushing waste, the vulgar-looking liver, the amazing, hectic heart— and I only half believed I housed such unlikely machinery.

"I loved coming to your office," I said, and I thoroughly meant it, although so much of that pleasure was inextricable from the attendant rewards, bracketed by that first sight of my mother waiting for me at school and the ride home hours later in the iridescent darkness.

"My appointments," he said. His voice was a little higher-pitched now and growing irritable.

"It was the end of the day," I reminded him. "Your appointments were over." I wanted to keep him on course—we were getting somewhere—but it was like trying to steer a large, unfamiliar vehicle through tricky traffic.

"Parksie," he said. He could have been summoning her, not just saying her name, and I found myself glancing around, as if I expected her to step soundlessly right out of the air to answer his command.

"She was always there when Mother and I came. I used to sit at her desk, drawing or working on the puzzles in *Highlights*." Her hand rested lightly on my head as I bent over the page. The colored pencils, newly sharpened, had a harsh, woody fragrance. The intercom near my writing hand muttered static. "You spoke to me over the intercom. You called me Miss Brill, and I pretended that I was your secretary, instead of Miss Snow. Do you remember?" I aspired to be a secretary then, or a waitress or a salesgirl, someone both officious and submissive, and with a pencil and a pad—so much for those inspirational models of the liver and the heart.

My father looked at me and put his fingers to his chin—an old, contemplative pose, the same one he'd struck for his official Bachrach portrait. "Take a letter, Miss Brill," he said, and I felt like whooping for joy.

"Dear Sir," I prompted, and found I had to swallow. "Dear, dear sir . . ." I leaned toward him in ardent conspiracy, but he was looking up into the foliage of the trees again. "Daddy," I said. *Wait a minute, don't go.*

He didn't answer, though; the trees had him in their green, leafy embrace. I stood up and released the brake on his chair. "Why don't we move," I suggested. "Let's get out into the sun." And I began wheeling him briskly in the direction we'd come from, away from the shadows where our reminiscences had stalled. But at the other end of the path, two familiar, bent figures were lurching toward us. One of them waved, fluttering a handkerchief or a scarf, and I veered abruptly onto the grass and kept on going.

My father grunted as the chair swerved, its wheels catching in the turf, tearing up blades of grass like a lawn mower. The seat belt must have grabbed him in the gut. "Sorry," I said, "so sorry," but I didn't slow down, even when I heard Marjorie Steinhorn's urgent soprano. "Alice! Yoo-hoo, Alice dear! Wait for us!" Instead I began running with the chair, bumping it over the uneven terrain, and my father's thin, fair hair flew up into a rooster's crest. "Hold on now," I told him, unnecessarily; his body was already stiffly braced and he was clutching the armrests.

A couple of minutes later, we were on another path, this one leading to the wide-open wings of the west gates, and I went forward at a steady but slower pace until we were through them and out onto the street. Only then did I stop long enough to look behind us. Marjorie and Leo were nowhere in sight. "We lost them," I said excitedly, like a criminal who'd cleverly eluded the police in a car chase. The police! I had entered my father's delusion. And it occurred to me then that I *was* a criminal, of sorts, that I had just kidnapped my father, springing him from the prison to which I'd also condemned him.

Except for his cataract surgery, he had only been away from the premises of the home once since he'd entered it, almost a year ago. Ev and I had picked him up by car one day in early March, when he still had frequent spells of lucidity. It was his birthday, and we took him to our apartment for lunch, where we served some of his favorite foods—smoked salmon and Brie and country pâté—at our family table, without the mess-hall racket of the home's dining room. Ev put a CD of Mozart on the stereo, and it played softly, lyrically all around us. It was a good day, an accomplishment, really. My father was alert and genial most of the time, and he ate with a genuine appetite, remarking on the silky sweetness of the salmon, the rough perfection of the pâté.

But on the way back to Riverdale, we got stuck in stop-and-go traffic on the West Side Highway. There was a grisly accident—an overturned SUV and a small, accordion-pleated sports car—that we approached at a funereal pace. My father was in the backseat of our car, craning to see, like everyone else, as we crawled past the glitter of ground glass, the sputtering flares.

When I turned around to reassure him, I saw the nervous glimmer of the emergency vehicle lights play across his pale, altered face. "I'm a physician, you know," he said, and his hands plucked fretfully at his seat belt. "Stop the car, driver," he ordered Ev, although we were at a complete standstill at that moment. He wanted to get out, to offer medical assistance.

It was something he'd done at least once before, in Chilmark, more than forty years ago, when he and my mother and I were coming back from a dinner party. There'd been a collision then, too, and the driver of one of the cars, a young woman, had suffered a crushed windpipe, which my father punctured with his pocketknife before inserting the empty tube of someone's ballpoint pen, enabling her to breathe until the ambulance arrived to take her away.

I'm sure I didn't see any of that—my mother would have shielded me from it—yet my recall of the scene is graphic in its detail. The impromptu surgery was done by flashlight, the victim's face dramatically lit, as in a Sargent portrait. She sounded as if she were gargling. This memory was probably fostered by my imagination and the excited stories I overheard at the beach the next day. My father was a great hero. For all I knew, he was responsible for the fiery sun and the flying clouds and the surf that crashed and sucked at our feet.

But that day after his birthday lunch, he was only a bewildered old man who'd been overstimulated and fed too much rich food. All the charm he'd managed to muster at the table had completely vanished. "Let me out of here!" he kept shouting, long after we'd gone past the accident. "Why am I being tied up? Untie me, you bastards!" And between these outbursts, he kept belching loudly, the way Scotty used to do at dinner to annoy Suzy.

Later on, Ev would speak ruefully of "our noble experiment" and say how sorry he was that I'd had to go through it—the excursion had been his idea in the first place—but then he was hunched anxiously over the wheel, muttering to himself as he drove, things like, "This is just great," and "Oh, fuck," while I alternately jabbered at my father as if he were actually listening, and wept, wiping my eyes and nose on the sleeve of my down jacket. It was the saddest event of my life, even though no one had died; maybe because no one had died. By the time we got to the nursing home, I wanted nothing more than to turn my father back over to his keepers. You would think there was a bounty on his head.

The neighborhood near the home is residential and upscale. As I pushed his chair along the street, a woman in a bathrobe came out of her house and collected her mail. Another woman had two beribboned poodles on leashes at the curb. "What are you waiting for, girls?" she said to them. "Don't you want to go shopping?" It was the sort of scene that would have amused my father once. But now his profile could have been on the prow of a ship, or on the face of a coin. His expression was fixed yet unfocused.

Still, I didn't concede defeat. When we came to a coffee shop a few blocks away, I tamed his hair and then mine with the same comb, and wheeled him inside. We were hot and thirsty from our adventure, and I ordered tall glasses of iced coffee with whipped cream for both of us. As he slurped his noisily through a straw, I said, "I wanted to continue talking to you, Daddy, without any interruptions."

He blotted his lips on a paper napkin and bent to the straw again. "You kept the door to your office locked sometimes, didn't you?" There were two doors, I remembered then, one in the reception area where Miss Snow sat, and the other in Parksie's office. He looked up at me, with foam dissolving on his lips, giving nothing away. I knew that I was being too direct, too impatient. The earlier rapport between us was totally gone, and I wasn't doing anything to reestablish it. I sounded more like a cop grilling a suspect—*that* metaphor again—than a daughter trying to revive nostalgic moments with her old dad. But it was already late in the day, and he looked exhausted. I was tired, too. Damn those trees. Damn the Steinhorns. "Your *office*," I repeated, insistently.

"Office," he echoed, and in a worried tone, "I don't have my keys." He patted the pockets of his windbreaker, carefully at first, and then frantically, as if he were frisking himself.

"That's right, you don't have any keys," I said sharply. "So just stop looking for them, okay?"

He put his hands obediently on the table, and I stroked them in a feeble attempt at conciliation. "But you used to," I said. A whole clangorous ring of them, denoting possession and authority. "Keys to the house on Morning Glory Drive and to the Lincoln. Keys to your vault at Chase. And keys to your offices at the hospital. Please try to remember, Daddy, won't you?"

But it was like tapping on all the windows and doors of an abandoned house. And I was losing my own connection to the dream-memory I wanted to evoke, the thing in my chest that refused to travel to my brain. I watched him finish his coffee, letting the ice melt in mine until it was un-drinkable. Then I wheeled him back to the home and turned him in again.

20

Michael still hadn't given me any new pages, despite all his talk about the major breakthrough I'd inspired. He seemed a lot more interested in me now than in his novel, with a level of attention I found unsettling. When he called one morning and said, in a husky, urgent voice, that he wanted to see me, it sounded like the kind of remark usually accompanied by a knowing wink. Ever since I'd blithely told Dr. Stern that I didn't think too much beforehand about the "visceral" thing between Michael and me, I had been thinking about it a lot, with a disagreeable mixture of guilt and apprehension. I told Michael that I'd meet him in the park, safely away from our sexual arena, and to please bring his copy of the manuscript.

The neighborhood children were back in school, but there were still plenty of babies and old folks around, along with the regular procession of dogs and their walkers. Even the homeless man who screamed was in place, quiet at the moment but ready to go off like a car alarm at the slightest perceived insult. They were all perfect distractions and perfect chaperones.

I'd been rereading the revised chapters of *Walking to Europe*. They were so much stronger than the first draft—why had he stopped? And why was I still displaying such saintly caution and tact when I was really growing impatient with Michael, with waiting for some resolution of the mysteries he'd raised? Those three tattoos of Caitlin's, for instance, and Joe's profession of guilt about her, that haunting but cryptic "What have I done?"

We were sitting on a bench facing the river, and when Michael started to put a proprietary arm across my shoulders, I moved away and said, irritably, "What *has* he done, anyway?"

"Who?" Michael asked.

"Joe, of course," I said. "He's been yakking about Caitlin's disappearance for almost two hundred pages, and he seems to take total responsibility for it. But we have no idea why. Obviously he knows something crucial—when are you going to let the rest of us in on it?"

"Why do you sound like that?" Michael said.

"Like what?"

"Like you're angry with me about something. It can't be about Joe."

"Why not?"

"Because he's a fictional character, Alice."

"I don't think so," I said. And I could swear that thought hadn't crossed my conscious mind until I heard myself say it.

Michael grew pale and his upper lip glistened with perspiration. Everyone around us had receded into the background. Even the homeless man, who had indeed begun to scream, seemed remote and innocuous. "I don't get this," Michael said.

"Yes, you do," I said.

"So now you're editing my life?" When I didn't answer, he said, "Could we just go up to your place?" He had a doggy look about him again, but it was more beseeching now than playful.

"What for?" I said. "It's over." I'd known that with certainty before

I'd even left the apartment. That's why I hadn't worn any makeup or perfume, and why my hair, which he'd once tangled around his wrist until my scalp prickled, was pulled back so severely now with a rubber band.

"Shit," he said, and reached for his cigarettes. When he absently offered me one, I took it. It seemed the least I could do.

But I inhaled too deeply and singed my throat. When I could speak again, I said, "Michael, I'm really sorry. I should never have let this happen between us."

"Why not?" he asked miserably.

Because I'm the grown-up here, I almost said. *And because it would be even more painful in the end if we continue, at least for me.* Instead I stamped out the cigarette—I'd probably just given up smoking, as well—and I clasped my hands in my lap, so I wouldn't try to take his hand or touch him in any other way. "Because it isn't appropriate. And it interferes with our professional relationship."

"And you're married," he said.

"Yeah, that, too," I admitted, thinking that he wouldn't have been such a good writer if he didn't have so much insight.

"Wasn't it okay?"

Okay. The understatement of the century, I thought. The term *raw sex* came easily to mind, for the obvious reasons, and as opposed to something gently simmered in the juices of a shared life. But I only said, "It was lovely," a deliberately prim, past-tense description of something that still reverberated in all my nerve endings.

"Shit," Michael repeated, which I took as kind of a halfhearted acceptance of things.

I waited awhile and then I said, "So, do you want to tell me about the manuscript?"

"I thought I'm not supposed to do that, that I might 'talk it out.'" He made exaggerated quote marks in the air as he spoke.

"You might," I said, trying to ignore both the sarcastic gesture and the bitterness of his tone. "But I think we'll have to take that risk. Come on, let's walk."

Once we were in motion, it became much easier to talk. Maybe that was because we could only look obliquely at each other, and because some of the nervousness we'd both been feeling was expended by our striding legs. I was also more direct with him, less afraid or superstitious about invading that sacrosanct creative field. I asked him when he'd started writing the book, and he said that it was begun—inside his stoned head, anyway—when he was still in high school. He thought about it obsessively, but he didn't write anything down for years.

"At first it was going to be a memoir," he said. "Do you want to hear the opening line? 'My sister Donna was named for a girl in a series of books my mother loved when she was young.'"

"Donna Parker," I said right away, "I loved them, too." I knew that I'd just recklessly crossed over the border into his parents' generation. That, and the corroborating fact of my naked face in sunlight, must have helped to ease the sting of my rejection. It didn't matter that those books had stayed in print for years and then been reissued; that Suzy had read them all, too, although not without considerable disdain. I was too old for him; he could surely see that now.

But Michael wasn't even looking at me; his mind was elsewhere. "I called her Donna Duck," he said, "because she waddled when she first learned to walk. We actually *were* sixteen months apart. I used to quack into her neck, and it broke her up."

"'Cake' was an imaginative leap, then," I said.

"Well, you triggered that. I was really happy when you wanted those kinds of backstory details about Joe and Caitlin. It reminded me of the truth, and it empowered me to be inventive at the same time."

"Is she dead, Michael?" I asked.

"Yeah," he said. "Yeah."

"And did she live with one abusive man after another, like Caitlin?"

Michael wobbled a little and stopped walking. We faced each other. "No," he said. "She never lived with anybody but me and our mother and father."

"What do you mean?" I thought of devastating disease, of retardation.

Michael was crying. I had to grab his hand and lead him to a bench. There was no one else there; we were at the last curve of the promenade before you come to Gracie Mansion. We sat down and this time I put my arm around him. "Wait," I said. "It's all right." And, "Take your time."

A tugboat pushed a long garbage barge slowly past us before Michael spoke again. "She died when she was four years old," he said. "It was my fault."

"How can that be?" I asked. "You were, how old—five? Six?"

"I was supposed to be watching her."

"Michael, that's crazy, you were just a baby yourself."

"But I was good at it," he insisted. "My mother had a migraine; 'the hammer,' as she called it, had conked her in the head, and she had to lie down in a dark room with a wet compress over her eyes. I made it for her. And I was used to watching Donna—it was like my job."

I needed a villain, someone besides this grieving man sitting next to me, still sheltering a grieving boy, and I felt a swell of rage at his mother, coddling her complaint in a darkened bedroom, relegating her own job to little children. But then she lost one of those children. "What happened?" I asked.

"It was August and hot as hell, normal for Pontiac, though. One of our neighbors had a round aboveground pool. It wasn't that deep, but there was a little ladder of three or four stairs leading to it. I went up them and Donna followed, the way she always did." Stepping on his heels. "The water was scummy, I remember that. Like cold soup with wrinkled fat on top. There was a white rubber ring—it said 'USS something'—floating around the edge of the pool. I could read."

I didn't need to hear the rest. I didn't want to hear it, either, but I had asked, so I was obliged to listen. "I leaned in and pushed the ring around with a stick for a while," Michael said, "and then I went down the stairs, past Donna, who was in my way. There were other kids in the yard, things going on. Wash hanging that we ran through like curtains, a tied-up dog that kept barking."

"It wasn't your fault. They told you that, right?" And I remembered "The Stone Boy," a story by Gina Berriault, in which a mother won't forgive her younger boy after he accidentally shoots and kills his brother. The boy stands naked outside her closed bedroom door, waiting vainly for the absolution of her love. "What about the tattoos?" I asked, because I needed to get away from the pictures in my head.

"The blue circle for the pool, the white bracelet for the life preserver, the yellow crescent for the moon reflected on her back," he recited quickly, in a monotone. "Although it was daytime and the moon was only a little sliver of white. I remembered being surprised that I could see it and the sun at the same time. Pretty corny symbolism, right?"

"I like the moon stuff, not the rest," I said, and we sat silently for a few beats, as if we were both merely contemplating editorial changes in the manuscript. And then I said, "In the book, you let Caitlin live to grow up. I think I understand that. But why did you give her such a terrible life?"

Michael shrugged. "I'm not sure," he said. "Maybe to show that she'd have been better off dying young?"

"Do you believe that?"

"No."

"Are you going to tell us that in the end? And that Joe invented her whole adulthood?"

"I don't know," he said. "Do you think I should?"

"I don't know, either," I confessed. "But it's something to think about, a possible way around what you're unable to write." Maybe it was the only way around it, but I had reverted to my old, careful nondirective self. It was his book, his life.

We stood up at the same time and started walking again, and after a while Michael escorted me back to my building. I thought about asking him to come upstairs with me once more, to try to make up for art's failure to console or even properly explain anything. But I was weary, and I imagined that I looked something like his mother when she was being pounded by one of her "hammers." In fact, I wanted to lie down in a darkened room, myself, with a soothing compress across my brow. So we hugged and parted.

There was a message on my machine from a woman named Ruth Casey. I'd contacted her, suggesting she call me about a manuscript she'd submitted, her account of raising a severely autistic child. The market was overrun with books on the subject, but this one was different. Ruth was a single mother, for one thing, and she was a professional writer. There was no self-pity in her writing voice, or false cheer. Her book, which she called *Perfection*, began, "It took seven years, three surgeries, and one in-vitro fertilization before David and I conceived Rose, so of course we expected the reward of perfection. But nothing is ever promised or owed." By the end of the manuscript, David is long gone and Rose is thirteen, her body relentlessly maturing while she remains emotionally undeveloped and unreachable. Ruth Casey lived with Rose in the city, on the Upper West Side. I scribbled a note to myself to call her back to discuss the project. Maybe I'd just offer some free publishing advice.

Then I went into Suzy's old room and scanned the shelves until I found my original dog-eared copies of the Donna Parker books. *Donna Parker in Cherrydale. Donna Parker in Hollywood. Donna Parker, the Mystery at Arawak.* That girl really got around. I closed the window blinds and got into Suzy's maidenly bed, along with a couple of the books, the ones that, miraculously, still had dust jackets, as frayed and faded as they were. Donna herself looked archaic, with her brunette version of the Doris Day flip and that dorky hair band.

I opened *Donna Parker in Hollywood* to the first page. Even with the blinds shut, there was enough afternoon light in the room to read by. "Donna Parker closed the lid of the suitcase triumphantly and looked around her bedroom." As soon as I began reading, I remembered how Violet and I used to act out the books, and that she had always insisted on being Donna, consigning the supporting role of Donna's best friend, Ricky West, to me.

I put up a protest each time—I didn't want to be a mere sidekick to the girl who won hearts and solved mysteries wherever she went, who could even feel triumphant after closing a suitcase—but Violet prevailed, as she usually did in our arguments, by firing a steady stream of logic at me, like an automatic pistol. Wasn't I a redhead, like Ricky, and didn't Donna have dark hair, just like herself? Besides, Violet had actually been to Hollywood once.

Never mind that she was only an infant on that trip, or that Violet's elec-trified frizz was nothing like Donna's smooth coif. My own counterlogic — my father and Donna's were both named Sam (her mother was mostly known as Mrs. Parker), and it was only fair to take turns — seemed weak, even to me. What bothered me more than anything was that Ricky's mother was dead. I couldn't bear to identify with that definitive fact of her life, even if it all was only make-believe, and not the most persuasive writing in the first place.

Later that night, I called Violet and asked her why we had loved those books so much, and she couldn't explain it, either. She wanted to know what made me bring them up, and I told her that this guy I was editing mentioned that his mother had loved them, too. I spoke carefully, like a drunk afraid of slurring her words, but for one panicky instant I wondered if I'd actually said, "this guy I was fucking."

The most peculiar thing was that Violet remembered letting me be Donna once in a while in our game. "But you didn't!" I cried. How could she edit memory that way?

"Well, you can be her now, if it's that important," Violet said drily.

"Thanks a lot," I said, "but it's a little late. I'm Ricky forever."

"I let you be Jane Eyre, though, remember?"

"Yeah," I said, "but that was so you could be Mr. *and* Mrs. Rochester."

Violet changed the subject then, as she does on those rare occa-sions she fails to have the last word. She asked about my progress on the art show essay, and then she told me, in an offhand manner, that Ev had offered to print the invitations to the opening and the catalogs, as a gift.

"That's nice," I said, trying to ignore the sudden commotion I felt in my chest. "So, is he seeing anybody?" I asked. If she could change the sub-ject, so could I.

There was an agonizing pause. What is it that lawyers say? Don't ask a question if you don't already know the answer. "How should I know?" Vi-olet finally muttered. "Why don't you ask him yourself? You are talking to each other, aren't you?"

"Sure," I said. "We're both civilized." As I said it, I pictured Ev, draped in a fur pelt and carrying a big club, dragging me by my hair across York Avenue. I let out a yipping laugh, and Violet said, "What's so funny?"

"Nothing," I said. "Everything." And right then both of those opposing assessments seemed true.

21

Ev and Al, Al and Ev. Our names had never been on everyone's tongues, like Helen and Sam's, except for our brief, scandalous fame in Iowa after that first kiss. Once, newly married, we were at a large party, and the host introduced us to another couple, who immediately reversed our names. That moment, in which we could have easily corrected them, flitted by. One of us still might have said something, but when the man turned to Ev, saying, "So, what do you do, Al?" Ev and I exchanged conniving smiles over his head, and let the mistake continue all evening. "So, what do you do, Al?" I said to him later, in bed. And he turned to me with a gaze of concentrated desire and said, "I do this, Ev, and this, and this."

We were rather smugly comfortable with our assigned genders and their complicated components. I'd already recognized what I thought of as the male, the "Ev" in me—that aggressive itch in arguments, my desire not to just defer to anyone louder or bigger. And Ev wasn't afraid to display what I saw as his feminine side, especially the nurturing kindness he was capable of in a crisis. I still cling to some of those easy sexist notions.

The next time I saw Dr. Stern, I told her about that long-ago party and our switched identities. I wasn't sure why I'd brought it up. There were so many things to talk about, so many events and incidents, dreams and memories. Our lives seem brutally short until you calculate all the crowded minutes and try to choose the ones that best define you. During that same session, I told her about ending the affair with Michael. Somehow I expected her approval for my good behavior, even though she had never evinced disapproval before. I guess I was spoiled by past rewards in my life—lavish praise for a childish poem, a big bonus for landing a big book.

But Andrea Stern appeared to be her usual neutral self. All she wanted to know was how *I* felt about terminating things with Michael. "Awful, if you want to know the truth," I said. "The sex was fantastic, like a poultice over all the places that hurt. You know, the perfect panacea for midlife angst. But when I let myself think ahead more than a day at a time, I became terrified, so I walked away while I could still walk. I mean, I knew we were never destined to go off into the sunset together." I sounded as if I were trying to convince myself, too, and I couldn't seem to shut up. "Probably because I'm a lot closer to the sunset than he is."

"It will get better," Dr. Stern said.

I was startled; that was the most direct, unsolicited statement she'd ever offered me. "Promise?" I asked.

She only smiled. "What about the manuscript?"

"The real business between us? That's still going forward. And maybe we'll have more time for it now." That last came out more wistfully than I'd intended.

Dr. Stern was interested in how Michael had masked his personal tragedy in fiction, and in my ability to figure it out. It boded well, she said, for an interpretation of my own psychological mystery.

"I went to see my father last week," I said, "speaking of mysteries." I recounted the highlights, or low moments, of my visit to the nursing home, the way I'd harassed my poor father about the past, to no avail. I could have throttled him when I was there, as if he were willfully withholding information, but he became an object of pity in retrospect. "I wish my children would ask me everything they need to know right now, before I lose it, too," I said. "Favorite recipes, where the family jewels are, all the big secrets."

"You see your father as the repository of family secrets?"

"Yes, locked and sealed forever. And he's swallowed the key."

"There may be other keys, other ways in," Dr. Stern suggested.

"You mean me?" I said. "But I only have little snippets of early memory. And I'm not sure I didn't make some of it up. I used to write fiction, re-member."

"Michael does, too," she said. "It's one way of processing the truth."

"So what do I do? Write the story of my life? Or maybe I ought to try free association—the Violet Steinhorn method of recovered memory." I was being sardonic, of course, but as I sat there, under Dr. Stern's steady, gently inquiring gaze, it began to seem like a reasonable idea. So I leaned back into the wings of the chair, shutting my eyes, and began.

It became a habit, something I could do at will almost anywhere and any-time, without anyone's awareness, the way I used to do the Kegel exercises for weeks after giving birth. On the checkout line at the supermarket, browsing in a bookstore, even talking on the telephone. I'd had a secret life under my skirt, and now there was one inside my head. The exercises gradually tightened my pelvic muscles, and, if nothing else, this new process let me know what was on my mind, which moved in a frantic zigzag, like a fly trapped between the panes of a window. Not all that free, really, and I wasn't ever sure if I was trying to get in or out.

I thought about Ev of Ev and Al, and about Ev alone. Then, unexpect-edly, of Ev with someone else. But I skittered away from that idea before it could turn into an image. The children were seen in riffled snapshots at all ages, an impatient glance through a family album. My mother, young and then dead, as if she'd barely lived at all—the life span of a fly? Geese flying in a vee over Central Park. The vee of my own crotch and Michael or Ev thrashing into me. And there were flashes, bulletins from childhood: bossy Violet as Donna Parker, as the Headless Horseman, Faye coming up the basement stairs, my father in his leather chair, with Beethoven pouring over everything, like honey in which to trap a fly.

One day I went to see where Ev was living. He wouldn't be there, I was certain of that, because Scotty had told me they were meeting at Ev's office at noon before going out to lunch. This news made me feel both pleased and envious—they had formed an alliance behind my back—but at least it gave me the opportunity to investigate Ev's new life without his knowledge. I took the subway to 42nd Street and then walked a few blocks south and west until I came to the address on the blue Post-it he had left on my computer.

The building was one of those generic postwar places. Ugly yellowish brick, a revolving door. A dentist and a podiatrist shared the office space on the street level—they might have advertised head-to-toe care. I looked up, counting the uniformly blank windows; Ev's sublet was on the tenth floor, apartment 10B, but I didn't even know which way it faced. I could see a doorman sitting at a desk in the lobby, reading a newspaper. I imagined walking right past him as if I belonged there, and taking an elevator up to the tenth floor. But then what?

There were two hired cars double-parked in front, their black-suited drivers slouched against the hoods, smoking. Fast-food and video rental places were conveniently situated across the street, and the neon SAME DAY SERVICE sign of a dry cleaner/laundry blinked beguilingly only a few doors down. It didn't feel like a neighborhood, although people obviously lived there. The revolving doors flashed in the sunlight. Two men with attaché cases went in. A woman in a leather mini skirt and big sunglasses came out and got into one of the hired cars. I felt like the spy that I was and, unaccountably, like a traitor.

"Need a ride?" someone said. I was so startled, you would've thought there was a gun at my back. But it was only the driver of the other double-parked car. Between fares, probably, or stood up by one of them.

As soon as my heart slowed, I realized that a ride was exactly what I needed, that I wanted to get out of there as quickly as possible. "Yes, I do," I said. "How much to Mount Sinai Hospital?" I truly hadn't planned to say that; I guess that's what happens when you leave yourself open to free association.

My father's offices had been on the twelfth floor of the old Klingenstein Building. My mother and I used to go in through the entrance on Madison Avenue, near 100th Street. The scene had changed, like everything else. I remembered a hot dog stand and someone selling Italian ices in the summer, but vendors lined the street now, offering everything from socks and watches to knockoffs of Gucci handbags.

Nuclear medicine took up the entire twelfth floor of Klingenstein. I was reminded of those dreams one has about places that are familiar, yet vitally changed: the school with an elusive homeroom, the house with a sudden, unexplored wing. The whole place must have been gutted and re-constructed, so I couldn't even locate my father's former space. It had been fairly close to the elevators—you made a left turn when you got off, and then veered right (my feet automatically followed an old path)—but I wasn't sure if the elevators were still in the same place.

A doctor in a red turban went by, and a young man on crutches. I wan-dered around, peering into offices where strangers sat at computers and the sick waited to have their fortunes told, the way they always have. There was no one anywhere resembling Miss Snow or Parksie, though, and no gilt plaque announcing the inner sanctum of Samuel Brill, MD. What-ever I had hoped to discover, or recover from the past, wasn't evident, and going there seemed like nothing more than a naïve and futile impulse. Yet I roamed the corridors awhile longer, hunched over and with one hand held against that distressed place in my chest; it's a wonder no one asked if I was looking for cardiology.

I walked all the way home afterward, and found that my knack for leapfrogging thoughts was impaired. All I could think about, obsessively and with a keening sadness, was Ev in his new quarters, feeling restless and displaced. It was easy enough to imagine the furnishings, as undistin-guished and anonymous as the building. The standard bed, sofa, end ta-bles, and easy chair you'd find in any mid-priced hotel suite. Wall-to-wall carpeting in some neutral, desert tone; plants that don't require that much water or light. Everything without particular character or charm, except for the handful of artifacts Ev had taken from home: his blue Clichy, the yellow catch-all bowl from the kitchen counter, some photographs of the kids.

Our apartment, on the other hand, had retained most of its idiosyn-cratic familial appeal, like a museum dedicated to our former lives. As I opened the door and stepped inside, I remembered the time Ev and I took the children to Sagamore Hill, Teddy Roosevelt's old summer residence on Long Island, and how those roped-off rooms still contained the furniture, the bedclothes, the rugs, the abandoned toys of that long-dead family. We visited the graves afterward, in case their tenants' absence from those rooms wasn't proof enough. Even the family dogs were buried there, which made Scotty cry. This was a melodramatically morbid comparison, I knew. Everyone who'd inhabited our rooms was alive and well, even if most of us lived somewhere else now. The place was spooky with domestic history, though, and ominously quiet.

When the phone rang, I dropped my purse on the bed before I answered it, and when I heard Ev's voice in my ear, I sat down beside the purse. My first, illogical thought was that he knew somehow about my spying mission, that he was calling to accuse or berate me. But it was only a friendly call; we *were* civilized beings, just as I'd told Violet, and there was ongoing family business between us. He told me that he'd had lunch with Scott, and that they'd had a pretty good time. "Scotty seems to have his head together," he said, which amounted to a rare paternal tribute from Ev.

"So, are you going to take him into the family business?" I asked. I was just trying to be funny, I suppose, to go along with what seemed like his own good humor.

But I encountered what I can only call a shocked silence. "I would never do that to him," Ev said finally. His voice had become cool and flat.

For the first time in a long while, I really contemplated his daily working life. I pictured him knotting his tie in the morning, stuffing his briefcase with papers, putting coins and keys and antacid tablets into his pockets. He'd taken the subway downtown most days, a claustrophobic, bone-rattling rush-hour ride. He would travel on a different line now, and for a shorter trip, but it would be a similar hustle to get to his office. And I saw the office itself, his desk covered with paper and font samples, and the bulletin board behind it a collage of annual reports, flyers, and bar mitzvah invitations.

The cousins Ev had grown up with, Barry and Lloyd, were stationed in identical cubicles across from his, two balding guys who shot rubber bands at their pretty Latina employees and talked loudly and incessantly on the telephone, making deals, haggling over prices. The printing business had undergone radical changes with the advent, the onslaught, of the computer. The founding uncles' noisy old presses were long gone, like the uncles themselves; it was all desktop work for their successors, and very competitive. They had to keep reinventing the operation, making it ever more high-tech and cost-effective, and Ev's vocabulary, which had once favored phrases like *moral imperative* and *narrative flow*, was infused now with references to thermography and digital output.

As if it were a natural segue of thoughts, I remembered our first apartment together, in Iowa—on the top floor of a Victorian frame house divided into student rentals—with its whining bedsprings and the determined clacking of our twin typewriters. I felt a charge of regret and longing, like the last surge of electrical power right before an outage. "I know that," I said, limply and too late. "I was just kidding. And, anyway, it's not as if you're Tony Soprano." *Alice, think before you speak!* When he didn't respond, I kept right on going. "I hear that you've volunteered to print the catalogs for Violet's group. That's really great—will they be in color?"

"I don't know," Ev said, still without affect.

I sighed. How long was he going to keep this up? I'd told him that I hadn't meant what I'd said, which was tantamount to an apology. And what right did he have to be so damned sensitive? Just like me, he knew that everyone is disillusioned in the end, especially the most ambitious among us. You just have to make the most of what happens, without taking it out on the people around you. "I have to go, Ev," I said.

"Yeah, I'm pretty busy here," he answered, as if it had been his own idea to hang up.

A couple of days later I took Scott to dinner at one of the Indian restaurants in his neighborhood. Over the appetizers, he told me that he was thinking of going back to school, that he and Ev had discussed it during their lunch date. He was going to look into a film program at the New School for the spring semester.

"What will you do with *that*?" I asked, although it was in keeping with the sort of schemes I used to dream up for him.

He shrugged. "I don't know, video editing maybe, or animation. Dad says they're, like, pretty hot fields."

"Uh-huh. And will you give up your job at Tower?" I asked, as if I were scandalized about his sacrificing such a plum.

"Yeah, probably," Scott said. "Dad says he'd bankroll me at first, and then maybe I could get a student loan or something."

Dad says, Dad says—*that* was a brand-new mantra. I bit into a samosa and burned my tongue. As I downed some ice water, it occurred to me that Ev must have been giving Scotty some recent handouts or loans. That was why he hadn't asked me for any money for a while. When the two of them had been at such inflexible odds with each other, I'd hoped and argued for just this kind of sympathetic connection between them. But now I felt usurped by it. Ev had called forth his soft, impractical alter ego, Al, to mother our prodigal son. And the residual Ev in me bristled with resentment. "Do you know anything about film?" I demanded. "Do you even go to the movies?" I wouldn't have been all that surprised if my voice deepened into a baritone, if dark hair sprang up on the backs of my hands. Scott leaned away from me, clutching his fork. "Oh, Scotty," I said. "I'm sorry, I'm really sorry. I don't know what got into me."

"It's okay, Ma," he croaked, still eyeing me warily. Mercifully, our main courses arrived then, in a theatrical production of sizzle and smoke, breaking the awful tension.

The next time I saw Dr. Stern, I found myself paraphrasing Celia. "All relationships are such stupid power struggles," I said. "Why does one of us always have to be on top, in bed and in the world? Why can't we ever just lie there peacefully, side by side? I mean, before we're dead."

22

Ruth Casey had submitted her manuscript, *Perfection*, to a few publishers before she'd sent it on to me, and she'd gotten it back quickly from all of them, and without comment. I suspected it had only been read by some very young editorial assistants who couldn't, or wouldn't, imagine the grim realities of autism she'd depicted. Or maybe it had just been buried in the slush pile and not read at all. I was going to refer her to an agent I knew who would probably put her in touch with a mature and sympathetic editor, but on a second read, I saw ways of making the manuscript better first, and more competitive in a crowded market.

The writing was very good, but she'd only done occasional short magazine pieces before, and she needed help with organizing her material and the general structure of the book. And I wondered if the narrative would be more appealing if the voice were a little warmer and less detached. But its main content, about the daily struggles of a couple with a wild yet unresponsive child, and the gradual loss of hope, was both arresting and appalling. Even the latest scientific findings, Ruth wrote, which took the onus off the parents of autistic children, with new suspects like epilepsy and a fragile X syndrome, couldn't relieve her and her husband of their sense of liability. "I didn't need Bettelheim to nail me," she wrote. "I gladly did it to myself. David took an even bigger hit." Despite the cool, tough tone of her prose, I expected Ruth herself to appear war-torn, starved for sensible company and a compassionate ear.

In person, though, she was merely an impassive and pallid dishwater blonde in her early forties. When I held out my hand, she took it, but hers was icy and limp and I quickly let go. In describing her to Violet later, I used the word *reserved*, but I actually thought she was a pretty cold fish. Maybe her disaffection enabled her to deal with her sad and strenuously difficult life; it also made her the ideal antidote to Michael for me. This was going to be a professional arrangement, pure and simple. No one would have to take off her clothes to get any work done.

I took on *Perfection*, and also an informed, but overwrought, novel of the Renaissance, glad to be kept busy and sidetracked from my personal problems. When I checked my e-mail one morning for new responses to my ad, there was a message from Thomas Roman. I realized that I hadn't thought about him much in the turmoil of the past few weeks. He wrote that he was coming to New York City soon for a few days, and wondered if we could meet for a drink or tea somewhere; he had something to give me. If that turned out to be a collection of my mother's love letters, I wasn't sure I wanted to see them.

So much had transpired since I'd started looking into her past. I remembered the tortured scrawl of my father's letter to "Darling," and I thought of his confusion when he accused me of bringing my "paramour" to the nursing home, and of my actual betrayal of Ev. It wasn't easy to trust love or any of its artifacts. And my desire to know everything was tempered by a need to protect certain aspects of memory and history. But maybe Thomas Roman had a poem of hers I'd never seen before, or only an innocent letter containing some of those early anecdotal details unavailable anywhere else. I wrote back, setting a time and place for us to meet.

That afternoon Michael and I met at a coffee shop to go over my notes on his recent revisions. We'd exchanged a few wary e-mails, but hadn't seen each other since the end of our affair. He was sitting in a booth when I got there, scribbling in a notebook.

"Hey," he said, jumping up and dropping his pen, but the kiss that landed near my chin was chaste and friendly. Dr. Stern was right; it was already a little better. As soon as we were settled in the booth, with the table between us, we ordered coffee and got right down to business.

He'd taken up the idea of Joe as the inventor of Caitlin's adult life, and had written a couple of long, new revelatory chapters in a kind of creative frenzy. It was wonderful work but somewhat sloppy, in the way of first, rapturous drafts. I was torn between slowing him down so that he would write more carefully, and urging him to simply go on and edit later.

Michael solved the dilemma himself by saying that he was bushed— he'd been working overtime at the factory—and needed to pause for a while and just polish his sentences. He also wanted to look at the new stuff in the context of the rest of the manuscript.

His decision pleased me, and so did the ease between us, the lack of sexual tension. I told him about the Gina Berriault story and said that he might want to read it, as much for its keen understanding as for its literary example.

I was getting ready to leave when a woman approached our booth and said hello to me. She was a tall, Nordic-looking blonde. For a discomfiting moment or two I had no idea who she was. Then I realized it was Imogene Donnell's girlfriend—who'd aroused such domestic yearning in me that day in Brooklyn—and her first name, Patty, fell into place, too.

After I introduced her to Michael, she began to talk about the upcoming art show, and how excited she and Imogene were about it. "Maybe you can make the opening, too," she said to Michael. "We'll need all the warm bodies we can get."

Michael wrote the information down on a paper napkin he'd pulled from the table dispenser. I felt only the smallest pang when I saw how he perked up at her invitation to be a warm body, and the way he looked her over. Well, he was in for a surprise.

There was a surprise for me, too, when I got home. The official invitation to the art show was in my mailbox. But it's too early, was my first thought. The return address on the envelope was the gallery's, but my name and address were in Ev's handwriting; this was a special, preview mailing. I didn't open the envelope until I was upstairs, in the kitchen, where I used the fish-boning knife to slit the top with surgical precision.

The invitation was stark and striking—bold black letters on a single page of heavy white stock. The heading was the word ANYWAY, which I'd finally come up with as a title for the show, with the artists' names listed alphabetically underneath, followed by the date, the time, and the place. I shook the envelope, hoping for a personal note, but nothing fell out. Then I propped the invitation against the coffeemaker, so I could see it from every angle in the room.

The title had occurred to me after I'd interviewed all of the artists, examined their slides, and considered and rejected several other possibilities. Then I remembered Imogene shrugging and saying that creating art didn't make much sense, given the way the world was, but that she did it anyway. I thought of Greta Gordon's valiant little "night lights," and about India, whose studio was once in the shadow of the World Trade Center and whose grandparents had been in Bergen-Belsen. The persistence of these artists, like Violet's, in the face of such dispiriting times and so few rewards, seemed to be at the core of their work.

The members of the collective met and voted unanimously to approve the title. They hadn't read the essay yet, because I was still refining it, incorporating my motivation for naming the show "Anyway" into the text. It felt good to write it, but less thrilling than when I used to write fiction. Maybe you're not supposed to be thrilled with your own writing; maybe that precludes the reader's delight. It was one more thing I might have discussed with my mother, if she had lived, or with Ev, if we hadn't been so locked in competition.

I'd made a reservation at the Palm Court at the Plaza for my tea with Thomas Roman, because it was a place my mother had liked so much. If Rumpelmayer's still existed, we might have gone there instead. I was the first to arrive and was shown to a table in that elegant, open room, facing the entrance, where I could watch out for him. "I'll be the oldest guy there," he'd written. "You'll know me by my decrepitude."

That didn't turn out to be hyperbole. He came toward me in slow motion, leaning on a wheeled walker, with a tiny, equally aged, but more nimble woman at his side. She seemed to be deliberately decelerating to keep in step with him. Tom Roman was stooped, but still tall; he reminded me of those white-crested wading birds we used to see at sunset at the beach in Chilmark. The woman was his wife, Emily, a "behind-the-scenes person," as she put it, at *Leaves*.

"My first reader," he amended. "She used to read *everything* that came in, even when there was postage due. She was always afraid she'd miss something." He looked amused and adoring. Why shouldn't he be? Emily obviously adored him, too, and she was abidingly radiant. It was hard to imagine her ever lampooning some awful submission to *Leaves*, just for kicks, the way the other summer interns and I often did at G&F.

"So you're little Alice," she said, beaming at me over her menu. "We were so fond of your mother."

"All those letters, back and forth," Tom said. "We felt like childhood friends. But we met only once, on the Vineyard," he added. "You were there, too, but I doubt you'll remember."

I didn't remember, although I scrambled through a mental montage of those distant summers, trying to dredge up a youthful version of this ancient pair. But I knew then, if you can ever know that sort of thing for certain, that my mother's friendship with Thomas Roman had never been more than that.

"How is the memoir coming along?" he asked.

I'd forgotten about that. All of my "harmless" lies were coming back to haunt me, one by one. My face flared, and I had to take a long sip of iced tea before I could answer. "I'm not actually writing a memoir," I said. "I'm just trying to find out some things for myself; you know, to sort out the past." I felt like one of those scam artists who prey on the elderly, as if I'd attempted to wangle their life's savings from them rather than simple information about my own family.

But neither of them seemed that surprised or perturbed by my confession. Then I took my mother's Central Park poem from my purse and handed it to Tom, asking if he'd ever seen it before. He read it carefully, at least a couple of times, before shaking his head and passing it on to Emily. She'd never seen it before, either. "This seems like a rough draft," she said. "Your mother did so many revisions before she sent anything out. Maybe she just didn't have time to work on this one."

"That last line is interesting, though," Tom said, "with its nod to Dickinson."

"And kind of mysterious," I said. "I was hoping you'd seen the poem before, or that my mother had spoken to you about it. I keep thinking that it's a clue to her history, and even my own."

Tom shook his head again, as if to clear his thoughts, and said, "I'm sorry, Alice." Then he reached into one of the flap pockets of his jacket and withdrew a small envelope that he handed to me. "But maybe this will help in recapturing the past."

There was a snapshot inside the envelope, one of those faded, scalloped-edged prints from my childhood. It was taken at the beach—a seagull swooped down above striped umbrellas toward some quarry in the water. I was in the center of the picture's foreground, squinting as I always did in the sun, and about waist-high to the four adults leaning together to fit in the frame of someone's Brownie lens. We were all wearing swimsuits.

I would never have recognized Tom and Emily; did they recognize themselves in those dark-haired, nervy-looking strangers? My father had one arm around my mother's waist and the other clamped to the top of my head, as if he were saying, through the clench of his smile, "Hold *still*, Alice." And he would have been right to restrain me. My left arm and leg were only a blur; I was already headed elsewhere, maybe into the future that was now. "God," I said.

"Yes," Tom Roman agreed.

"Your father was so much fun," Emily said. "We laughed and laughed that day."

Fun! It wasn't a word I would have associated with my father, but as if the snapshot were only the freeze-frame of a movie, I envisioned our pose broken by the click of the shutter, and then all of them in motion behind me along the shoreline, their eruptions of laughter generated by some-thing witty my father had just said.

"That's for you," Tom said, when I tried to hand the snapshot back to him, and I thanked him and tucked it into my purse, alongside my mother's poem.

We argued briefly over who would pay the check, but my relative youth and alacrity helped me to prevail. They were staying at a hotel downtown, someplace cheaper and more modest than the Plaza, and I put them into a taxi before I started walking home. Floating, almost.

23

I'm standing at the door to my father's consultation room. There's a
tremendous sense of urgency; someone is ill or injured, maybe me. I'm
clutching a book to my chest to stem the rising pain there. Yes, I'm the one
who's ill and my father's door is locked. I make a fist with my free hand to
bang on the door, and then I jiggle the knob and call out to him. I can hear
muffled voices and music coming from inside — it sounds like a cocktail
lounge — but he doesn't answer. I run around a street corner and try another door and it swings open much too easily, as if it's fallen off its hinges.
The room it leads to is completely white. I can't see anything except that
whiteness, like the brilliant glare in an operating room. The book is gone;
I must have dropped it in the street. "Daddy!" I cry, and then I wake up.

The next day, at Andrea Stern's, I tried to make meaningful associa-
tions with the images in the dream. Even before I got there, it came to me
that the book I'd held to my breast represented my mother — her poetry,

the pain in her own breast, her wish to calm the feeling in mine. Didn't I still carry her everywhere, and wasn't she lost?

I wondered if the whiteness of the room stood for purity, virginity, for something bridal, or maybe it was a kind of void, like the blank pages of another book, the one I hadn't written. I told myself that my father didn't come to the door because he couldn't, because he was senile and confined to a wheelchair. Except he was in his office in the dream, completely restored to his old vigor from the sound of things, and I was a child again.

Dr. Stern stayed on the sidelines, offering encouragement and affirmation as I stumbled toward interpretation, but not pressing me into making connections. I felt so restive, the way I did when I was in labor, with a desire to pace or to just push the damned thing out. At the hospital, they'd made me wait until the baby began to descend, getting ready to present itself to the world. Suzy, especially, took her sweet time. Now I was the one stalling, unwilling or unready to let go. "This is like having a baby," I groaned, and Dr. Stern said, "Yes, it's hard work."

"But maybe it's only false labor," I told her, just as I kept telling the doctor in the delivery room, when I wasn't screaming. There was no backing out then, but before my hour in Dr. Stern's office was up, I had veered away from the subject, and the most vivid details of the dream began to recede and fade.

I went to Violet's studio later that day for coffee and a second opinion, and, as I had anticipated, she was far more directive and confrontational. "You women with kids are always looking for analogies to childbirth in everything," she said. "In your writing and your painting, even in reading your own dreams—it's such a cliché."

I glanced at the canvas on her easel; there was certainly nothing life-giving there. "Well, they're all hard work," I said, a dull echoing of Andrea Stern.

"Yes, but you have to be more creative in your thinking," Violet said, "and more radical."

"So what do you think it means?"

"No, what do *you* think? And get your mind out of the stirrups for a minute."

"I think I'm going nuts," I said. "My marriage, my life, is wrecked, and all I can dream about are my parents. It's as if I'm arrested at about the age of ten."

"Ten," Violet said thoughtfully. "What happened then?"

"You were there, too. You tell me."

"It's your dream, Alice. It's your life." She wasn't that directive, after all. And hadn't Jeannette Joie said something similar about the nagging feeling in my chest?

"That was the year I went to Dr. Pinch," I told Violet. "His name inspired me, you know. I used to pinch myself, hard, while I was in his office, so I wouldn't blink."

Violet laughed. "Did it work?" she asked.

"Of course not."

"What else?"

"Wait a minute," I said. "Wait."

"What?"

"My birthday."

"What about it?"

"I don't know. I can see the whole date printed out somewhere, on a calendar or something." Violet's birthday was only two weeks later, and we always had back-to-back celebrations. "Did we do anything special at our parties that year?"

"I can't separate them from one another anymore. Was it the year of that manic clown, or was it when you had the magician with the balloons? Poor Allie, you were so afraid of those balloons."

"I still am, a little. That awful rubbery squeak when he knotted our party favors. Cute little dachshunds for the girls, airplanes for the boys."

"Sexist bastard," Violet said mildly. "We should have reported him to NOW."

"Actually," I said, "I preferred the dachshunds. They *were* pretty cute. Yet I was never prepared for when they popped—the bang and that sudden deflation."

"Yeah, don't you just hate that deflation."

"Women like you," I said, "are always looking for sexual metaphors."

"Well, when you can't get the real thing . . ." Her voice trailed off, and the smile she tried on was feeble. Then she told me that she'd broken up with her married doctor a few weeks before, after she'd seen him walking past Framework one afternoon with his wife and child.

"But you knew that they were part of the deal," I said.

"Yes, of course." Violet said. "And I could handle them in theory, just not in the flesh."

Flesh, I thought, the word evoking nakedness, in a sexual sense, and in the sense of being exposed and undefended. And I knew that my own fleshy presence in the world would keep Violet and Ev from ever getting together, easing a fear I hadn't even let myself acknowledge before this.

Then I thought of Michael, and of the startling possibility of Violet and Michael—that's what comes from free association—but she was too old for him, really, just as I had been, and she probably wasn't even his type or the right temperament. Part of my resistance to the idea, I knew, came from an old, subliminal rivalry between Violet and me, the darker side of our devotion. For an only child, I seemed to have an endless supply of would-be siblings.

"I'm sorry," I told Violet.

She shrugged. "I'll live," she said. "Now back to you. Where were we? You were ten, right?"

But the fused odors of turpentine and linseed oil in the studio, which I'd always thought of with pleasure as Violet's particular fragrance, had begun to seem suffocating. "Let's not do this right now," I said. "We're not getting anywhere, and it's creepily like Donna and Ricky trying to solve one of their little mysteries. Besides, I really have to go." I realized that I'd just given one reason too many, that fatal move of bad liars. I looked at my watch, as if to back up my sudden restlessness with a hint at having actual plans.

The only place I needed to go, though, was home. And once I got there, I wasn't sure of what to do with myself. It was that transitional time of day you might mark with cocktails and music when you lived with someone else, putting up a cheerful unified front against the onset of darkness. I didn't feel like drinking alone, but I put a CD on the stereo, the soundtrack from *Sleepless in Seattle*, with all those gorgeous, sentimental old ballads.

When Jimmy Durante's raspy, vital voice crackled through the speakers, singing "As Time Goes By," I closed my eyes and began to slow-dance with an invisible partner around the living room. After a couple of turns, I bumped into the sofa, and I opened my eyes and sat down, overwhelmed by feelings I couldn't exactly name. I remembered dancing with Ev, of course—swaying in place, really—and, long ago, watching my bathrobed parents glide across the floor together to the music of Les Brown or Charlie Spivak. Like the embracing dancers suspended inside my mother's perfume bottle. Was any of that, or maybe all of it, the source of the music in my dream? The whole thing was becoming curiouser and curiouser. And then I saw myself, barefoot, perched on my father's black leather slippers, being whirled around the room, too, with my head flung back, until I was dizzy with delight and vertigo.

I shut off the stereo and went into the bedroom, where I took out my mother's folder. I lay across the bed and opened it, reaching for the letter from the *New Yorker* editor in its separate pocket. There was the date—November 18, 1963—my tenth birthday, on the envelope's postmark, not on an old calendar, as I'd suggested earlier to Violet. This was surely just a coincidence, but it seemed weighted with some significance I didn't understand.

Later, when I was in bed again, absently watching the news on television, it occurred to me that the whiteness in my dream was a presence more than a void or an absence. But I couldn't elaborate on that impression, and I fell asleep soon after that, still thinking about the dream, and hoping for and dreading a rerun, or even a sequel.

The next morning I realized that I hadn't dreamed at all, at least not that I could remember. It was as if my head had been erased, leaving only chalky traces of what had been written there. I had a date to meet Suzy near Bloomingdale's for lunch, and to go shopping with her afterward for bedding. Unlike Suzy, I've never liked shopping very much. It's always seemed to be as much of a time-killing social ritual as a simple convention of free enterprise. But now I had plenty of time to kill; it made me contemplate how many hours of most couples' lives are expended on ordinary domestic matters, like cooking meals and eating them, making love or plans or conversation.

As often as not lately, I ate directly from take-out cartons, sometimes standing at the kitchen counter, and I didn't usually even go out to pick stuff up anymore; I had it delivered from one or another of the million ethnic places in the neighborhood: a noodle dish or something with chicken or tofu—they all tasted pretty much the same after a while—topped by an unpeelable complimentary orange or a packet of fortune cookies. *Your honesty will be its own reward.* Yeah. *The winds of opportunity sew the seeds of success.* Oh, the mysterious East Side!

So many people are on their own in the city. That's why those bicyclists with plastic bags hanging from their handlebars are always crisscrossing the streets in the paths of taxis and pedestrians. I felt exposed in my aloneness every time the doorman announced over the intercom that I had a food delivery, and by the obviously modest size of my order. Dinner for one. I could swear that my skin was starting to smell like soy sauce, and every few days I threw out another refrigerated carton of petrified rice, a congealed version of what's thrown at the newly married for luck.

At a bistro on Third Avenue, Suzy observed that I looked a little drawn, before she launched into a kind of joyous operetta about George and herself while she slid the red Bakelite bracelet up and down her arm. Somehow she also managed to finish everything on her plate. Then we went off to Bloomingdale's.

There was a white sale in progress, and as soon as I saw the sign at the head of the escalator, I was reminded of my dream. I thought of telling Suzy about it, but I was afraid its hidden meaning might turn out be too intimate to share with her. Maybe Violet's sexual metaphors were as common as rice, and maybe Freud was mistaken when he maintained, as Violet once informed me, that not all dream material was necessarily sexual. It was imperative not to lose my real place in my children's lives by trying to become their friend.

While I was thinking all of that, Suzy worked her way determinedly along the sales racks, riffling through packaged sheets and pillowcases as if she were looking for something she'd misplaced. Even from a few feet behind her, I could hear her murmured exclamations about the superiority of one shade of parchment white over another, or about thread counts that seemed to reach into infinity.

When Ev and I first lived together, in Iowa City, our bed linens were a colorful assortment from our hastily merged households. His dark percales were permanently scented by a floral fabric softener, yet a stray sock or two often clung to them with static tenacity. I'd usually wake up with a rash on my cheeks, which might have come from the marathon kissing we did, or an allergy to the fabric softener. Or maybe we had a dangerously low thread count. But the only thing that mattered then was how recklessly we threw ourselves down onto those scruffy, mismatched sheets for love or sleep. They could have been clouds or cacti for all we noticed.

"So, what do you think, Mom?" Suzy asked. "Manila or alabaster? Lauren or Charisma?"

I grabbed her arm. "Listen," I demanded. "You're still happy, aren't you?"

Suzy looked nervously around us. "Of course I am!" she exclaimed. "What's the matter with you? Haven't you been listening to me?"

I glanced around then, too, releasing her arm. I was embarrassing my children, one by one, in public places. "Of course I have," I said. "I just wanted to make sure, that's all. Lauren. Manila."

The following Wednesday I told Dr. Stern that I hadn't had the dream again. "I'm worn out from thinking about it," I said. "And yet I feel remiss, as if I haven't completed an important homework assignment." Afterward, I started to walk home through Central Park again, despite my lingering lassitude, and the fact that I wasn't dressed for the sudden, unseasonable chill. Leaves blew around my feet, and the birds near the reservoir pecked disconsolately or huddled together in their inflated feathers.

This walk was the starting point of the resolution I'd made that morning to be more active and hopeful. I had been lying around the apartment too much—brooding about everything, sleeping in sudden, uneasy little installments, and not getting enough exercise. I planned to begin eating healthier foods, too, and maybe even join a gym. On the main floor of Bloomingdale's the other day, Suzy had urged me to have a makeover, or at least buy a new lipstick, and I'd reluctantly agreed. But when the beauty consultant approached, wearing a white lab coat and a dazzling professional smile, I had a moment of panic and headed for the doors.

The park wasn't crowded this time, maybe because of the unsettled weather. There were several empty benches along the water, and I sat down on one of them to rest for a few minutes. I must have fallen asleep instantly, my brand-new talent, and I woke to something stinging my face. I couldn't have been out very long; I was much too guarded to take a real nap in the middle of the park. But I seemed to have slept into winter.

It was snow that was stinging my face — pelting it, really — in a deluge of colossal flakes flying out of a thick sallow sky. There were already sugary little piles on my lap and on my open-toed shoes. I glanced at my watch; I hadn't been asleep for more than ten minutes or so. I could hear people shouting to one another in the distance, and a dog barking raucously somewhere. This was an event, a phenomenon, a freak snowfall on an ordinary October afternoon.

I stood and brushed myself off, but new flakes kept coming swiftly from every angle, onto my bare head and my eyelashes. I had to blink them away. Everything — trees, benches, birds — appeared blurred, and it was the most surreal sensation, like being trapped inside a snow globe shaken by a hyperactive child. How could I be sure I wasn't just dreaming again?

But when I resumed walking, the true dream began to surface, unbidden, behind my eyes. I was at my father's office door once more, demanding, begging to be let in. The book was securely in my arms, and I heard the music and those voices — still tinny and unclear. Then I was around the corner at that other door, the one that gave too readily at my touch, and there was that great blaze of whiteness, a nothingness that was something, like the blinding snow of an unexpected storm. Miss Snow.

24

I turned and headed in the other direction, back toward Andrea Stern's, feeling slightly disoriented, and skidding and slipping in my ridiculous shoes. Before I was halfway there, the bizarre little storm abruptly ended. Only a few more feathery flakes drifted down, and I glimpsed the sun through that dense sky, like the first bit of fruit uncovered in a cup of yogurt.

It seemed to bring me to my senses. What had I been thinking? The patient right after me would still be in the office, spilling out *her* story, and given all the human misery and mystery around, the rest of Dr. Stern's schedule was probably filled, too.

When I got home, I called and left a message on her machine, saying that I needed to talk to her, it was urgent. Then I sat on the bed with my hands in my lap and waited for her to call me back. The pride I'd taken that summer in my independence, in my ability to cope with anything, fell easily before the fear of dealing with this alone. But I couldn't stop my goose-stepping thoughts and the panoply of pictures going by in my head.

I knew that I wasn't ever going to be certain of what I'd seen more than forty years ago in my father's office. Andrea Stern wasn't a magician; she couldn't just pluck an irrefutable memory from my brain, like a living dove from her sleeve. Some events are forever lost, except for the evidence of souvenirs—the outing at the beach with Tom and Emily Roman, for instance—or else skewed into fantasy.

Children are famous for that, for recalling what they'd only imagined and holding on to it as some sacred truth. When Jeremy was three or four, he told me he remembered being in my belly, how dark it was, and how he had to grab at bits of food that went by after I ate them. Suzy once swore that she was a flower girl at Ev's and my wedding, which struck me as an intuitive lie, since she had been there, all right, but still on the inside. And then there's the whole Rashomon of family argument, with all those competing, sworn testimonies.

I was only ten years old on that fateful day, and a relatively protected, innocent ten, except for my exposure to Violet, who always seemed to know so many more things than I did. I was a cherished child who fed gourmet bread crumbs to the birds in the park, and still half believed it was possible to find your way back home from anywhere, following a path of similar, carefully strewn crumbs.

As I sat there waiting for the phone to ring, I kept seeing myself rapping politely on one door to my father's consultation room, before going to the other one and turning the knob. No one was around, none of the usual nurses or secretaries, not even Parksie or Miss Snow. I didn't pound with my fist and I didn't call out, except in the dream, where I'd attempted to be a hero. I never ran down to the street, either, and the door didn't fall off its hinges; it just opened.

She was sprawled across his desk, her thighs parted by his trousered leg. He could have been sawing her in half with it. Where was his silver clock, the onyx inkstand, the photograph of my mother and me? I don't think there was ever any music; I probably invented that part to cover up the sounds I must have heard: the farmyard grunts, the swish of serge against nylon. Just as I began blinking to hide everything unbearable to see.

By the time the phone rang, I'd replayed those moments so many times, they became almost ordinary, the way appalling images on the news sometimes do. Dr. Stern was between appointments; we could speak for only about ten minutes, but she'd had a cancellation for the next afternoon at four, if I'd like to come in. I said that I would and then I told her as quickly as I could what had happened: sleep, storm, revelation. Ten minutes, it was like a meter running.

"How do you feel?" she asked.

"Shocked," I said. "*In* shock. As if I've lost a lot of blood. How could I have forgotten something like that? And how can I be sure it's even true?"

"You can't be," she said. "You just have to trust yourself, and the process of remembering."

"I don't know that I do," I murmured. Maybe I was the ultimate unreliable narrator.

"Why do you think you were there alone?" Dr. Stern asked.

"That's a good question," I said. "But I can only guess at the answer. I imagine it was the end of the workday, with the typewriters covered and the patients all gone. And my mother may have gone somewhere, too, for a few minutes, just around the corner or to the gift shop to get something. She might have put me on the elevator first."

"Would she do that?"

"Maybe. She struggled against being overprotective. There would have been at least a few other people, and an elevator operator who knew us, and where I should get off." I paused. "But my father couldn't have been expecting us, could he? It must have been a surprise visit. Some surprise."

"Yes," Dr. Stern said, "I'll bet it was. But I'm going to have to go now. I'll see you tomorrow."

"There's more," I said, that old delaying tactic, the one I'd used so often as a child to put off bedtime. "I have to tell you something," I'd say to my mother, after the last kiss, one more sip of water, the final words of the story she'd been reading to me. And I'd win her back for a few extra minutes, a dozen extra kisses. But there really was more now; I could feel it crowding out that tired scene at my father's office door. I had to remind myself that I was an adult, someone who could take no for an answer and postpone gratification, or at least pretend to. "But it can wait until tomorrow," I said, and we hung up.

I said, "I have to tell you something," and my mother turned in the doorway to face me. Her dark hair was haloed by the light in the hallway, and I could barely make out her features.

My father was waiting for her downstairs—I could hear dance music, the plaintive growl of horns, a throbbing bass. Her voice was mild, though, and only slightly impatient. "What is it now, Alice?"

In the past I'd groped for stories to keep her there: Violet had been mean to me at lunch, the art teacher liked my red sweater, we'd learned four new vocabulary words and the principal exports of Bolivia. I was too old for bedtime stories by then, so we'd only had our usual little end-of-the-day chat, and I'd already expended all of my inconsequential daily news.

The other thing, the extraordinary thing I had seen or believed I'd seen in that other doorway, had been flickering on and off in my mind for weeks, like a lightbulb that needed tightening. While we ate dinner somewhere the evening it happened, and on the ride home. And before that, right after I left my father's doorway and ran down the corridor to the patients' restroom, where I peed and washed my cold hands and burning face, and stared into my eyes in the mirror to see what might still be reflected in them. Someone knocked on the door after a while, and I held my breath, waiting, until there was more knocking and I heard my mother call, "Are you in there, Alice?"

I wasn't supposed to use public toilets without her permission—it had something to do with safety and hygiene—but she hadn't been around to be consulted. "Can't I ever have any privacy?" I barked, and I heard her walk away.

By the time I came out, my mother was in my father's private restroom, "fixing her face," as he called it, and he was sitting a few feet away at his desk, wearing his pristine lab coat and writing into a patient's folder. Everything was in place: the clock, the photograph, the inkstand, the plaster models of the kidneys and the lungs. Only Miss Snow was missing. As I watched he dipped his pen into the inkwell and wrote something inside the folder.

"Well, look who's here," he said, putting his pen down, and beckoning to me.

Can you dream when you're awake? I went to him, and he kissed the part in my hair and retied the ribbon that tamed it into a ponytail. He always pulled it tighter than my mother did.

I said, "I have to tell you something," and my mother said, "What is it now, Alice?" It was weeks or even months later. Dr. Pinch was already in the picture. My mother's hand was on my bedroom doorknob, the music was pulling her away. And I said, "Daddy was kissing Miss Snow on his desk." Did I actually say those words? The part about the desk would be critical, because otherwise I could have been mistaken. He might have just been taking a speck from her eye, or examining her throat, if they were standing up.

Somehow I'd turned the feral act I'd witnessed into kissing, smooching, something playful and tender. Whenever I revisited that moment, his mouth was buried in her neck, like a vampire's. They were struggling fiercely against each other, and she appeared to be losing the battle.

My mother's face was still in shadow, but I could see the shift in her expression. More of the whites of her eyes were showing, and there may have been a glint of her teeth. "What are you talking about?" she said.

"Come lie down with me," I said, whimpered, really.

But she didn't come. Her hand was on the door frame, keeping her there, blocking even more of the light. The music went on and on. "Alice, is this a story you're telling me?" That was one of our euphemisms for lying. *Exaggerating* was another, and so was *stretching the imagination*.

She'd given me an easy way out. "April fool!" I could have cried, if it were April 1. Or, "I was only kidding." I didn't say any of that, though. I was rolling downhill; there was no way to stop. "No!" I said. "Daddy was kissing her neck, and he was holding her down."

It felt like a lie as I said it, but it had the impact of the truth. "Go to sleep right now," my mother said, and she closed the door. The ordinary, scary darkness was a blessing of sorts. It let me fall asleep quickly, just as my mother had commanded me to do.

"So," I said to Dr. Stern. "That's everything, I think." She waited, watching me. "I don't feel any better," I said, and I laughed.

"Did you expect to?" she said.

"Not really. Violet always prepares me for the worst, you know. She said . . . what did she say, again? Oh, yes, that you aren't a trauma doctor."

We sat in silence for a few seconds and then she said, "Do you think you stopped blinking after you told your mother?"

"Maybe," I said. "Probably. That would make sense, wouldn't it? I didn't have to look at that scene in my head anymore, because I'd passed it on to her."

"And were you relieved?"

"I suppose so. This is all conjecture, though, isn't it?" Or hocus-pocus, I was thinking. I *had* expected to feel better, and I felt worse, really anxious, and the pressure in my chest had become urgent.

"Tell me what you're thinking," Dr. Stern said.

"That you're a fake," I blurted. "Oh, God, I'm sorry."

"Don't be, it's fine. You're disappointed in me."

"We got this far," I said. "I mean, we dug all this crap up, and what good is it? Now I know that I finked out my father and hurt my mother." I'd done more than that; I had broken her heart, the very thing I had once sworn that I would never do. "She must have been furious with me."

"You were a child," she said. "*Her* child. Do you really think she was angry with you?"

"Yes, at least for that moment, but she knew enough not to kill the messenger. So she killed something else instead."

"What?" Andrea Stern asked. She was leaning forward slightly in her chair.

"Her ambition," I said. "Whatever desire she'd had to become a known poet."

"I thought your father did that," she said.

"Not single-handedly," I told her, and myself. "We were in it together."

"Why would you do such a thing?" she asked.

I could only guess. "Because I wanted to be the writer in the family?" I saw myself hammering away at the keys of my silver Olivetti. My father once stopped outside my room and said, "Christ, Alice, you're going to break that thing."

"You know, the queen is dead, long live the queen. Or maybe it was just the old Oedipal triangle. He was the first man in my life, right? I don't know, *you* tell *me*."

But she clearly wasn't going to do that. Instead she said, "Your mother kept on writing, anyway, but you stopped."

"I didn't do it to punish myself," I said. "I just wasn't very talented. And my mother may have kept writing, but she gave up on finding a larger readership. She'd threatened my father with her potential and he got back at her, with my help."

"Why are you so sure that's what happened?"

"Because I know writers, and the drive behind even the quietest, most selfless-seeming ones." I sighed. "The proof is in her folder. There are no more notes from *The New Yorker,* and no evidence that she ever put a manuscript of her poems together."

"Do you think she confronted your father with what you'd told her?"

"I have no idea, but I doubt it. I mean, life continued. Helen and Sam, Sam and Helen. I grew up and went off to college." The goose ate that feathered thing and flew away. "She died." I fumbled in my purse for a Kleenex, but I didn't seem to need it. "I'd like to kill him," I said quietly.

All the weeping I'd done in that room, and now I was dry-eyed, stony. And I was feeling antsy. I began tapping my fingers on the armrest of my chair, and I took a peek at my watch. Where was the next patient, anyway?

Afterward, I walked to Broadway and went into a bar, thinking: there goes my resolution to be healthy and happy. But I couldn't go home just yet, where the facts of my life lay in wait for me. It wasn't quite five o'clock, and there were only a couple of men inside the bar, drinking beer and staring up at one of the news channels on the muted TV. I garnered an appraising glance or two before their gaze returned to the screen.

The bartender came and I ordered a dry martini. After it arrived, I looked up at the television set, too, in time to watch the eerily soundless aftermath of a synagogue bombing in Turkey. Other news, about sports, health, entertainment, and politics, crawled relentlessly across the bottom of the screen. One of the men slipped off his bar stool and came and stood next to me. "Some world, huh?" he said.

How could I respond to a remark like that? Like the news crawl, it seemed to cover everything and nothing at once. It was much easier to imagine myself screwing this stranger somewhere, at his place or in a hotel room, in total silence. He was in his forties or fifties and nice looking enough, and clean. He was probably sane, probably as lonely as I was. I wondered if my heated fling with Michael, and what I'd rediscovered about my father and Miss Snow, had undone all my old romantic notions about love and sex. I took a long, last gulp of my drink and said, "Yes, but I have to be going."

At home I picked up the telephone, but there was nobody I wanted to call, not even Ev, or Violet. Ruth Casey's manuscript was on the night table next to the phone and I turned randomly to a page somewhere in the middle and willed myself to concentrate on the text. It was a scene in which Ruth tries to get her autistic child to make eye contact with her— first by talking softly, then by raising her voice, louder and louder, until she's yelling, and finally by grabbing the girl's face hard and forcing it toward her own. "But she was still defiantly indifferent," Ruth wrote, a seeming contradiction in terms that worked surprisingly well. And the editing I'd done so far—mostly trimming and cutting and pasting—had helped to make the manuscript tighter and more coherent. But Ruth was defiant, too, resisting my suggestions to "warm up" her prose.

Maybe it didn't matter; I'd begun to reluctantly see that there would probably still be resistance by most publishers to such a sad story that refused to be a tearjerker, or attempt to either inspire or console. Was I obligated to tell Ruth that, when she hadn't asked? In her book proposal, she'd stated her intentions clearly. "This isn't one of those success stories about bringing a child out of the wilderness of her affliction," she'd written. "And it isn't a spiritual guide for other parents, or a breast-beating diatribe against fate. It's a report of what can happen to anybody, of what happened to us." Perhaps this was only another dance in which I should let the writer lead.

I put the manuscript aside and opened my mother's folder. Sitting at my desk, I read and reread her Central Park poem until I'd committed it to memory, until the words hardly made sense anymore. I took the letter from *The New Yorker* and put it into the zippered compartment in my purse. Now I knew why there were no other letters like it.

I went to the mirror and tried to cry. Nothing doing. Then I looked at photographs of my parents—their wedding portrait, the snapshot that Thomas Roman had given me, dozens of others in one of my mother's carefully arranged albums. My father smiled for the camera a lot, I noticed, and he squinted into the sun, like me. Emily Roman had said that he was so much fun. I remembered the smell of surgical soap, the way his black torpedo of a car sliced into the night.

The martini may have helped to deaden my feelings, but even hours afterward, when the alcohol had surely worn off, I was impassive rather than murderous. "I'd like to kill him," I'd told Andrea Stern, but my heart wasn't really in it. I was cool enough to be a hired assassin, or a surgeon.

A couple of weeks later, when Mrs. Hernandez called from the home, I was working on a manuscript, and I was annoyed by the interruption. I hadn't visited my father for a while, but I hadn't completely abandoned him, either. I still did what had to be done: promptly sending the checks for his care, approving haircuts and visits to the podiatrist. There had been other, recent calls about him. A toothache had to be attended to, and his hearing aid replaced for the second time. "What is it now?" I asked irritably, jarred by this echo of my mother's question to me.

Miss Hernandez cleared her throat. "Dear," she said. "I'm afraid I have some sad news."

25

I decided on a graveside service. There would probably be only a few people in attendance, and I wanted to get it over with as quickly as possible. My father had never had much tolerance for lengthy ceremonies, either. "Keep it short and sweet," he'd advise before any public event at the hospital, even when he was about to receive an award. I felt perfectly efficient and composed as I made the plans for his funeral. My only real concerns were about the tone of the service, and that it might rain.

I'd asked the Jewish chaplain at Mount Sinai to officiate. He was fairly young and new to the job, and had never met my father. "Tell me something about him," he said, as we sat in his office. I was struck dumb for what seemed like a long time, and he leaned toward me, making a steeple of his hands, and said, "Well, he was a surgeon, right? So maybe we shouldn't give God top billing." Oh, a comedian, I thought. My father would have had him yanked offstage with a vaudeville hook.

As it turned out, I was wrong about everything. I'd put a notice in the

Times, and a respectable crowd appeared at the cemetery: my own family, of course; a couple of distant paternal cousins; and a few friends, including Parksie and Violet and her parents. But several of my father's old colleagues and patients showed up, too. The survivors. *Old* was the operative word. Some people leaned on canes or walkers; the occasion must have surely given them pause. I was sorry that I hadn't provided chairs, and what was my big rush to get my father underground?

His coffin was there when we arrived. The freshly dug hole awaiting it seemed almost vulgar beside my mother's tidy little verdant plot, the result of something called Perpetual Care. Ev once said after writing the annual check that it was like renting a tuxedo to be buried in.

I used to go to the grave site regularly and pull up a few rogue weeds myself, and tamp the disturbed earth back down, until my mother's unremitting silence, and my own, made those excursions painfully pointless. The last time I was there, I remembered, a man at a neighboring grave kept muttering, as if he were carrying on his end of a long-standing argument with his dead wife. But maybe he was just praying.

There were no visitors' stones or pebbles placed, like primitive calling cards, on the white mantel of my mother's tombstone. I picked up a small handful from the path between the avenues of graves and slipped them into my jacket pocket, intending to set them out later. The largest one was as round and smooth as a worry stone, and I worked it with my fingers inside the pocket.

It was an unseasonably mild November afternoon. That freaky little October snowstorm seemed like nothing more than a cosmic joke now. There was enough of a breeze to lift a couple of yarmulkes, which my boys chased down and returned to their elderly owners. The clouds moved swiftly above that miniature marble skyline, allowing the sun to appear and disappear over and over again in a veritable light show, like a last, spectacular performance of weather on earth.

Rabbi Singer was wonderful. When the time came, he wasn't inappropriately funny, or inappropriately maudlin, either. To my relief, he didn't speak in a voice "like a statue," as the rabbi does in a Philip Roth story, and he didn't use any of the standard eulogizing words, like *beloved* and *ador-*

ing. He seemed to have gleaned the essential Samuel Brill from what I was finally able to tell him—the arrogant, gifted doctor; the uxorious husband; the elusive, seductive father; the good grandfather. Music lover, food enthusiast, avid swimmer. He even mentioned my father's red hair, "that persistent, recessive trait," with a nod to Jeremy and me, and we exchanged misty, empathetic smiles.

Ev stood next to me and held my elbow, an escort's courteous gesture, even after I willed him to move his hand to my neck, which ached to be touched. The last thing the rabbi said, before intoning the Hebrew prayer for the dead, was that my father had served the body and that my mother, as a poet, had served the soul, the *neshumah.* That was a little too flowery for me, but I was glad that he'd mentioned her, other than as an appendage of my father's life. And it made me wonder if my father had ever privately pitted his calling against hers—Science against Art—with his own coming up short. Never, I decided; he was much too complacent for that. Medicine enabled you to live, he would have concluded, poetry only suggested how.

Then one of his former patients, whose years my father had apparently extended, tottered to the edge of the open grave and began to extol him. His voice was too loud at first, and then too soft. We might have all been on a subway platform, trying to listen to an announcement crackling over the PA system. Only a few phrases were clearly discernible—"brilliant surgeon," "my life," "eternal gratitude"—before he broke into sobs. Ev took his arm and led him back from the brink. How my father would have loved the tribute and despised the emotional display.

The coffin was lowered into the grave. Careful, careful, I wanted to say, when it pitched a little on the way down, just as my mother would caution the men carrying a new piece of furniture into our house. Someone handed me a child's red plastic shovel, like the ones I'd had in Chilmark, and I scooped up a little earth with it and threw it onto the coffin before handing the shovel to Ev, who did the same before passing it on to Suzy. And so on down the straggly line of mourners that had begun to form.

If it weren't for the gravediggers standing by, four burly men leaning on their man-sized shovels, it might have taken days to cover him over. As people approached, one after the other, to perform this symbolic duty, I tried not to think about the times I'd buried my father's feet in the sand, and how he had always bounded up from that frangible prison and run into the foaming surf. I rubbed the worry stone in my pocket until it grew warm, and then I pressed a sharper pebble under my fingernail, the way I'd once pinched myself to keep from blinking.

At home Esmeralda came to the door wearing a black dress and a sheer white apron I had never seen before. While we were gone, she had let herself into the apartment and arranged an elaborate buffet lunch. Surely I hadn't ordered this much food when I'd anticipated only a small turnout. Esmeralda hadn't seen Ev for a long while, but for once she only had eyes for me, the principal mourner, the grand hostess of this funeral feast. When she gripped my hand and said *"Lo lamento mucho,"* I didn't need a translator.

The children all hovered near me at first, as they used to when they were little and felt shy among strangers. "Go talk to the cousins," I told Suzy, giving her a little shove in their direction. "Fix a plate for the rabbi," I instructed Scotty, who was eyeing the food anyway. When I touched Jeremy's hair, he drifted away, too, toward Celia, who was standing alone on the other side of the room.

They were still living together, in that unknowable way of other couples. Maybe their music bound them, or maybe that was what threatened to pull them apart—what Celia meant when she'd referred to a "power struggle." In a review of a concert their chamber group gave in Philadelphia that summer, the critic had lauded her technical brilliance and Jeremy's sensitive interpretation of the music. Did such praise simply indicate their innate harmony, or somehow set them against each other, like shades of Ev and me?

Violet brought me a cup of coffee and said, "So now you're an orphan."

"I'm a little old for that, aren't I?" I said, refusing to acknowledge the wrench I felt.

Then I noticed that Parksie was hanging back like a wallflower at the entrance to the living room, even though she knew several of the people there, and I went to speak to her. We had the usual postmortem conversation, about how lucky we were that the threatened rain had never materialized, and what a surprise it was to see so-and-so again after all these years. Neither of us mentioned my father. Both of us were thinking about him.

She looked considerably older than the last time I'd seen her, only months before, at the nursing home. I noticed a slight, nodding head tremor now, as if she were agreeing with everything I said. And her real eyebrows seemed to have vanished and been replaced by twin arches penciled in by a cartoonist to depict surprise.

I felt a rush of affection and pity, and I said I had a gift for her that I wanted to deliver personally. The idea had just occurred to me, and I chalked it up to sentimental impulse. She invited me to have lunch at her place on Roosevelt Island the following week. "I'd love to," I said, certain that I'd come up with something of my father's to bring to her when the time came.

A line had formed at the buffet table, similar to the one at the cemetery. Life goes on, as Marjorie Steinhorn had whispered hotly in my ear earlier, and I was starting to feel hungry, myself. The platter of smoked fish was so artfully arranged, and I could smell something sweet, coffee cake or doughnuts, being heated in the oven. Things had been very different right after my mother died. I'd been such a wellspring of tears then, and nothing had seemed appetizing to me until Ev appeared in the Cedar Rapids Airport with those bagels.

At last everyone was gone, except for Ev and the children, and we all gathered in the living room. Esmeralda had washed the dishes and put them away; there was nothing left to do. I took off my shoes and lay down on one of the sofas. Suzy plopped down next to me and began to massage my feet. "George and I are staying here with you tonight," she announced.

As soon as she said it, I realized that it was an offer I'd been hoping Ev would make, and I avoided looking at him when I said, "You don't have to, Suze. I'm really wiped out, and I have a pill to take."

"Mom," she said firmly, "our stuff is already in my old room." She yawned, and that served as a cue for everyone else, except George, to get up and prepare to leave. I urged them to go to the refrigerator first and take some of the leftovers, the same speech I made after almost every family dinner. But I just lay there as I said it, and soon I began yawning, too, and my eyelids fluttered.

When I awoke, I was still on the sofa, with a blanket tucked around me. I felt bewildered for a few moments. The room was dark, but I had no idea of the time, and I had to let the events of the day seep back into my mind. *Orphan*, I thought in chilling wonder. And then I found myself slipping even farther backward, to the phone call from Mrs. Hernandez, telling me that my father had died in his sleep, during an afternoon catnap in his wheelchair.

I'd called Ev right away, and he came from his office to drive me to Riverdale. It was a good, peaceful death, the resident doctor assured us, even though my father had been alone when it happened. We were asked if we wanted to view the body. *Body!* What an intimate term for a stranger to use about such a reserved person. And *view* struck me as odd, too, as if we were being invited to a film or a museum exhibit, where we would be able to keep the critical distance of spectators. "Yes," I said, daring them to prove it.

My father was still in his room, but they had laid him out on the bed, with the gray cashmere throw pulled up to his chin. The sun hadn't set yet, and I glanced nervously at the window before I thought: it's all right to be lying down at this hour, you're dead. Now the word *dead* didn't seem quite right, either, although he was tallow-faced and still. *Absent* was more like it. Why did the nuances of language matter so much to me, even at a time like this? Was I trying to edit my father's death? I put my hand on his cold brow. Somehow the title "Daddy" still fit this carapace, if not the middle-aged woman who'd used it. Stop thinking, I commanded myself, but it didn't work. Old gander, I thought. Cheating bastard. *Herr Doktor*. My love.

We went directly from there to the funeral home, where I chose a coffin — the most grown-up act of my life — and made arrangements for the pickup and delivery of the body. Then Ev drove me back home, with a small carton of my father's belongings on my lap. "Do you want company for a while?" he asked, when we pulled up to the building.

Language, again. I turned to look at him, but his face was unreadable, aside from the sympathy that had been there all day, and didn't seem nearly enough at that moment. "No, thanks," I said. "I'm fine, really."

"Well, try and get some sleep, Al," he said. "I'll call the kids. They can call everybody else." The motor was still running and the heater was on. He kissed me on the cheek, and then he reached across me to open my door, and his arm grazed my breast and my shoulder. I couldn't have felt worse if he'd tossed me from the car while it was moving.

Now I threw off the blanket and got up creakily from the sofa to go down the hallway to the bathroom. The apartment was quiet; Suzy's door was closed. "Is that you, Mom?" she called out drowsily. "Do you need anything?"

"No, dear," I said. "Shh. Go back to sleep," something I was certain I'd never do again, myself. After I used the toilet and brushed my teeth, I put on a nightgown and got into bed, leaving the light on. There were a few books on my night table shelf that I'd been meaning to read, and I opened one, and then another, but I couldn't become engaged. When I closed the last book, I expected to be haunted by images of the funeral, or of the day my father died. Instead, Miss Snow stepped into my head, the way she used to step into my father's office, tall and blond and elegant, with one manicured hand to the pearls around her neck, and the other holding her steno pad. I realized that I hardly knew anything about her, beyond her appearance and her secretarial service to my father. She was like a movie star who could only be identified by the role she played. It was then that I understood my impulse to visit Parksie.

I got out of bed and went to the closet, where I'd put the carton of my father's things. There wasn't much. I'd already given his watch to Jeremy, who'd first learned to tell time with it, and divided various medical awards — the medallions and plaques — among all the children. Some personal items, like his clothing and toiletries and the new hearing aid, I'd left to be distributed to other, indigent inmates of the home. And my mother's ancient jade plant now stood in fluorescent light on the counter of the nurses' station of the Alzheimer's floor.

The carton in my closet held only the silver clock, still ticking; the framed photograph of my mother and me; and the medical book with its transparent overlays. What would I bring to Parksie the following week?

The photo was out, so it was a toss-up between the book and the clock. And I finally chose the clock because it was a more substantial and valuable object—it came from Georg Jensen—and it seemed to better represent the man Parksie knew, with the grandeur of its silver casing, the austere face, and that faint but determined pulse. My decision was also selfish, because I loved the book, with its monogrammed caduceus bookplate and those layered pages that could be peeled back, one at a time, to reveal the heart of the matter.

26

The tram ride to Roosevelt Island, that swift glide over the river between bridges and buildings, is one of the lesser-sung charms of the city, although Violet referred to the island itself as a kind of middle-class penal colony. She was such a cynic, but on the bus from the tram to Parksie's house, I began to see what she meant. I was struck by the institutional look of the high-rises, how generically alike the storefronts were. And the streets were practically empty; where were all the people? Even the tram and the bus had only a few other passengers.

Yet this was a safe and comfortable place for Parksie to live during this late stage of her life. The rents are lower than in Manhattan, and every-thing she needed—market, pharmacy, church, laundry, library—was within walking distance, or only a five-minute bus ride away.

I had put the clock in a gift box and wrapped it with silver paper and matching cord, and I'd made a detour to Payard for some pastries on my way to the tram. Parksie lived on the twentieth floor of her building. Her

one-bedroom apartment was rather small, but she had only a slightly ob-
structed water view, and a clear view of a pretty little park. The furnishings
reminded me of a bed-and-breakfast Ev and I had once stayed at in Vermont. This place was just as persistently busy and cheerful, with Laura
Ashley floral patterns everywhere, creating an illusion of eternal spring,
and lots of pillows and dishes of potpourri. An oversized ledge in the living
room that might have been a great window seat was devoted to a display of
framed photos of Parksie's family and a few of her departed cats. Two living tabbies blinked indifferently at me from a padded basket nearby.

She'd made shrimp salad and deviled eggs for our lunch—the fluted
eggs must have been squeezed through a pastry tube—and the dining table,
in an L-shaped extension of the living room, had been set with enormous
care. Pristine place mats, shining silverware. The gold-rimmed plates were
clearly from her good china, and the white linen napkins, folded into
peaks, resembled the old-fashioned nurses' caps Parksie once wore. She
was in mufti today, dressed up in a boxy, powder-blue pantsuit with matching eye shadow. I was touched by all the preparations she'd made for my
visit, and by the exuberance of her greeting. "You're here!" she cried,
opening her arms to enfold me, as if I'd just rowed myself across the river.

During lunch we chatted about Suzy's engagement and the various ex-
ploits of Parksie's numerous nieces and nephews. This one was in medical
school, that one was a computer whiz. They lived in Idaho, Alaska,
France! Everyone was growing up so fast, weren't they? Where did time
go? It was familiar rhetoric, but I thought she looked a little frightened
when she said it. I'd considered telling her about Ev and me, but decided
against it. It was a burden she could live without, and I guess I didn't want
to damage her sense of me as a successful person.

After dessert, I handed her the gift-wrapped clock, and she painstak-
ingly unknotted the cord and undid the paper without tearing it—she
would use them both again. After she opened the box and pulled the tissue apart to reveal the clock, a gasp escaped her. Then the room grew so
still, I could hear the clock's steady ticking from my seat across the table.
This is where time goes, it seemed to say. "Alice!" she exclaimed. "Oh, but
I couldn't . . ."

"Of course you can," I said. "Why, it was something you saw every day."

"But shouldn't it stay in the family? Wouldn't Suzy and her fiancé like to have it? Or one of the boys?"

"No, they wouldn't. It's yours, I want you to have it. And I'm sure my father would want you to have it, too." I could see her waiting, poised to receive his signal to approach, in the office, at the nursing home.

"Thank you, dear," she said. "This means a great deal to me." She'd begun scanning the room, trying to settle on a place to put the clock. There was no natural spot for it, no desk or mantelpiece, and every table-top was already crowded with knickknacks. She stood, finally, and walked to the windowsill photo gallery, where she moved a few frames from the center to each side, and settled the clock in the space she'd made. "There," she said, with satisfaction, and stepped back to admire it.

"Yes, perfect," I agreed, envisioning the dark mahogany gleam of my father's desk. I got up and began to clear the dishes.

Parksie went to the sofa and sat down, patting the cushion beside her. "Come," she said. "Just leave those, I'd much rather visit with you."

"Me, too," I admitted. I sank into my designated seat and said, "This is so cozy. And I loved the tram—those little red seats—it was like an elegant amusement park ride."

"And so convenient," Parksie said. "Look how it's brought you here to me."

Of course that made me feel guilty; why hadn't I ever come to see her before? And I was reminded of the specific purpose of this visit. "Do you know who I've been thinking about lately?" I said. "Miss Snow."

She was startled. "Diana?" she said.

I'd forgotten her first name, that she'd even *had* a first name. Diana— it was imbued now with an aura of royalty and tragedy. "Was she as pretty as I remember?"

"Oh, yes. But she was a type. Cool, you know, with that blond pageboy, that pale, pale skin. And she could have used a few extra pounds on her bones."

"Her last name certainly fit, though, didn't it?" I glanced around at the flowers and flounces in an effort to get that flurry of whiteness out of my head.

"When she got married, she became Diana Loach," Parksie said.

"Really? That's not quite as evocative, is it? I've often wondered what became of her." I had thought of Miss Snow, occasionally, over the years, but she was fixed in my mind as I'd once known her. I was really unable to imagine her growing older, and in a domestic setting. "Do you know where she is now, what she's doing?"

"I'm afraid not. We haven't been in touch for years. They moved to Pennsylvania before the children were born. She had three of them, just like you. Walter's, her husband's, firm relocated, you know. They manufactured paper cartons. She sent announcements: new address, babies' births, that sort of thing. Family photographs at Christmas. And I always wrote back." She paused. "But you know how it is, Alice, everyone's busy and it's hard to keep track of people." A polite way of saying she'd been dropped. "What made you think of her?" Parksie asked. "Oh, of course, your father's death. We should have tried to notify her . . ." She trailed off, looking somber and preoccupied.

"Well, yes, perhaps," I said, patting her hand. "But I was thinking about her even before that, going over those times Mother and I came to the hospital to meet Daddy. While we waited for him, I would sit at your desk or at Miss Snow's, drawing and coloring, do you remember?"

"Of course I do," Parksie said. "How could I forget? I used to hang some of your little pictures in my office." Her expression was dreamy and nostalgic, and her head bobbed, as if she were saying, *Yes, yes, I remember everything.* Dear Parksie. She was the one I loved, even as I'd idolized Miss Snow.

"But what was she like, Miss Snow?" I asked. "I mean, personally?"

"She was an excellent secretary, as I recall. Extremely accurate, and she typed fifty-five words a minute."

What an odd detail to have held all these years, and it certainly wasn't the sort of information I was fishing for. I wanted to know if she was aggressive, vain, passionate, reckless. If she had a sense of humor, or of fairness, and if other women liked her, or just the men. Yet I could almost hear Miss Snow's fingernails tapping briskly on her metal typewriter keys, and see the way each page in her steno pad was divided neatly down the middle by a narrow red line. Then I thought of the "letter" my father had scrawled that day in the nursing home. "Darling," he'd written, clearly, before making all those frantic, senseless markings. Weren't they something like the mysterious squiggles and strikes, the symbols of Miss Snow's short-hand?

Parksie's eyes were closed. She might have been reminiscing, too, or maybe she'd just dozed off.

"Parksie, listen," I said. "There's something I want to ask you."

Her eyes flew open, like a doll's. "What?" she asked.

"I don't know how to say this," I said.

One of the cats uncoiled itself from the basket at that moment and sprang onto Parksie's lap. "Oh, Cynthia," she said, "you want to join the conversation," and she ran her hand along the purring engine of the cat's throat.

I was grateful for the distraction, but very soon Parksie was looking at me again, with curiosity and concern. Was I only imagining something else, a flicker of alarm? "It's about Miss Snow," I said.

She resumed stroking the cat. "Oh. What about her, dear?"

"I have this one disturbing memory of her. It's almost like a dream."

Parksie sat forward and the cat spilled off her lap. "Yes?" she said.

I took a deep breath and let it out slowly. "This is pretty awful," I said. "And I want you to understand why I'm telling you about it. It's not to gossip or to blacken anyone's name. It's just that I've been feeling troubled lately, and I wasn't sure why until I remembered something that happened a very long time ago. Or at least I *think* I remember it. Anyway, I have to know now, just for my own peace of mind, and I hoped that you might be able to help me out."

"What in the world are you talking about, Alice?" Parksie said.

"Okay, here goes. One day, when I was about ten, I opened the door to my father's office at the hospital, to his consultation room, and they were in there."

"Who was?" she said.

"My father and Miss Snow. Diana," I said, trying it out.

Parksie's hand was pressed against her own throat. She might have been measuring the pulse leaping there. "Was she taking dictation?" she asked, but she didn't seem to have much confidence in her question.

"No. She was lying across my father's desk, and he was lying on top of her."

"That's impossible!" Parksie cried. Her hand dropped beside her on the sofa cushion with a little thud.

"That's what I thought at first, too," I said. "But now I can't get that picture out of my mind. He was kissing her neck; his leg was between hers. There's no question about what they were doing."

I'd seen it as a struggle then, but her arms were wound around his back, not pushing against his chest to free herself. I'd knocked at the other door, but they couldn't have heard me over the uproar of their own breathing. "It was so strange, it was completely white in there, like a blizzard," I said.

Parksie groaned, and I let my gaze wander toward the window across the room, feeling irritable, and with a sudden longing for the real, clamorous life of the city. What was *wrong* with her? She was what my father used to call, with amused derision, a "maiden lady," but she was also a trained nurse, for God's sake. When I finally looked back at her, her eyes were fixed on me.

Then I was in that doorway again, on the threshold of everything. My father battered against Miss Snow, whose white-stockinged legs opened to let him in, while her plump white arms clutched at his back. But why was Miss Snow wearing white stockings? She wouldn't—her hosiery was always sheer, and in that flesh-toned shade they still call Nude. And I saw that the woman on the desk was the blizzard herself, dressed entirely in white—even her shoes and her little winged cap—like a bride, a vision, a nurse. She turned her head then because *she'd* heard me at the door, even if he hadn't, and her kohl-rimmed, blue-shadowed eyes were the same eyes that were looking at me now, with the same consuming horror and despair.

How had I have ever confused her with Miss Snow? I felt dizzy and sick to my stomach. I could have easily given my entire lunch up right then: shrimp salad, deviled egg, pastry, coffee. And I would have taken back everything I'd said, in return, rewound the entire day. Oh, Alice, think before you speak.

Parksie hadn't moved. Even when one of the cats leapt onto the sofa to investigate, nudging its head against her arm, she stayed as still as stone. What if she'd had a stroke, died? In some ways, this was worse than when

I'd told my mother. At least I was a child then, *her* child, as Dr. Stern had pointed out. Now, here, I was simply an emissary from the past, of the dead. I glanced across the room at the silver clock, some cruel jokester's version of the gold watch given for a lifetime of service.

I swallowed a few times and wet my lips before I began my retreat. "I guess you never knew anything about it," I said. "Or maybe it *was* just my imagination. You know how children are, and Daddy used to always say I let mine run away with me. And it doesn't really matter in the long run, does it? I mean, he's dead—and Mother, too—and Miss Snow, well, she's Mrs. Loach now, isn't she, and who knows what's happened to her in all this time." I was finally able to shut up, to simply sit there and listen for Parksie's breathing.

When I could detect it again, it sounded shallow and rapid. "Look at the time," I said, without consulting my watch or that relentless clock. "The tram leaves on the quarter hour, right? I'd better be going, I have so much to do." Drink hemlock, I thought, put my head in the oven, jump off a bridge.

Parksie stood up, too, and I linked arms with her on the way to the door. "What a lovely lunch that was," I said. "But I didn't mean to upset you with my story."

"Oh, no, dear," Parksie managed to say.

"Well, good, then," I said. "Because that was all ages ago, anyway."

"Yes," Parksie said.

I held her longer than I should have, trying to gauge whether she was really hugging me back or simply tolerating my embrace, and, at the same time, testing the resiliency of my affection for her. It felt so good being in her arms, I knew that my feelings, at least, were still intact. All of it *had* happened ages ago, in what seemed right then like another lifetime. "Let's you and I never lose touch," I said. My voice was as plaintive as it had been when I'd asked my mother to come and lie down on my bed with me.

"Of course not," Parksie replied. But maybe that only meant birthday cards and a photograph at Christmas of the cats curled in their basket.

I just missed the next tram going back to the city. Several passengers had disembarked, carrying briefcases and shopping bags. There was a woman in a wheelchair and someone wheeling a bicycle. The bus taking them home was going to be crowded, too. A few people had started walking, and when I looked back at the grid of buildings behind me, I saw that lights had gone on in random patterns in all those anonymous high-rises, that people lived there, just as they did everywhere. Some of them would be watching the evening news by now, preparing supper, returning phone calls. And in a little while I would be home, too.

27

There's a certain thrilling authority to an art show opening, even in a co-op gallery. It's like a party given by the friends of a writer for a book that's been self-published, or published by some tiny, obscure press. There won't be any reviews, and sales will be minimal, but the party room is always crowded with well-wishers, and the cheap wine is poured freely and goes to everyone's head so that the noise level is high and celebratory. Even the platter of American cheese chunks and grapes is decimated, and all the copies of the book on display are grabbed up, giving the illusion that they're in demand in the real world, too.

The excitement at One Art had spilled out into the street, where a few people were standing around smoking and talking in loud, animated voices, while a group of others, including me, went past them into the industrial building, and then slowly up the five flights in the cranky, padded freight elevator. I felt self-conscious and nervous during the ascent. This would be my first public event, my first social outing, since my father's death and the improbable shock I'd sustained, and had seemed to almost *will*, in Parksie's apartment.

"Maybe children can be forgiven," I'd told Dr. Stern on my next visit. "But I'm a grown woman now, on my way to becoming an *old* woman, and I'm still running around spreading unhappiness."

"You feel pretty terrible about this," she said. "But you didn't really get to the truth until you'd spoken to Parksie about it, did you?"

"Not until she looked at me that way. I'll never forget that look. But why did I ever even think it was Miss Snow? They hardly resembled each other."

"You're the one who made the switch," Dr. Stern said. "Any ideas?"

"It was obviously convenient, with the whole whiteness thing. And I suppose I just couldn't accept that it was Parksie. She must have been in her thirties back then, yet I'd never thought of her, even retrospectively, as a sexual being. The way Faye didn't seem to have a self outside her role in my family's life. Ev is right. What a spoiled brat I was. Am."

"And Miss Snow was easier to accept?"

"I guess so. She was more expendable, for one thing. I mean, she was there, but she wasn't a *fixture*. I think everyone always knew she would get married and go away. And when Parksie referred to her the other day as a 'type,' that really resonated with me. I'd perceived Miss Snow as glamorous, which I guess was just an unsophisticated child's take on sexy." I took a couple of deep breaths.

"Would your mother have found Miss Snow more expendable, too?"

I hesitated; that seemed like such a crucial question. "I don't know," I finally said. "Maybe. Yes, I think so. As wounded as she was about my father and Miss Snow, it probably would have been much more hurtful to know that it was Parksie. She'd have felt more betrayed, all around, I think, angrier with my father, and even more threatened."

Dr. Stern didn't say anything. She sat there, letting me absorb the implications of what I'd just said. "Are you trying to let me off the hook?" I asked.

"No, I'm just trying to help you to see the whole picture."

The whole picture kept playing in my head the rest of the day—in the supermarket on my way home from Dr. Stern's, as I attended a meeting at

G&F in the afternoon about Michael's book, and on the subway that evening going downtown to the opening at One Art. But once I was there, the images on the walls gradually replaced the ones in my head.

The gallery was mobbed and vibrantly humming; where had everyone come from? I remembered helping Violet mind that other show months before, and how almost no one had shown up while we were there. I'd invited a few people myself this evening, as a hedge against a poor turnout, but I didn't spot any of them when I came in.

These were probably mostly relatives and close friends of the artists. Aunt Lil and Uncle Bernie, who had signed the guest book that other time, cousins, neighbors. Opening night! The allotted fifteen minutes of fame. I saw the Steinhorns talking to an antediluvian woman in a wheelchair, sporting a corsage. There was a cluster of beautiful young girls; a couple of babies, riding like rajahs in back carriers; and a Jack Russell terrier struggling for release from a woman's arms. A toddler ran gleefully between Imogene's pillar-like sculptures and through the forest of legs, with a man chasing after her, calling, "Alexandra, you're going to get hurt!" Only a few people were actually looking at the artwork.

I went to the wall of Violet's paintings first. They were as familiar as old friends—gloomy, difficult old friends who stop you, like the Ancient Mariner, and insist on telling you their dark, convoluted story. A young couple, dressed in gothic black and with a lot of body piercing, stood next to me, gazing at one of Violet's canvases. "Wow," he said, which could have meant anything, and she said, "Yeah." They guzzled their wine and drifted away, as Violet came up beside me and said, "Well?"

"I'm impressed," I said. "And I'm not the only one. Do you see that guy with all the nose rings? He just looked at these and said 'Wow.'"

"That's my cousin Ralph's son, Peter. He's completely insane."

"Well, insane people can still be very astute critics."

"So which one do you want?" Violet asked.

"Oh, come on," I said. "You know that isn't necessary."

"That was our deal, remember? Did you see the catalog?"

"I got one in the mail. It looks nice," I said, happy to veer away from the issue of a reciprocal painting. Ev had sent the catalog to me, just as he'd sent the invitation, without a note. He really had done a fine job, though.

The graphics were beautiful, and there were no typos in my essay. Well, how could there be? Everything's printed from a computer disc today. I could see a little pile of catalogs on a desk in the corner, surrounded by half-empty plastic cups and crumpled cocktail napkins. The runaway toddler, still at large, had a catalog in each of her grubby fists.

"Nice?" Violet said. "*Nice?*" She grabbed my arm, pinching the skin between her fingernails. "It's fucking wonderful, Alice, and so is he."

"Violet, listen," I began, pulling away from her grasp, but she cut me off.

"No, *you* listen. That whole business with Scott?" she said. "Ev was right. The kid was screwing up again."

"What do you mean?"

"I mean he was lifting stuff from Tower, maybe selling it."

"He was not!" I rubbed my arm hard where she had pinched it, trying to deflect the pain I felt everywhere else. "How do *you* know?"

"Because he told me."

"Who did?"

"Scotty."

"You're making this up," I said, but I remembered the special bond Violet, the perfect not-parent, had always had with my kids, and that Scotty did have a kind of compulsion to ultimately confess, to cleanse his conscience without really altering his habits. "But why didn't you tell me?"

"Because you would have said I was making it up, like you just did. Because you're deliberately blind when it comes to Scott. So I told Ev instead."

I'd been betrayed by everybody. "Thanks a lot," I said angrily. And then, "What did he do to him?"

"Ev? I don't know. He probably yelled and then talked to him. And I think he made him pay for the stuff he took and quit the job."

I thought of my dinner with Scott at the Star of Bombay, of his sudden interest in filmmaking, his uncharacteristic deference to Ev. "I don't believe this," I said, but I believed it all completely.

"Ev handled it," Violet said. "He saved Scotty's ass. But that kid should be in treatment."

"You think everyone should."

"Why not?" Violet said, reasonably.

I glanced around the room, eager to escape our conversation. "Oh," I said. "There's Ruth Casey." She had just stepped off the elevator, as if to provide me with an excuse for fleeing. "I'll speak to *you* later," I warned Violet, and I made my way through the crowd.

"Ruth, I'm so glad you could make it," I said. Actually, I was completely surprised to see her there. The last time we'd met, a few days before, at my apartment, we'd worked together on one of her final chapters, in which her husband leaves and she finds herself rocking in place for hours alongside her daughter. It was a terrific and terrible scene. "This is very good," I told her. "The whole book is."

She seemed to wait. As always, she was pale, calm, inscrutable.

Then, in a burst of honesty, I said, "But I'm not sure about the market for it. The way things are, the sales departments make the big decisions, and they all seem to be hung up on happy endings. They probably wouldn't take *Madame Bovary* today, unless she paid off her library bill and took an antidote."

Ruth smiled, but not bitterly. What was a publishing disappointment in light of all the other catastrophic events of her life?

"You could change it, I suppose," I said. "Make it more *encouraging,* somehow, or play up to the reader's sympathies . . . But that would violate your intentions, wouldn't it?" Before she could answer, I went on, "Listen, we might still be able to get it into the right hands." A good doctor always told the patient the truth, but without destroying all hope.

"Okay. Thanks," Ruth said.

There was a clumsy silence then. I noticed the invitation to the art show opening on the coffee table, next to Ruth's manuscript, and I picked it up and handed it to her. "My friend is going to be in this art show," I said. And I chattered a little about Violet's co-op group, and how the artists in it didn't compromise, or sacrifice their integrity to public taste, either. "You might like to take a look at their stuff. Why don't you come to the opening?"

It had been a pretty perfunctory invitation, the filler for an awkward conversational pause, but now here she was. Maybe she just needed to get out for a change, to be among animated, social beings. Like me. "Would you like a glass of wine?" I asked. "Or some club soda?"

"Sure," Ruth said. "Red, if they have it." And she stepped away and began looking at the artwork.

I headed in the direction of the refreshments table, past Greta Gordon's night-light collages. There were red dots next to two or three of them, indicating that they'd been sold. I made a quick survey of the room and saw that there were dots alongside a few other works, too, mostly the smallest, and likely the least expensive, ones. God bless relatives and friends.

Marjorie Steinhorn stepped up and blocked my path. "Alice," she said. "How are you?" Her eyes ate me up and spit me out. "Where's Everett?" she wanted to know.

So Violet hadn't told her about the separation, or maybe she had; it was hard to tell. "He's around," I said, gesturing vaguely behind me. "Isn't this lovely? Well, my congratulations to you and Leo."

"For what?" she asked. Then she glanced in the direction of Violet's paintings. "Oh," she said.

"Excuse me, Marjorie," I murmured. "There's Ev." It wasn't him; I didn't see anyone I knew at that moment, but I'd gotten away. Before I could reach the wine, though, someone took my arm and said, "You're Alice, right?" It was the photographer, India. She was holding a single rose wrapped in wet paper towel, a thorny tribute from an admirer.

"India, hi. I was about to go look at your photographs."

"They're over there," she said, pointing to the left of where I'd been heading.

She was still gripping my arm, the same one Violet had held, and I let myself be steered toward the wall she shared with an elderly landscape painter. The landscapes, fuzzy bucolic scenes—the painter's vision was poor, like Monet's—looked even more discreet next to the enlargements of India's bold and witty work. I wondered who'd decided to pair these particular artists, and how it felt to stand clothed in a public place beside images of one's self in the nude. India didn't appear to be uncomfortable or concerned. "They look great," I said sincerely.

"Thanks," she said, and suddenly she seemed shy. "I like what you wrote in the catalog about them. You understand what I'm trying to do."

"Yes," I said. "At least, I hope so." I felt uncommonly pleased and flustered. When someone came up behind India, covering her eyes and saying "Guess who?" I took the opportunity to slip away.

The elevator door opened, discharging even more people—although I could have sworn there wasn't another drop of space—and Michael was among them. I'd forgotten that Imogene Donnell's girlfriend had invited him to the opening. What had she told him again? That they needed all the warm bodies they could get.

I had called Michael that afternoon, right after the meeting at G&F, but I'd reached his voice mail. "It's Alice," I said. "I have some great news! Call me." But when he did, I was on another call. "Oh, no, I missed you," he'd moaned. And we continued to play phone tag for the rest of the day.

Now here he was, a warm body walking into my real life. "Michael," I called. He looked around and waved when he saw me, and began to stride through the crowd. I was never going to get a drink.

The response to *Walking to Europe* at G&F had been even better than I'd hoped. The sales manager, who'd seen the completed manuscript beforehand and invited me to the meeting, asked me to read the first two pages aloud, and there was applause afterward, something I'd never heard there before. They'd offered a really generous advance for a first novel— although it was still easier to get money for someone new than for a seasoned writer with a bad sales record. And they wanted me to be the editor, freelance. Most importantly, they'd talked about positioning the book prominently, with a big first printing and a sizable promotional budget. He'd need an agent now, to set up the deal, and I had a couple of names to give him.

I broke all the news to Michael in the midst of that racket—I had to shout a little to be heard, and he kept whooping and laughing and hugging me. I glanced around uneasily to see who might be watching us. It would be just my luck to have Marjorie Steinhorn as the star witness for the prosecution. She wasn't in sight, but Ev was.

He was talking to Violet, near her paintings, and he had a cup of wine in his hand. How long had he been standing there? And what were they

saying? Neither of them was looking at me, and I went from feeling conspicuous to an eerie sense of invisibility. Even Michael's attention was beginning to wander—all those lovely, long-haired young women—and I
said, "Why don't you take a look at the show. I'll catch up with you later."
And once again, I was weaving through the crowd. It felt as if I were in the
midst of another dream, the kind where you're struggling to get somewhere, but never arrive. I'm walking to Europe, I thought.

The "whole picture" that Dr. Stern had held up for me to view that
morning finally included my own marriage, not just my parents', and the
effect that idealizing one had probably had on the other. I'd concluded
that most marriages are complicated by the addition of children, in more
than the usual ways; that without meaning to, we turn them into little foot
soldiers for our separate causes. I had worked both sides for my parents,
like a double agent, and poor Scotty was caught in the crossfire between
Ev and me. When I spoke about Ev, I realized that the feeling in my chest
was still there, that the bad news it had first delivered last April was layered
and complicated, that it was about the past, certainly, but it was about the
future, too.

I finally did make it across the gallery floor to where Ev was standing.

"Alice," he said as Violet walked away, looking anxiously back at us before she disappeared.

I was preparing to confront him about Scott, but I surprised myself by
saying instead, "The catalog looks great."

"I've been meaning to call you," he said. My heart bumped; he was finally going to tell me about Scotty, and I braced myself for an argument.

"About your essay," Ev said.

"Oh?"

"It's really fine. I mean the writing. It's the best you've ever done."

"Thanks" was all I could manage. If he'd said any more, I might have
become suspicious. Any less, and I would have been bereft. As it was, I felt
stunned, as if he'd put his hand out and touched my bare skin. Yet I waited
for a qualification, for something negative.

Years ago, when we were still workshop adversaries, he once complained that I didn't hear the implicit praise in his criticism. Like what, I'd
thought sullenly—that I'm not completely illiterate, that I have a nice ass?

Which wasn't exactly fair: I'd never caught him checking me out back then; had I wanted him to? Now he didn't say anything else, and I said, "How have you been?"

"I've been better. And you?"

"All right."

"Have you been writing anything else?"

"Not really," I said, and there was an uncomfortable pause. But I knew how to fill it. "Have you?" I asked.

"I've been messing around a little. A couple of stories."

"Oh, well, that's good, I guess," I said.

"Yeah. No pressure now, you know. It's almost fun."

He was looking directly at me, and it was difficult to look back, or away, for that matter.

"Maybe you'll take a look at some of it, sometime," he said. "I could use a little feedback."

"From me?" I scoffed. "When did you become a masochist?"

Then someone going by jostled him, hard, and his wine splattered onto my white shirt. Red wine, naturally. Why did I feel slightly faint when I glanced down at it?

"Shit," Ev said. "I'm sorry, Al." He took his jacket off and put it around my shoulders, covering the stains. The jacket smelled like him.

"I'm sorry, too," I told him.

"Why don't I get us a couple of drinks," Ev said. "Or we could go somewhere else if you want to."

Before I could answer, a child began screaming. It was that toddler, Alexandra, who, as her father had prophesied, had finally gotten hurt. Perhaps the dog had bitten her; it had gotten loose, too. Her father carried her into the elevator and the door slid closed behind them. Then I saw Michael across the room through a corner of my vision. He was talking to someone, a blond woman, offering her his disarming smile the way he used to offer me cigarettes.

It took long seconds before I realized that the woman was Ruth. That was because she looked so different now. There was a little color in her face for once, and her usual cool demeanor had evaporated. One hand was on her hip, the other on her neck, and then she switched hands, as if she didn't quite know what to do with them. When the elevator came back, she and Michael got into it together.

Of course. But why hadn't I thought of introducing them? It had nothing to do with a sense of competition, as it had when Michael and Violet occurred to me, and I really was able to let go of him now. Maybe I'd unconsciously equated the heat of attraction with joy, without even considering it as a palliative for grief. I guess I'd forgotten how Ev and I finally came to be together, and that love was always a reasonable prospect.

28

April, again, and Esmeralda was helping me with the usual spring chores. She was on the kitchen step stool, swiping a wet rag across the highest cabinet shelf, and I was in the bedroom emptying my closet, throwing articles of clothing onto the various piles I'd started to assemble on the bed: hand-me-downs, thrift shop, dry cleaners. In the living room between us, Diana Ross and the Supremes were belting out one of their greatest hits.

Years ago, when I lived with my parents in Riverdale, spring cleaning was always a major production. It involved rug beating in sunlight, turning mattresses, pruning trees, and the clearance of dead leaves and broken branches from the gutters and flower beds. The whole enterprise signified renewal—some of the perennials were already poking their heads up through the ground—and that we were going to live forever, or at least into another cycle of seasons.

Now we were just getting rid of another layer of city dust and pruning some of my possessions. The stink of mothballs had given way over time to the sachet of cedar blocks, and life was counted out more cautiously now, with one eye on the horizon. Still, I felt reasonably happy, even hopeful, and readily willing to let go of that soft yellow sweater, of last year's favorite skirt. Then I came to my loden jacket, an in-between garment that I mostly wore on warmer autumn days and brisk ones in early spring. It felt oddly heavy on the hanger. I reached into one of the pockets to see what was weighing it down and found the stones I'd gathered at the cemetery the day of my father's funeral, which I'd intended to set out on the shelf of my mother's monument.

There were just a handful of them, and they weren't really heavy at all. Perhaps I'd only been propelled by memory to look in that pocket. I sat on the bed, between piles of clothing, and poured the stones back and forth between my hands. A little grit sifted down onto my lap, and then I came across the smooth worry stone that I'd worked with my fingers during my father's service.

As I touched its cool, satiny surface, something broke in me and I flung myself facedown on the bed, onto the loden jacket, and began to sob. The thing was, I couldn't seem to stop, or even hold down the volume of my wailing. If it weren't for the Supremes, I'm sure Esmeralda would have come running in to see what was wrong. The jacket was roughly wet with tears and snot; its wooden toggles pressed into my forehead and my cheeks, and still I kept on. I hadn't cried like that since my mother died. Maybe I had never cried quite like that.

Of course my face was a mess of blotches afterward. I splashed it with cold water and put my sunglasses on. Then I filled two large shopping bags with the clothes that I'd set aside for the thrift shop. I called goodbye to Esmeralda and went downstairs. The worry stone was in the pocket of my jeans as I walked toward Third Avenue under the pale, still-folded leaves of the trees.

The thrift shop was doing a lively business. Women, mostly, bent over the jewelry cases, breathing on the glass, fixed on finding treasures. A couple of men picked through the ties with less enthusiasm, less of an apparent sense of a mission. This was one of the better places, staffed by helpful volunteers supporting a good cause. It didn't smell of death and damp basements, the way some of the others did, and the merchandise was generally of a high quality.

"These things come from *rich* dead people," Violet once observed. "It's all designer stuff, and the sizes are so small." She was the one who had taught me to wear other women's used clothing, to get over any squeamishness I'd had about it. She said it was a natural thing, this recycling of belongings. "Someone else will even live in our houses someday," she pointed out. In my case, they already did, at least in the house of my childhood.

I turned the bags over to a volunteer, an elderly woman who looked pretty well heeled, herself. She peeked inside one of them and said, "Oh, nice," and I had a momentary misgiving about my yellow sweater. Usually, I'd browse through the racks and the paintings after I dropped off a donation, but I was unable to concentrate on those material goods this time, and I found myself out on the avenue again in a few minutes. My hand went automatically to the stone in my pocket, and then I raised my other arm and hailed a taxi.

The turbaned driver, thousands of miles from his native home, didn't look too pleased at the prospect of driving to Cypress Hills. After some dickering, I made a deal with him, for twenty-five dollars over the meter and the usual tip, if he'd wait for me and take me back to the city. We didn't speak again all the way to Queens, although his two-way radio kept squawking strangled words in a language I didn't understand.

I had to get directions to my parents' plot from a clerk in the cemetery office. The driver had turned off his radio by the time I got back to the cab. I pointed, and we drove slowly, in silence, down the narrow road, until I said, "Turn here." Then, after a while, "Wait. This is it, I think." And it was.

My father's gravestone had been installed a few weeks after the funeral, without ceremony. I hadn't been back to see it before this. Its posture was erect next to my mother's matching stone, which I realized, with this new frame of reference, had sunk a little over the years. It tilted very slightly toward his, reminding me of the way she used to tilt toward him in conversation. Still, there was more symmetry now.

I ran my editorial eye over his chiseled inscription, checking it for

errors. Once, someone at work told me that the writer Isaac Bashevis
Singer's monument says WINNER OF THE NOBLE PRIZE, and that his widow
had ordered it engraved that way to get even with him for his infidelities.
It's probably an apocryphal story; it has the bittersweet aspect of something
he might have written himself.

Here are my parents lying in their twin beds, I told myself, under their
living green coverlets. But no amount of metaphor could make me roman-
ticize the work of nature going on down there. Years ago, after much discussion, Ev and I both decided to be cremated. "Do me on a low flame,
just in case," he'd said the day we put it in writing, and I'd laughed, but all
those jokes are hollow when you think about them. Helen and Sam, Sam
and Helen. Ev and Al. Everything else falls away.

I dug the worry stone from my pocket and placed it on the ledge of my
mother's tombstone. I found a similar one, though not quite as smooth or
white, on the path near their graves, and I placed it on my father's. Then I
opened my purse and took the letter from *The New Yorker* out of the zippered compartment. I slipped it under the worry stone, which served as a
paperweight now in the mild April breeze, but I could still read the words
"Try us again!" before I turned away.

When I got back into the cab, the driver turned in his seat and looked
at me with beautiful, dark liquid eyes. "Mother?" he asked. "Father?"

"Yes," I said, and he shook his head.

"And *your* family?" I asked.

"There," he said, solemnly, gesturing through the cab window, and he
could have meant Pakistan or India or heaven, or just another section of
Queens.

Esmeralda was gone when I got back to the apartment. She'd left a row
of emptied bottles of cleaning supplies on the kitchen counter, my signal
to buy refills. I made a shopping list and put the empties into the bin in the
trash compacter room. Then I began to prepare dinner, using some of
those healthful ingredients said to help stave off decline and cremation.

As I sliced radishes for the salad, I thought of my mother's poem
"Minor Surgery," and of what it might mean to have a bloodless heart. It
was, in effect, what I'd accused Ev of back in the workshop, and later in

our arguments about Scott, after all the nights of that organ's steady beating against my own. But it wasn't true, even metaphorically. And he was wrong about me, too. My passion wasn't simply willed, it was a product of my history.

Ev and I had originally come together in haste, in a state of heightened emotion, and for a while it seemed that we'd parted that way, too. But I think now that our separation was probably in the making during all those years, the way a pearl forms inside an oyster, one grain of irritation at a time.

So we were very cautious about trying to get back together. That we'd both said we were sorry that night at One Art was merely an overture, a show of goodwill and a demonstration of our mutual loneliness. But we were able to sustain that détente for a while as we reveled in Suzy and George's wedding plans, and worried over Jeremy and Celia, who still gave off sparks of tension the way they'd once radiated happiness.

"I thought they were okay," Ev said sadly, "that they'd patched things up. What's going on?"

"I'm not sure," I told him. "Some clash between love and art, I suspect, don't you?" And we traded rueful little smiles. "Maybe they'll work it out, though," I offered. We were like longtime business partners going over the ledgers together, marking the profits and losses.

But soon after that, we fell into arguing again, with each of us assigning blame for some things and assuming it only reluctantly for others. Of course, Scotty came up in the venting of our grievances, and after a storm of shouting and tears we finally agreed on joint responsibility for his failures, with our alternating fits of indulgence and control, and that he did need outside help. Dr. Stern referred him to someone downtown. God knows what he says there, or how long it's going to take to undo whatever we've unwittingly done to him.

Ev and I spent hours and hours talking, too, in mediation, until one particular evening, when we came to an impasse. We were in the apartment, our first time there together since the day of my father's funeral, and I had just told Ev about my recent discovery about my father and Parksie, and what I had told my mother. It was a way, I thought, of letting him back

into my head, into my life. I expected him to be sympathetic—even to try
to absolve me—like the old Ev, who'd rubbed my feet whenever the world
was unkind.

And he did say some of the right things: that I was only a kid when it all
happened, and that my mother had still been happy in many ways. But he
seemed more distracted than moved by my news of the past, and in a little
while he said, "How about you?"

"What about me?"

"You know," he said. "*Your* love life."

I didn't know what he meant at first, and then I got it. He wanted to
know if I was my father's child, if I had screwed around, too, in his absence. It felt like such a violent break in the careful diplomacy of our rene-
gotiations, like a bomb going off at an embassy.

I'd discussed the possibility of confession with Dr. Stern only the week
before. All she'd said was that I'd have to try to understand my motives for
telling Ev about Michael, and consider the possible consequences. One of
them was that I'd probably learn about any extramarital affairs Ev might
have had. Quid pro quo. Did I want to know about that? I decided I didn't,
that too much honesty would be an unbearable burden for the fragile
bones of our attempted reunion.

Still, I felt hurt and angry that he'd asked so bluntly about something
that sensitive, especially in the context of what I'd just told him about
my mother and father. Why did their marriage always seem to be such a
ghostly presence, and a pall over my own? Begone! I ordered, the way I'd
once implored them to stay. And I almost blurted out the truth to Ev, just
to hurt him back, but then I didn't. I only said, "There's nothing to tell,"
which was really just another version of the truth, because the facts weren't
for telling, not then, anyway.

And I didn't go on to say, "How about you?" even when I was still
goaded by anger, because of an abiding sense of fairness, and the dread of
finding out. When I'd finally let myself imagine Ev with someone else, it
was that woman in the leather miniskirt and big sunglasses I'd seen leave
his building the day I went there as a spy. She seemed anonymous enough,
impermanent, a phantom now, just like Michael.

The danger we'd just avoided led us, inevitably, into bed. Something was bound to before too long. Ev kept declaring his love, the way he used to, and married lust is a fine, polished thing, but it doesn't exactly drive you crazy, or push you into making sudden, rash, long-term arrangements. So we had to slip back together again slowly and soberly, over several weeks, looking through both ends of the telescope at our lives.

Later on the night of the day I'd gone to my parents' graves, after Ev and I had eaten our wholesome dinner, we sat in the living room and listened to the evening news. Then he shut off the radio and took some pages from his briefcase. Positioning himself in the chair next to the brightest lamp in the room, he began to read aloud from a story he'd been working on. I sat adjacent to him, doodling on a pad in my lap as he read, writing down things like "God-like omniscience," "so *bleak*," and "what is at stake here?" I might have been commenting on Violet's painting, on the wall behind Ev's head.

While he continued to read, his voice rising and falling in waves, I scribbled over some of my words with little sketches of idealized men and women, seen in profile, like the ones Violet and I used to draw in high school during long assemblies, and then I covered the profiles with Escher-like optical designs.

When Ev finished reading, he gathered his pages, cleared his throat expectantly, and looked up at me. I waited a few thoughtful beats before I said some of what I'd written down, leavening my harshest comments and questions with scattered offerings of sincere praise—applying that blend of honesty and charity that our teacher, poor Phil Santo, used to vainly press us to try in the workshop—while Ev kept jotting down what seemed to be earnest notes.

Then we changed places. I carried my notebook to the easy chair near the good light, and put on my reading glasses, so at first I was in his shadow, and then he was in mine.

ABOUT THE AUTHOR

HILMA WOLITZER is the author of several novels, including *Hearts, Ending,* and *Tunnel of Love,* as well as the nonfiction book *The Company of Writers.* She is a recipient of Guggenheim and NEA fellowships, and an Award in Literature from the American Academy and Institute of Arts and Letters. She has taught writing at the University of Iowa, New York University, and Columbia University. Hilma Wolitzer lives in New York City.

ABOUT THE TYPE

This book was set in Electra, a typeface designed for Linotype by W. A. Dwiggins, the renowned type designer (1880–1956). Electra is a fluid typeface, avoiding the contrasts of thick and thin strokes that are prevalent in most modern typefaces.